METRO GIRL

METRO GIRL

Janet Evanovich

HarperCollins*Publishers*

METRO GIRL. Copyright © 2004 by Evanovich, Inc. All rights reserved. Printed in the United States of America. No part of this book may be used or reproduced in any manner whatsoever without written permission except in the case of brief quotations embodied in critical articles and reviews. For information, address HarperCollins Publishers Inc., 10 East 53rd Street, New York, NY 10022.

HarperCollins books may be purchased for educational, business, or sales promotional use. For information, please write: Special Markets Department, HarperCollins Publishers Inc., 10 East 53rd Street, New York, NY 10022.

FIRST EDITION

Designed by Nicola Ferguson

Printed on acid-free paper

Library of Congress Cataloging-in-Publication Data is available upon request.

ISBN 0-06-058400-9

04 05 06 07 08 ❖/RRD 10 9 8 7 6 5 4 3 2 1

METRO
GIRL

ONE

Just because I know how to change a guy's oil doesn't mean I want to spend the rest of my life on my back, staring up his undercarriage. Been there, done that. Okay, so my dad owns a garage. And okay, I have a natural aptitude for rebuilding carburetors. There comes a time in a girl's life when she needs to trade in her mechanic's overalls for a pair of Manolo Blahnik stilettos. Not that I can afford a lot of Manolos, but it's a goal, right?

My name is Alexandra Barnaby, and I worked in my dad's garage in the Canton section of Baltimore all through high school and during summer breaks when I was in college. It's not a big fancy garage, but it holds its own, and my dad has a reputation for being an honest mechanic.

When I was twelve my dad taught me how to use an acetylene torch. After I mastered welding, he gave me some spare parts and our old lawn mower, and I built myself a go-cart. When I was sixteen, I started rebuilding a ten-year-old junker Chevy. I turned it into a fast car. And I raced it in the local stocks for two years.

"And here she comes, folks," the announcer would say. "Barney Barnaby. Number sixteen, the terror of Baltimore County. She's coming up on the eight car. She's going to the inside. Wait a minute, I see flames coming from sixteen. There's a lot of smoke now. Looks like she's blown another engine. Good thing she works in her dad's garage."

So I could build cars, and I could drive cars. I just never got the hang of driving them without destroying them.

"Barney," my dad would say. "I swear you blow those engines just so you can rebuild them."

Maybe on an *un*conscious level. The brain is a pretty weird thing. What I knew was that on a *conscious* level, I hated losing. And I lost more races than I won. So, I raced two seasons and packed it in.

My younger brother, Wild Bill, drove, too. He never cared if he won or lost. He just liked to drive fast and scratch his balls with the rest of the guys. Bill was voted Most Popular of his senior class and also Least Likely to Succeed.

The class's expectation for Bill's success was a reflection of Bill's philosophy of life. *If work was any fun, it would be called play.* I've always been the serious kid, and Bill's always been the kid who knew how to have a good time. Two years ago, Bill said *good-bye* Baltimore and *hello* Miami. He liked the lazy hot sun, the open water, and the girls in bikinis.

Two days ago, Bill disappeared off the face of the earth. And he did it while I was talking to him. He woke me up with a phone call in the middle of the night.

"Barney," Bill yelled over the phone line. "I have to leave Miami for a while. Tell Mom I'm okay."

I squinted at my bedside clock. Two AM. Not late for Bill who spent a lot of time in South Beach bars. Real late for me who worked nine to five and went to bed at ten.

"What's that noise?" I asked him. "I can hardly hear you."

"Boat engine. Listen, I don't want you to worry if you don't hear from me. And if some guys show up looking for me, don't tell them anything. Unless it's Sam Hooker. Tell Sam Hooker he can kiss my exhaust pipe."

"Guys? What guys? And what do you mean, don't tell them anything?"

"I have to go. I have to . . . *oh shit.*"

I heard a woman scream in the background, and the line went dead.

Baltimore is cold in January. The wind whips in from the harbor and slices up the side streets, citywide. We get a couple snowstorms each year and some freezing rain, but mostly we get bone-chilling gray gloom. In the midst of the gray gloom, pots of chili bubble on stoves, beer flows like water, sausages are stuffed into hard rolls, and doughnuts are a necessity to survival.

Miami, it turns out, is *hot* in January. I'd taken the midday flight out of BWI, arriving in Miami midafternoon. When I left home I was wrapped in a quilted down-filled coat, cashmere Burberry scarf, fleece-lined boots, and heavy-duty shearling mittens. Perfect for Baltimore. Not great for Miami. On arrival, I'd crammed the scarf and mittens into the medium-size duffel bag that hung from my shoulder, wrapped my coat around the duffel bag handle, and went in search of the taxi stand. Sweat was soaking into my Victoria's Secret Miracle Bra, my hair was plastered to my forehead, and I was sucking in air that felt like hot soup.

I'm thirty years old now. Average height and average build. I'm not movie-star gorgeous, but I'm okay. My hair is naturally mousy brown, but I started bleaching it blond when I decided to stop being a grease monkey. It's currently platinum and cut in a medium-length shaggy kind of style that I can punk up with paste if the occasion arises. I have blue eyes, a mouth that's a little too big for my face, and a perfect nose inherited from my Grandma Jean.

My parents took Bill and me to Disney World when I was nine. That's the extent of my in-the-flesh Florida experience. The rest of my Florida knowledge consists mainly of horrific bug stories from my mom's friend Elsie Duchen. Elsie winters in Ocala with her daughter. Elsie swears there are cockroaches as big as cows in Florida. And she says they can fly. I'm here to tell you, if I see a cow-size cockroach fly by, I'm gone.

I gave Bill's address to the cabdriver, and I sat back and watched Miami roll past the window. In the beginning there was a lot of concrete road stretching forward into a confusing jumble of intersections and turnoffs. The turnoffs spiraled away to super highways. And the super highways flattened and went on forever. After a few minutes the Miami skyline appeared in the distance, in front of me, and I had the feeling I was on the road to Oz. Palm trees lined the road. The sky was azure. Cars were clean. Exotic stuff for a girl from Baltimore.

We rolled across the Causeway Bridge, leaving Miami behind, moving into Miami Beach. My stomach felt hollow, and I had a white-knuckle grip on my bag. I was worried about Bill, and my anxiety was increasing as we drew closer to his apartment. Hey, I told myself. Relax. Pry your fingers off the bag. Bill's okay. He's always okay. Like a cat. Lands on his feet. True, he wasn't answering his phone. And he hadn't reported in for work. No reason to panic. This was Wild Bill. He didn't always prioritize in the normal fashion.

This was the guy who missed his high school graduation because en route to the ceremony he found an injured cat on the side of the road. He took the cat to the vet and wouldn't leave until the cat was out of surgery and awake. Of course, he could probably still have made the ceremony if only he hadn't felt the need to seduce the vet's assistant in examining room number three.

The troublesome part about my late-night phone call from Bill was the woman screaming. This was a new twist on Bill's usual call. My mother would freak if she knew about the call, so I'd said nothing and boarded a plane.

My plan was to somehow get into Bill's apartment and make sure he wasn't lying on the floor dead. If he wasn't dead on the floor and he wasn't hanging out watching television, my next stop would be the marina. He was on a boat when he called me. I thought I might have to find the boat. Beyond that, I was clueless.

The Causeway Bridge fed into Fifth Avenue in South

Beach. Fifth was three lanes in each direction with a grassy island in the middle. Businesses lined both sides of the road. The driver turned right at Meridian Avenue, went one block, and pulled to the curb.

I was in a neighborhood of single-family bungalows and blocky two-story stucco apartment buildings. The lots were small. The vegetation was jungle. Cars were parked bumper to bumper on both sides of the two-lane street. Bill's apartment building was yellow with turquoise and pink trim and looked a lot like a cheap motel. There were wrought iron security bars on the windows. In fact, most of the buildings on the street had barred windows. In Baltimore, bars on windows would be found in conjunction with gang graffiti, street garbage, burned-out crack houses, and broken-down cars. None of those things were present in this neighborhood. This neighborhood looked modest but neatly maintained.

I paid the driver and trudged up the walkway that led to the apartment entrance. Moss grew between paving stones, overgrown flowering bushes and vines spilled onto the sidewalk and raced up the yellow stucco building, and the air smelled sweet and chemical. Bug spray, I thought. I was probably a step behind the exterminator. Best to keep my eye out for the cow-size cockroach. Lizards skittered across the walk in front of me and clung to the stucco walls. I didn't want to prejudge Miami Beach, but the lizards weren't doing a lot for me.

The building was divided into six apartments. Three up and three down. Six front doors on the ground level. Bill lived in an end apartment on the second floor. I didn't have a key. If he didn't answer his doorbell, I'd try the neighbors.

I rang the bell and looked at the door. There were fresh gouges in the wood around the lock and the dead bolt. I tried the doorknob and the door swung open. *Damn.* I'm not an expert on criminal behavior, but I didn't think this was a good sign.

I pushed the door farther open and looked inside. Small entrance foyer with stairs leading up to the rest of the apartment. No sounds drifting down to me. No television, talking, scuffling around.

"Hello?" I called. "I'm coming up, and I have a gun." This was a big fat lie shouted out for a good cause. I figured in case there were bad guys going through the silverware drawer this would encourage them to jump out the window.

I waited a couple beats and then I cautiously crept up the stairs. I've never thought of myself as being especially brave. Aside from my short career at racing stocks, I don't do a lot of wacky, risky things. I don't like scary movies or roller coasters. I never wanted to be a cop, firefighter, or superhero. Mostly my life has been putting one foot in front of the other, moving forward on autopilot. My family thought it took guts for me to go to college, but the truth is, college was just a way to get out of the garage. I love my dad, but I was up to here with cars and guys who knew nothing else. Call me picky, but I didn't want a romantic relationship where I was second in line to a customized truck.

I got to the top of the stairs and froze. The stairs opened to the living room, and beyond the living room I could see into the small kitchen. Both rooms were a wreck. Couch cushions had been thrown onto the floor. Books were pulled off shelves. Drawers had been wrenched out of cabinets, and the drawer contents scattered. Someone had trashed the apartment, and it wasn't Bill. I'd seen Bill's style of mess. It ran more to dirty clothes on the floor, food stuck to the couch, and a lot of empty beer cans, everywhere. That's not what I was seeing here.

I whirled around and flew down the stairs. I was out the door, on the sidewalk in seconds. I stood facing the building, staring up at Bill's apartment, gulping air. This was something that happened in movies. This didn't happen in real life. At least it didn't happen in *my* real life.

I stood there trying to pull myself together, listening to the steady drone of traffic a block away on Fifth. There was no visible activity in the apartment building in front of me. No doomsday cloud hanging overhead. An occasional car cruised by, but for the most part, the street was quiet. I had my hand to my heart, and I could feel that my heartbeat was improving. Probably it had even dropped below stroke level.

All right, let's get a grip on what happened here. Someone tossed Bill's apartment. Fortunately, they seemed to be gone. *Unfortunately,* Bill seemed to be gone, too. Probably I should go back and take another look.

The voice of reason started yelling at me inside my head. What are you, nuts? Call the police. A crime was committed here. Stay far away.

Then the voice of the responsible older sister spoke up. Don't be so cowardly. At least do a walk-through. Bill's not always so smart. Remember the time he "borrowed" Andy Wimmer's classic GTO from the garage so he could take his buddies on a joyride and ended up in jail? And what about the time he "borrowed" a keg from Joey Kowalski's bar for his Super Bowl party. Maybe you don't want to get the police involved right away. Maybe you want to try to figure out what's going on first.

Good grief, the voice of reason said.

Shut up, or I'll bitch slap you into tomorrow, the sister voice said to the voice of reason.

Bottom line is, the sister voice grew up in a garage in Baltimore.

I blew out a sigh, hoisted my duffel bag higher on my shoulder, and marched back into the apartment building and up the stairs. I set my bag on the floor, and I studied the room. Someone had been looking for something, I decided. They'd either been in a hurry or they'd been angry. You could conduct a search without making a mess like this.

It wasn't a big apartment. Combination living room and dining room, kitchen, bathroom, and bedroom. The door to the medicine chest was open in the bathroom but not much else was touched. Not much you can do when tossing a bathroom, eh? The top to the toilet tank was on the floor. No stone unturned.

I crept into the bedroom and looked around. Clothes were strewn everywhere. The drawer from the small chest beside the bed was on the floor, and condoms, still in their wrappers, were scattered across the carpet. *Lots* of condoms. Like the entire drawer had been filled with condoms. Yep, this was Bill's apartment, I thought. Although the number of condoms seemed optimistic, even for Bill.

The television and DVD player were untouched. Scratch drug-induced burglary off the list of possibilities.

I went back to the kitchen and poked around, but I didn't find anything of interest. No address book. No notes detailing criminal activity. No maps with an orange trip line. I was feeling more comfortable in the apartment. I'd been there for fifteen minutes and nothing bad had happened. No one had rushed up the stairs wielding a gun or a knife. I hadn't discovered any bloodstains. Probably the apartment was really safe, I told myself. It's already been searched, right? There's no reason for the bad guys to come back.

The marina was next up. Bill worked on a corporate boat owned by Calflex. The boat's name was *Flex II,* and it sailed out of Miami Beach Marina. I'd gotten a map and a guidebook at the airport. According to the map, I could walk to the marina. I'd be a puddle of sweat if I walked in my present clothes, so I changed into a short pink cotton skirt, white tank top, and white canvas tennis shoes. Okay, so I'm a bleached blond and I like pink. Get over it.

I'd looked for a second set of keys while picking through the mess on Bill's kitchen floor. I wanted to leave my duffel bag in the apartment when I went to the marina. I hoped the front door could still be locked. And if I could get it to lock I'd need a key to get back in.

Normally, people keep extra keys on hooks in the kitchen or by the door. Or they were kept in kitchen or bedroom drawers with a collection of odds-and-ends junk. Or, if you. were frequently hung over and tended to lock yourself out in your underwear when you stepped off the stoop to retrieve your morning paper, you might hide the keys outside.

I slipped my purse over my shoulder and went downstairs, carefully leaving the door open behind me. At home we kept our emergency keys in fake dog poop. My father thinks fake dog poop is hilarious. Tells everyone. Half of Baltimore knows to look for fake dog poop if they want to burgle our house.

I snooped under an overgrown bush to the right of the front stoop and *bingo*. Fake dog poop. I removed the keys from inside the pile of poop. A house key and a car key. I tried the house key, and it fit Bill's front door. I locked up and followed the path to the sidewalk. I pressed the panic button on the remote gizmo attached to the car key, hoping to find Bill's car among the cars parked there. Nothing happened. None of the parked cars responded. I had no idea what Bill drove. No logo on the key. I aimed the remote toward the other end of the street and didn't get a hit there either.

I set off on foot and found the marina four blocks later. It was hidden behind a strip of condos and commercial real estate, barely visible from the road. I crossed a parking lot, aiming the remote around the lot as I walked. None of the cars beeped or flashed their lights. I crossed a small median of grass and flowers and stepped onto a wide concrete sidewalk that ran the length of the marina. Palm trees lined both sides of the walkway. Very neat. Very pretty. Wood docks with slips poked into the channel. There were maybe ten docks in all, and most of the slips on those docks were filled. Powerboats at one end. Sailboats at the other end.

The huge cranes that serviced container ships off-loading at the Port of Miami were visible directly across the channel. Because I'd studied the map, I knew Fisher Island sat offshore, at the mouth of the harbor. From where I stood I could see the clusters of white stucco high-rise condos on Fisher. The orange Spanish tile roofs sparkled in the sunlight, the ground floors were obscured by palms and assorted Florida greenery.

There were white metal gates at the entrance to each of the marina docks. The signs on the gates read NO ROLLER-BLADING, SKATEBOARDING, BICYCLE RIDING, FISHING, OR SWIMMING. OWNERS AND GUESTS ONLY.

A small round two-story structure perched at the end of one of the docks. The building had good visibility from the second floor, with green awnings shading large windows. The sign on the gate for that dock told me this was Pier E, the dockmaster's office. The gate was closed, and yellow crime scene tape cordoned off an area around the dockmaster's building. A couple cops stood flat-footed at the end of the dock. A crime scene police van was parked on the concrete sidewalk in front of the white metal gate.

Ordinarily this sort of thing would generate morbid curiosity in me. Today, the crime scene tape at the dockmaster's office made me uneasy. I was looking for my missing brother, last heard from on board a boat.

I watched a guy leave the dockmaster's office and walk toward the gate. He was midthirties, dressed in khakis and a blue button-down shirt with sleeves rolled. He was carrying something that looked like a toolbox, and I guessed he belonged to the crime scene van. He pushed through the closed gate and our eyes made contact. Then his eyes dropped to my chest and my short pink skirt.

Thanks to my Miracle Bra there was an inch of cleavage peeking out from the scoop neck of my tank top, encouraging the plainclothes cop guy to stop and chat.

"What's going on out there?" I asked him.

"Homicide," he said. "Happened Monday night. Actually around three AM on Tuesday. I'm surprised you didn't see it in the paper. It was splashed all over the front page this morning."

"I never read the paper. It's too depressing. War, famine, homicides."

He looked like he was trying hard not to grimace.

"Who was killed?" I asked.

"A security guard working the night shift."

Thank God, not Bill. "I'm looking for the Calflex boat," I said. "I don't suppose you'd know where it is?"

His gaze shifted to the water and focused one dock down. "Everyone knows the Calflex boat," he said. "It's the one at the end of the pier with the helicopter on deck."

That was the boat Bill was working? It was the largest boat at the marina. It was gleaming white and had two full decks above water. The top deck held a little blue-and-white helicopter.

I thanked the cop guy and headed for *Flex II*. I ignored the gate and the sign that said owners and guests, and I walked out onto the wood-planked pier. A guy was standing two slips down from *Flex II,* hands on hips, looking royally pissed off, staring into an empty slip. He was wearing khaki shorts and a ratty, faded blue T-shirt. He had a nice body. Muscular without being chunky. My age. His hair was sun-bleached blond and a month overdue for a cut. His eyes were hidden behind dark sunglasses. He turned when I approached and lowered his glasses to better see me.

I grew up in a garage in the company of men obsessed with cars. I raced stocks for two years. And I regularly sat through family dinners where the entire conversation consisted of NASCAR statistics. So I recognized Mr. Sun-bleached Blond. He was Sam Hooker. The guy Bill had said could kiss his exhaust pipe. Sam Hooker drove NASCAR. He'd won twice at Daytona. And I guess he'd won a bunch of other races, too, but I didn't pay close attention to NASCAR anymore. Mostly what I knew about Sam Hooker I knew from the dinner table conversation. He was a good ol' boy from Texas. A man's man. A ladies' man. A damn good driver. And a jerk. In other words, according to my family, Sam Hooker was typical NASCAR. And my family loved him. Except for Bill, apparently.

I wasn't surprised to find that Bill knew Hooker. Bill was the kind of guy who eventually knew *everybody*. I was surprised to find that they weren't getting along. Wild Bill and Happy Hour Hooker were cut from the same cloth.

The closer I got to *Flex II,* the more impressive it became. It dominated the pier. There were two other boats that came close to the *Flex* in size, but none could match it for beauty of line. And *Flex II* was the only one with a helicopter. Next time I had a billion dollars to throw away I was going to get a boat like *Flex.* And of course it would have a helicopter. I wouldn't ride in the helicopter. The very thought scared the bejesus out of me. Still, I'd have it because it looked so darned good sitting there on the top deck.

There was a small battery-operated truck at the end of the pier, and people were carting produce and boxes of food off the truck and onto the boat. Most of the navy blue and white–uniformed crew was young. An older man, also in navy blue and white, stood to the side, watching the worker bees.

I approached the older man, and introduced myself. I'm not sure why, but I decided right off that I'd fib a little.

"I'm looking for my brother, Bill Barnaby," I said. "I believe he works on this boat."

"He did," the man said. "But he called in a couple days ago and quit."

I did my best at looking shocked. "I didn't know," I said. "I just flew in from Baltimore. I was going to surprise him. I went to his apartment, but he wasn't there, so I thought I'd catch him working."

"I'm the ship's purser, Stuart Moran. I took the call. Bill didn't say much. Just that he had to leave on short notice."

"Was he having problems?"

"Not on board. We're sorry to lose him. I don't know about his personal life."

I turned my attention to the boat. "It looks like you're getting ready to leave."

"We don't have any immediate plans, but we try to stay prepared to go when the call comes in."

I thought it might be helpful to talk to the crew, but I

couldn't do it with Moran standing watch. I turned away from the boat and bumped into Sam Hooker.

Hooker was just under six foot. Not a huge guy, but big for NASCAR and built solid. I slammed into him and bounced back a couple inches.

"Jesus Christ," I said, on an intake of breath. "Shit."

"Cute little blonds wearing pink skirts aren't allowed to take the Lord's name in vain," Hooker said, wrapping his hand around my arm, encouraging me to walk with him. "Not that it matters, you're going to hell for lying to Moran."

"How do you know I was lying to Moran?"

"I was listening. You're a really crappy liar." He stopped at the empty slip. "Guess what goes here?"

"A boat?"

"My boat. My sixty-five-foot Hatteras Convertible."

"And?"

"And it's gone. Do you see a boat here? No. Do you know who took it? Do you know where it is?"

The guy was deranged. One too many crashes. NASCAR drivers weren't known for being all that smart to begin with. Rattle their brains around a couple times and probably there's not much left.

I made a show of looking at my watch. "Gee, look at the time. I have to go. I have an appointment."

"Your brother took my goddamn boat," Hooker said. "And I want it back. I have exactly two weeks off before I have to start getting ready for the season, and I want to spend it on my boat. Two weeks. Is that too much to ask? *Two friggin' weeks.*"

"What makes you think my brother took your boat?"

"He told me!" Hooker's face was flushing under his tan. He had his glasses off, and his eyes were narrowed. "And I'm guessing he told you, too. You two are probably in this together, going around ripping off boats, selling them on the black market."

"You're a nutcase."

"Maybe selling them on the black market was pushing it."

"And you have anger management issues."

"People keep saying that to me. I think I'm a pretty reasonable guy. The truth is I was born under a conflicting sign. I'm on the cusp of Capricorn and Sagittarius."

"Which means?"

"I'm a sensitive asshole. Whatcha gonna do?"

It was a great line, and I really wanted to smile, but I didn't want to encourage Hooker, so I squashed the smile.

"Do you follow NASCAR?" he asked.

"No." I hiked my bag higher on my shoulder and headed for the concrete walk.

Hooker ambled after me. "Do you know who I am?"

"Yes."

"Do you want an autograph?"

"No!"

He caught up with me and walked beside me, hands in his pockets. "Now what?"

"I want a newspaper. I want to see what they said about the guy who was murdered."

Hooker cut his eyes to the dockmaster's office. "I can tell you more than the paper. The victim was a forty-five-year-old

17

security guard named Victor Sanchez. He was a nice guy with a wife and two kids. I knew him. They found his body when he didn't check in as scheduled. Someone slashed his throat just outside the dockmaster's building, and then the struggle got dragged inside. The office wasn't totally trashed, but logbooks and computers were wrecked. I guess the guard didn't go down easy."

"Anything stolen?"

"Not at first look, but they're still going through everything." He grinned. "I got that information from the cops. Cops love NASCAR drivers. I'm a celebrity."

Not too full of himself, eh?

Hooker ignored my eye roll. "Do you want to know what I think? I think the guard saw something he wasn't supposed to see. Like maybe someone was smuggling in drugs. All right, I didn't think of that all by myself. That's what the cops told me."

I'd reached the path at the water's edge. The marina stretched on either side of me. There were several high-rises in the distance. They were across from Fisher Island, looking over the harbor entrance. I turned and walked toward the high-rises. Hooker walked with me.

"Are there really boats bringing drugs in here?" I asked him.

Hooker shrugged. "Anything could come in here. Drugs, illegal aliens, art, Cuban cigars."

"I thought the Coast Guard intercepted that stuff."

"It's a big ocean."

"Okay, so tell me about my brother."

"I met him a couple months ago. I was in Miami for the last race of the season. When the race was over I hung around for a while, and I met Bill in Monty's."

"Monty's?"

"It's a bar. We just passed it. It's the place with the thatched roof and the pool. Anyway, we got to talking, and I needed someone to captain the boat for me down to the Grenadines. Bill had the week off and volunteered."

"I didn't know Bill was a boat captain."

"He'd just gotten his certification. It turns out Bill can do lots of things . . . captain a boat, steal a boat."

"Bill wouldn't steal a boat."

"Face it, sugar pie. He *stole* my boat. He called me up. He said he needed to use the boat. I said 'no way.' I told him *I* needed the boat. And now my boat's gone. Who do you think took it?"

"That's borrowing. And don't call me sugar pie."

The wind had picked up. Palm fronds were clattering above us, and the water was choppy.

"A front's moving in," Hooker said. "We're supposed to get rain tonight. Wouldn't have been great fishing anyway." He looked over at me. "What's wrong with sugar pie?"

I gave him a raised eyebrow.

"Hey, I'm from Texas. Cut me some slack," he said. "What am I supposed to call you? I don't know your name. Bill only mentioned his brother Barney."

I did a mental teeth-clench thing. "Bill doesn't have a brother. I'm Barney."

Hooker grinned at me. "You're Barney?" He gave a bark

of laughter and ruffled my hair. "I like it. Sort of Mayberry, but on you it's sexy."

"You're kidding."

"No. I'm getting turned on."

I suspected NASCAR drivers woke up turned on. "My name is Alexandra. My family started calling me Barney when I was a kid, and it stuck."

We'd reached one of the high-rises. Thirty-five to forty floors of condos, all with balconies, all with to-die-for views. All significantly beyond my budget. I tipped my head back and stared up at the building.

"Wow," I said. "Can you imagine living here?"

"I *do* live here. Thirty-second floor. Want to come up and see my view?"

"Maybe some other time. Places to go. Things to do." Small fear of heights. Distrust of NASCAR drivers . . . especially ones that are turned on.

The first drops of rain plopped down. Big fat drops that soaked into my pink skirt and splashed off my shoulders. Damn. No umbrella. No car. Four long blocks between me and Bill's apartment.

"Where's your car parked?" Hooker wanted to know.

"I don't have a car. I walked here from my brother's apartment."

"He's on Fourth and Meridian, right?"

"Right."

I looked at Hooker, and I wondered if he was the one who had trashed the apartment.

TWO

"I don't like the way you're looking at me," Hooker said.

"I was wondering what you're capable of doing."

The grin was back. "Most anything."

From what I knew of him, I thought this was probably true. He'd started driving on the dirt tracks of the Texas panhandle, scratching and clawing his way to the top. He had a reputation for being a fearless driver, but I didn't buy into the fearless thing. Everyone knew fear. It was the reaction that made the difference. Some people hated fear and avoided the experience. Some people endured it as a necessity. And some people became addicted to the rush. I was betting Hooker fell into the last category.

The wind picked up, the rain slanted into us, and we ran to the building for cover.

"Are you sure you don't want to visit the casa de Hooker?" Hooker asked. "It's not raining in the casa."

"Pass. I need to get back to the apartment."

"Okay," Hooker said. "We'll go back to the apartment."

"There's no *we*."

"Wrong. Until I get my boat back *we* are definitely *we*. Not that I don't trust you . . . but I don't trust you."

I was speechless. I felt my mouth involuntarily drop open and my nose wrinkle.

"Cute," Hooker said. "I like the nose wrinkle."

"If you're so convinced my brother stole your boat maybe you should report it to the police."

"I did report it to the police. I flew in yesterday and discovered the boat was missing. I tried calling your worthless brother, but of course he isn't answering. I asked for him at *Flex II* and found out he'd quit. I tried the dockmaster, but they have no freaking records left. Blood on everything. How inconvenient is that? I called the police this morning and they took my statement. I expect that's as far as it'll go."

"Maybe someone else took your boat. Maybe the guy who killed the night guard took your boat."

"Maybe your brother killed the night guard."

"Maybe you'd like a broken nose."

"Just what I'd expect from a woman named Barney," Hooker said.

I turned on my heel, crossed the lobby, and exited through the door to the parking lot. I put my head down and slogged through the wind and the rain, walking in the direction of Fourth Street. Just for the hell of it, I pointed Bill's car remote in a couple directions, but nothing beeped or flashed lights.

I heard a car engine rumble behind me, and Hooker rolled alongside in a silver Porsche Carrera.

The driver's-side window slid down. "Want a ride?" Hooker asked.

"I'm wet. I'll ruin your leather upholstery."

"No problem. The leather will wipe dry. Besides, I'm thinking of trading up to a Turbo."

I scurried around to the passenger side and wrenched the door open. "What do you expect to gain by following me around?"

"Sooner or later, your brother's going to get in touch with you. I want to be there."

"I'll call you."

"Yeah, right. That's gonna happen. Anyway, I haven't got anything better to do. I was supposed to be out on my boat this week."

I wanted to get rid of Hooker, but I didn't have a plan. Truth is, I didn't have a plan for *anything*. Alexandra Barnaby Girl Detective was stumped. Just pretend it's a transmission, I thought. You take it apart. You see what's broken. You put it back together. Really go through the apartment. Bill was friendly. He didn't have a well-developed sense of secret. Surely, he talked to someone. You have to find that someone. You found the key in the dog poop pile, right? You can find more.

Hooker made a U-turn on Meridian and pulled into a spot in front of Bill's building.

"Thanks for the ride," I said, and I hit the ground running. Okay, not exactly running, but I was moving right along. I was hoping to get into the apartment and close and lock the door before Hooker could elbow his way past me.

I got one foot on the sidewalk, and I was yanked back by my purse strap.

"Wait for me," Hooker said.

"Here's the thing," I told him. "You're not invited in."

"Here's the thing about driving NASCAR," Hooker said. "You learn not to wait for an invitation."

When I reached the front door I tried opening it without the key. If the door had opened, I would have sent Hooker in first. The door didn't open, so I unlocked it and stepped inside.

"Someone broke into this apartment," I told Hooker. "You can see where they pried the door open. It was unlocked when I got here this afternoon. I don't suppose it was you?"

Hooker looked at the doorjamb. "I was here around four o'clock yesterday and again this morning. I rang the bell, but I didn't try the door. I was so pissed off I could barely see. No, it wasn't me." He followed me up the stairs and gave a low whistle at the mess. "Bill's not much of a housekeeper."

"Do you think I should call the police?"

"If something's been stolen and you need a report to put in an insurance claim, yes. Otherwise, I can't see where it does much good. I don't see the boat police out searching for my Hatteras."

"I can't tell if anything's been stolen. This is the first time I've visited. The television and DVD player are still here."

Hooker strolled into the bedroom and gave another whistle. "That's a *lot* of condoms," he said. "That's a NASCAR amount of condoms."

"How about giving the NASCAR thing a rest," I said.

He returned to the living room. "Why don't you like NASCAR? NASCAR's fun."

"NASCAR's boring. A bunch of idiots, nothing personal, driving around in circles."

"What's *your* idea of fun?"

"Shopping for shoes. Having dinner in a nice restaurant. Any movie with Johnny Depp in it."

"Honey, that's all girl stuff. And Depp's done some pretty weird shit."

I was going piece by piece, picking through the clutter on the floor. I was torn between wanting to put things away and restore order, and feeling like I needed to keep the integrity of a crime scene. I decided to go with restoring order because I didn't want to believe something terrible had happened.

"Maybe you shouldn't be touching this stuff," Hooker said. "Maybe there's something bad going on."

"I'm doing denial," I told him. "Try to be supportive. Help me look."

"What are we looking for?"

"I don't know. A place to start. An address book. A name scribbled on a piece of paper. Matchbooks he picked up in bars."

"I don't need matchbooks. I know the bars Bill liked. We went out drinking together."

"Do you know any of his friends?"

"It looked to me like Bill was friends with everyone."

An hour later, I had everything put away. Couch cushions were back in place. Books were neatly shelved. Knives, forks, assorted junk, and condoms were returned to drawers.

"What have we got here?" I said to Hooker. "Did you find anything?"

"A black lace G-string under his bed. Your brother is an animal. What have you got?"

"Nothing. But he made that phone call to me and he cleaned out his refrigerator. The only thing left is a can of Budweiser."

"Barney, that doesn't mean he cleaned his refrigerator. It means he had to go shopping for more Bud."

"These days most men call me Alex."

"I'm not most men," Hooker said. "I like Barney. Tell me about the phone call."

"Bill said he had to leave Miami for a while. I could hardly hear him over a boat engine. He said if some guys showed up looking for him, I shouldn't talk to them. And, he said I should tell you to kiss his exhaust pipe. I heard a woman scream and the line went dead."

"Wow," Hooker said.

It was six-thirty, and it was getting dark. It was still raining, I didn't have a car, and all that was standing between me and starvation was a single can of Bud. What's worse, I suspected if I opened it I'd have to share it with Hooker.

"Do you have any ideas?" I asked Hooker.

"Lots of them."

"About how to find Bill?"

"No. I don't have any of *those* ideas. My ideas run more to food and sex."

"You're on your own with the sex. I wouldn't mind hearing your ideas about food."

Hooker took his car keys out of his pants pocket. "For starters, I think we should get some."

I did a raised eyebrow.

"Some *food*," Hooker said.

We went to a diner on Collins Avenue. We had beer and burgers, French fries and onion rings and chocolate cake for dessert. There was healthier food on the menu but we weren't having any of it.

"The all-American meal," Hooker said.

"Did you ever eat here with Bill? Do you think anyone knows him here?"

"Pick out the prettiest waitress and I bet she knows Bill."

I had a photo with me. A picture of Bill smiling, standing beside a big fish on a big hook.

The waitress dropped our check on the table and I showed her the photo.

"Do you know him?" I asked.

"Sure. Everyone knows him. That's Wild Bill."

"He was supposed to meet us here," I said. "Did we get the time wrong and miss him?"

"No. I haven't seen him in days. I haven't seen him hanging out at the clubs, either."

We left the diner under clear skies. The rain had stopped and the city was steaming itself dry.

"You're getting better at lying," Hooker said, when we were belted into the Porsche. "In fact, you were frighteningly convincing."

He turned the key in the ignition and the car growled to life. When you grow up in a garage you learn to appreciate machinery, and I got a rush every time Hooker revved the Porsche. As vocal as I was about hating NASCAR, I've been to a couple races. Last year I was at Richmond. And the year before that I was at Martinsville. I wouldn't want to admit to anyone what happened to me when all those guys started their engines at the beginning of the race, but it was as good as any man had ever made me feel in bed. Of course, maybe I was just sleeping with the wrong men.

"Now what?" Hooker wanted to know. "Do you want to flash that photo some more tonight?"

It had been a long, exhausting day with a whole bunch of terrifying moments, starting with the takeoff from BWI. Nothing had turned out as I'd hoped. My sneakers were wet, my skirt was wrinkled, and I needed a breath mint. I wanted to think that the day couldn't get any worse, but I knew worse was possible.

"Sure," I said. "Let's keep going."

We were on Collins, heading south. The art deco buildings were lit for the night and neon was blazing everywhere. There were surprisingly few people on the street.

"Where's the nightlife?" I asked. "I expected to see more people out."

"The nightlife doesn't start until midnight."

Midnight! I'd be comatose by midnight. I couldn't remember the last time I stayed up that late. It might have been New Year's Eve three years ago. I was dating Eddie Falucci. I was a lot younger then. I pulled the visor down to take a look at my hair in the mirror and shrieked when I saw myself.

Hooker swerved to the right, jumped the curb, and skidded to a stop.

"Ulk," I said, flung against the shoulder harness.

"What the hell was that?" Hooker asked.

"What?"

"That shriek!"

"It was my hair. It scared me."

"You're a nut! You almost made me crash the car! I thought there was a body in the road."

"I've seen you drive. You crash cars all the time. You're not going to pin this on me. Why didn't you tell me my hair was a wreck?"

Hooker eased off the curb and cut his eyes to me. "I was worried it was *supposed* to look like that."

"I need a shower. I need to change my clothes. I need a nap."

"Where are you staying?"

"At Bill's apartment," I told him.

"You're kidding."

"I've thought it through, and it's perfectly safe. It's already been searched. What are the chances of the bad guys returning? Low, right? It's probably the safest apartment in South Beach." I almost had myself convinced.

"Do you have club clothes with you?"

"No."

"I can probably come up with something."

Hooker eased the Porsche to a stop in front of Bill's building. "I'll be back at eleven," he said.

• • •

The last thought in my head was of Hooker scrounging a dress for me. He probably had a bunch of them under his bed, rolling around like dust bunnies. It was still in the front of my mind when I woke up. It didn't stay there for long.

I opened my eyes and stared up at a very scary guy. He was at the side of the bed, snarling down at me. Hard to tell his age. Late twenties to midthirties. He was maybe six foot four, and his muscles were grotesquely overdeveloped, making him look more science fiction creature than human being. He had a thick neck and a Marine buzz cut. A ragged white scar ran from his hairline, through his right eyebrow, down his cheek, and through his mouth, ending in the middle of his chin. Whatever had slashed through his face had taken out his eye, because his right eye was fake. It was a big shiny glass orb, larger than his seeing eye, inexplicably terrifying. His mouth was stitched together in such a way that the upper lip was always held in a snarl.

I stared at him in stupefied horror for a heart-stopping second, and then I started screaming.

He grabbed me by my shirtfront, picked me up off the bed like I was a rag doll, and gave me a shake.

"Stop," he said. "Shut up or I'll hit you." He looked at me dangling at arm's length. "Maybe I'll hit you anyway. Just for fun."

I was so freaked out my mouth felt frozen. "Wha do wha whan?" I asked.

He gave me another shake. "What?"

"What do you want?"

"I know who you are. I know lots of stuff and I want your brother. He has something that belongs to my boss. And my boss wants it back. Since we can't find your brother, we're going to take you instead. See if we can't swap you out. And if your brother won't deal, that's okay too, because then *I* get you."

"What does Bill have that belongs to your boss? What's this about?"

"Bill has a woman. And it's about fear and what it can do for you. And about being smart. My boss is real smart. And someday he's going to be real powerful. More powerful than he is now."

"Who's your boss?"

"You'll find out soon enough. And you should cooperate or you'll end up like that night watchman. He didn't want to tell us nothing, and then he tried to stop us from going into the dockmaster's office to get the occupancy list. What a dope."

"So you killed him?"

"You ask too many questions. I'm gonna put you down now, and you're gonna walk out with me, and you're not gonna give me any trouble, right?"

"Right," I said. And then I kicked him as hard as I could in the nuts.

He just stood there without breathing for a couple beats, so I kicked him again.

The second kick was the home run because the big guy's glass eye almost fell out of his head. He released his grip on my shirt and went to his knees. He grabbed his crotch, threw up, and then went facedown into the mess he'd just made.

I fell back on my ass and scrambled away crab style. I got

to my feet and bolted, out of the bedroom, through the living room, down the stairs. I was on the sidewalk, ready to start running and not stop until I reached Baltimore, when Hooker pulled to the curb in the Porsche.

"B-b-big guy," I said. "B-b-big guy in Bill's apartment."

Hooker felt under his seat, brought out a gun, and got out of the car.

This did nothing to make me feel safe. If anything, it added to the panic.

"Don't worry about the gun," Hooker said. "I'm from Texas. We give guns as baptism presents. I knew how to shoot before I could read."

"I don't like g-g-guns."

"Yeah, but sometimes you need them. Lots of people need to shoot varmints in Texas."

"Like coyotes?"

"That would be in the country. In my neighborhood it was mostly pissed-off husbands shooting guys in their naked ass as they jumped out bedroom windows." Hooker looked to the open door and then up to the windows. "Tell me about this big guy."

"He was big. Real big. Like he didn't even fit in his skin. Like the Hulk, except he wasn't green. And he didn't have a neck. And he had a scar running down the side of his face into his mouth where he was all drooly and snarly. And his eye . . . his eye. Actually he didn't have an eye. Only one. The other one was fake, but it was a cheap fake. Like it was sort of too big for the *real* eye. And it didn't move. No matter what the real eye did, the one big cheap fake eye just stared out at me. Didn't blink, or anything. It was . . . frightening."

"Did he have a name?"

"I'm calling him Puke Face."

"Did Puke Face say anything interesting? Like why he was in Bill's bedroom?"

"He said Bill had a woman who belonged to his boss, so he was going to trade me. And that his boss was smart, and that this was all about fear and what it can do for you."

A blind was slightly pulled aside at one of Bill's windows. Hooker aimed his gun at the window. The blind dropped back into place, and a moment later we heard a crash from the other side of the apartment building. "Unh," someone said. And then there was the sound of receding footsteps. *Ka thud, ka thud, ka thud.*

"Sounds to me like he just jumped out Bill's window," Hooker said. "And he's limping."

"I kicked him in the nuts."

"Yeah, that might make him limp. Do you still want to do the club scene?"

I nodded. "I have to find Bill."

Hooker beeped the Porsche locked, and he tossed a shimmery scrap of material at me. "I hope this fits. It was the best I could do on short notice."

"It's still warm."

"Yeah, you probably don't want to know all the details."

I held the dress up by its little string straps. "There's not much here."

33

"Trust me, you don't want a lot of dress. This is Miami. They really mean it when they say *less is more*."

I followed Hooker back into the apartment, and we cautiously looked around.

"I'm a little flustered," I said.

"Perfectly understandable. If you need help getting into the dress . . ."

Yeah, right. Not that flustered.

"This is disgusting," Hooker said, upper lip curled at the mess on the rug.

"He threw up after I kicked him the second time."

Hooker instinctively put his hands to his package. "I could throw up just thinking about it."

I dragged myself and the dress into the bathroom. I did some deep breathing and got myself calmed down enough to keep going. Hooker was out there with his gun, and I was safe in here, I told myself. Just get changed and get out.

I stripped my clothes off and exchanged my bikini undies for a thong. I dropped the dress over my head and tugged it down. It was silver metallic with some spandex. It had a V-neck that plunged halfway to my doodah, and the skirt fell two inches below my ass. I swiped some mascara on my lashes, sprayed my hair into a style that looked like maybe my brain had exploded, and I tarted up my mouth. I'd brought two pairs of shoes with me . . . the sneakers and a pair of silver strappy sandals with four-inch stiletto heels. Shoes for every occasion. I slid my feet into the sandals and swung out of the bathroom.

"Holy cow," Hooker said.

"Too short?"

"Now *I'm* flustered."

Hooker had his hair gelled back. He was wearing black linen slacks, a short-sleeve black silk shirt patterned with fluorescent purple palm trees, and loafers without socks. He had a Cartier watch on his wrist, and he smelled nice.

"Easy to see how Puke Face got in. The door is completely broken," Hooker said. "If there's anything of value here, you should hide it or take it with you."

I gave Hooker the photo of Bill to put in his pocket. "The only thing of value is the television, and it's not that great."

I followed Hooker down the stairs and out to the Porsche. Hooker drove a block and a half over to Washington and valet parked the car in front of a club.

"We could have walked," I said.

"Boy, you don't know much. You probably think owning a Porsche is about power and bling. Okay, power and bling is part of it, but it's mostly about valet parking. It's about the sucking up and the ogling and the envy. It's about the *arrival,* baby.

He was being funny, but there was some truth to what he said. There were about a hundred people milling around outside the club. These were the people who weren't thin enough, young enough, rich enough, or famous enough to get on the A list. None of them had arrived in a Porsche. And none of them had given the doorman enough money to compensate for their shortcomings.

The doorman smiled when he saw Hooker and motioned him forward. I guess being a famous NASCAR guy has its compensations. The smile widened when he saw me attached to Hooker. I guess having legs that went from my ass all the way down to the ground had its compensations, too.

We took a moment to adjust to the dark and the lights and the pulse from the DJ. The women dancing onstage were all wearing feathers. Big feather headpieces, feathered G-strings, feathered bikini tops on their big fake boobs. The feathers were peach and aqua and lavender. Very South Beach avian.

"You do the men," Hooker yelled at me over the music, pressing the photo of Bill into my hand. "Hit up the bartenders and security guys. I'll do the women. I'll meet you at the exit in a half hour. If you see Pukey, get up on a table where people can see you and start dancing."

If you want to chat with someone in a club you have to yell in their ear or hope they read lips. I found a bunch of guys who knew Bill but none who knew where he was. A bartender gave me a cosmo. I felt a lot more relaxed after I slurked it down. I even started to feel a little brave. I met Hooker in a half hour and we left together.

"Did you get anything?" he asked.

"A cosmopolitan."

"Anything else?"

"Nope. That was it."

"I didn't get a lot either. I'll fill you in later."

The valet brought the car around. We got in and drove three blocks to another club. The experience was almost identical, except this time the women performing were dressed like Carmen Miranda. Lots of fruit on their heads, colorful rumba ruffles on their G-strings, and rumba ruffles on the bikini tops that held up their big fake boobs. I drank another cosmo. And I found out nothing.

"Do you suppose it's possible that we're being followed?" I asked Hooker. "I keep seeing this same guy. Someone different from Puke Face. He's all in black. Slicked-back hair. He was in the diner. And now he's here in the club. And I think he's watching me."

"Sugar, everyone's watching you."

We hit a third club, and I belted back my third cosmopolitan. I screamed at a couple guys, asking about Bill. And then I danced with a couple guys. I had part of a fourth cosmo, and I danced some more. I was liking the music a lot. And I was feeling very unconcerned over Puke Face. In fact, I was feeling pretty darned happy.

In this club, the women onstage were men. They were all dressed in a jungle theme, and they were excellent, except I'd gotten used to seeing a lot of big fake boobs and it felt like something was missing here.

I'd stopped worrying about the time, worrying about meeting Hooker at the designated exit. Probably a half hour had passed, but for some unexplainable reason the numbers on my watch had gotten blurry. Actually, it occurred to me that I might be just a teensy drunk.

Hooker plastered his hand against the small of my back and he guided me off the floor.

"Hey," I said. "I was dancing."

"I noticed."

He maneuvered me out the door and into the warm night air. He gave the parking attendant his ticket and ten dollars.

"So," I said to him. "What's up?"

"I've been watching you dance in this little dress for the last half hour, and you probably want to rephrase that question."

"Are we going to another club?"

"No. We're going home." He looked down at my shoes while we waited for the car to be brought around. "Don't your feet hurt in those shoes?"

"Fortunately, I lost the feeling in my feet an hour ago."

I woke up in Hooker's guest bedroom with the sun pouring in on me. I was still wearing the little dress. I was alone. And I was pretty sure I hadn't done anything romantic before I fell asleep. Hooker had refused to drive me back to Bill's. He said it wasn't safe. I guess he could be right, but it didn't feel safe here either.

I rolled out of bed and padded barefoot across the room to the window. I looked down and had a moment of vertigo. The ground was *w-a-a-ay* down there. Now here's the thing . . . I don't love *high*. Hurtling around a race track at 120 mph, in a metal enclosure resting on four wheels, feels natural to me. Being shot up thirty-two floors in an elevator does not. And the thought of dropping thirty-two floors turns everything in my intestines to liquid.

I carefully backed up and made my way out of the room, down a short hall, and into a large living-dining area. An entire wall of the living room and dining room was glass. I could see a balcony beyond the glass. And beyond the balcony was air. And a seagull flying backward.

The kitchen opened off the dining area. Hooker was lounging against a kitchen counter with a mug of coffee in his hand.

The kitchen was very white with splashes of cobalt blue. The living room and dining room mirrored the white-and-blue color scheme. Very contemporary. Very expensive looking.

"Why is that seagull flying backwards?" I asked Hooker.

"Wind. We've got a front blowing through."

And then I noticed it. The sway of the building.

There was a loud *crash,* and I turned to the window in time to see a seagull bounce off the glass and drop like a rock onto the patio.

"Omigod!" I said.

Hooker didn't blink. "Happens all the time. Poor dumb buggers."

"We should do something. Will he be okay? Maybe we should take him to a vet."

Hooker walked over and looked out. "He might be okay. Oops. Nope, he's not okay." Hooker drew the curtains. "Vulture food."

"You're kidding! How awful."

"It's the chain of life. Perfectly natural."

"I'm not used to being this far off the ground," I said. "I don't really love being up this high." Alexandra Barnaby, master of the understatement.

Hooker sipped some coffee. "It didn't bother you last night. Last night you loved *everything.* You tried to get me to take my clothes off."

"I did not!"

"Okay, I'm busted. You didn't. Actually, I volunteered but you'd already passed out."

I cautiously crept to the kitchen and poured myself a mug of coffee.

"Why are you walking like that?" Hooker wanted to know.

"It's spooky being up here. People weren't meant to live way up here. I feel . . . insecure."

"If God didn't intend for people to live up here he wouldn't have invented reinforced concrete."

"I'm not much of a drinker. My tongue feels like it's stuck to the top of my mouth."

"You keep talking dirty like that and I'm going to get excited."

"You get excited, and I'm leaving."

"It would help if you weren't wearing that dress." His eyes moved north to my hair. "Although, the hair is enough to make most men go limp. Not me, of course. But *most* men."

I could hear flapping and scuffling sounds coming from the patio. "Is that the seagull?" I asked

Hooker pulled the drape aside and peeked out. "Not exactly." There were some loud angry bird sounds, and Hooker jumped back and pulled the drape shut. "Food fight," he said.

There was a breakfast bar separating the kitchen from the dining room. Four stools lined up in front of the bar. A photo in a silver frame sat on the far end of the breakfast bar. It was a picture of a boat.

"Is this your boat?" I asked, picking the picture up to see it better.

"It *was* my boat. Prettiest boat ever made. And fast . . . for a fishing boat."

"Last night I talked to a bunch of guys who knew Bill, and

the consensus is that Bill made a last-minute decision to take off. Apparently, *Flex II* had just returned from a trip to the Bahamas. Bill went clubbing the night he got back, but he was supposed to sail the following morning, so he cut out early. Around one AM. And that's the last anyone's seen him."

"When did he call you?"

"Around two AM."

"So he comes back from a trip to the Bahamas," Hooker said. "He goes clubbing until one AM. He calls me at two AM. And he calls you right after he hangs up with me. He's on a boat. *My* boat!"

"*Maybe* he's on your boat."

"It's the only boat missing in the goddamn marina. I checked. He tells you some guys are going to be looking for him. A woman screams. That's the last we hear from him. An hour later, someone kills the night watchman."

I told him about the night watchman conversation I had with Puke Face. "So what does all this mean?" I asked Hooker.

"Don't know, darlin'."

"I need to go back to Bill's apartment. I left my duffel bag there. I wasn't thinking clearly."

Hooker palmed a set of keys off the bar. "I can help with that. NASCAR Guy to the rescue. After we get you out of the dress and into some shorts we can get on with the Bill search."

I followed him out the door, into a foyer with two elevators. Hooker pushed the button and looked at me.

"Are you okay? You just went white."

That's because my heart stopped pumping when I saw the elevators. "I'm fine," I said. "A little hung over."

41

We stepped into the elevator, Hooker hit the lobby button, and the doors closed. I sucked in some air and squinched my eyes shut. I didn't whimper or yell out "we're gonna drop like a rock and die." So I was sort of proud of myself.

"What's with the closed eyes?" Hooker wanted to know.

"I don't like to see the numbers changing."

Hooker slid his arm around me and hugged me close to him. "Cute."

Hooker parked the Porsche in front of Bill's apartment building, and we both got out. Bill's front door swung open when I pushed it. No key necessary. Definitely broken.

We went upstairs and froze at the entrance to the living room. The apartment had been tossed. Again. Not trashed, like the first time, but clearly searched. Couch cushions were slightly askew. Drawers weren't entirely closed. My duffel bag wasn't exactly as I'd left it.

"Why would someone go through twice?"

"Maybe we've got two different people."

We walked through the bedroom and bathroom. Nothing appeared to be missing. The Puke Face mess was sort of caked into the rug and not smelling too good.

"Give me ten minutes to shower and change my clothes. And then I'm out of here," I said.

I took a fast shower, blasted my hair with the hair dryer, and got dressed in shorts, T-shirt, and the white sneakers.

Hooker wasn't in the apartment when I came out of the bathroom, so I slid the duffel bag strap over my shoulder and went downstairs to look for him. I found him talking to one of Bill's neighbors. Smart. NASCAR Guy had a brain. Not to give him too much, I thought motivation helped. He really wanted his boat back.

It was late morning, and the sky was a glorious blue, no clouds in sight. The wind had cut back to a gentle stirring of air. The pale stucco buildings with the peach and aqua trim sparkled in the sunlight. Flowers were blooming everywhere, on trees, on vines, on bushes. Lizards rustled in the undergrowth. I was keeping guard for the cockroach.

Hooker left Bill's neighbor when he saw me emerge from the building. He walked over to me and took the duffel bag off my shoulder. Fine by me. No reason to get carried away with women's rights.

"I didn't want to interrupt," I said. "I assume you were asking about Bill?"

"Yeah. I've been going door to door. Most were no answers. I found the super's unit and told him about the broken lock. I said Bill was cruising, and you were here on vacation. He's going to take care of it. I also suggested he get someone in to shampoo the rug. The guy I was just talking to is retired and stays home all the time. His name's Melvin. His wife doesn't let him smoke in the house, so he's out on the front porch a lot. Said he has trouble sleeping and lots of times he just sits out and smokes."

I smiled at Hooker. "And he saw the guys who broke into Bill's apartment?"

"Both times."

THREE

Hooker dropped the duffel bag into the back of the Porsche. "According to Melvin, the first break-in occurred around eleven, Tuesday night. He said there were two guys. He didn't see them go in. He just saw them leave. He said he thought they were Bill's friends. It turns out Bill has lots of parties. Big surprise, hunh? He said they got into a black Town Car when they left. He didn't know any more than that."

"He give you a description of them?"

"It was dark. He couldn't see much. Medium build. Average height. He thought they were Cuban."

"And the second time?"

"He said they were Caucasian. Two guys again. This time, one went in and one stayed out. Dark slacks. Dark short-sleeve shirts. He was pretty sure they weren't wearing uniforms, but the *Flex* crew wears navy, so I'm not ruling that out. He said the one guy had slicked-back hair like a gangster."

"That sounds like the guy in the diner and the club. Remember I told you he was watching me?"

"It also sounds like half the guys in Miami. Melvin said the one guy walked right in, like he was expected."

"The lock was broken."

"Melvin didn't know about that. Melvin said he saw us leave. And then about five minutes later, the guys in black showed up. Melvin figured Bill was home. I think he felt bad that he didn't report it."

"Did Melvin see Puke Face just now?"

"No. Melvin was inside watching TV."

"Melvin isn't too smart."

"Melvin is at least three hundred years old."

"There seem to be a lot of people involved in this."

"We have the guys who tossed the apartment the first time. We have Puke Face. And we have the guys who tossed the apartment the second time."

"Unsettling."

"Yeah, but don't worry. I could clean their clocks if I had to."

"Because you're the clock cleaner?"

"Because I'm NASCAR Guy!"

"Frightening."

"Get in the car," Hooker said. "I'm taking you to breakfast at the News Café. *Everyone* eats breakfast at the News Café."

Five minutes later, we were on the sidewalk in front of the outdoor eating area of the News Café. We were waiting for a table, and we weren't alone. There were lots of people waiting for tables. We were all milling around on the sidewalk, gawking at the lucky people who had food, gawking at the people across the street who were rollerblading in thongs.

"This is Ocean Drive," Hooker said. "And as you can see, across the street there's a small green belt with a bike path, and beyond the green belt is the beach and the ocean."

"Would you rollerblade in a thong?"

"I wouldn't rollerblade in body armor."

"What happens when someone falls?"

"I move in closer to get a better look," Hooker said. "There's usually a lot of blood."

Hooker waded into the diners, stopping here and there to say hello and ask about Bill. He made the rounds, and he came back to the sidewalk. "Nothing," he said.

After ten minutes of waiting, we got a table. Hooker ordered eggs, a stack of pancakes, sausage, juice, and coffee. I got a bran muffin and coffee.

Hooker poured syrup on his pancakes and looked over at my bran muffin. "Yum," he said.

"If there's one thing I can't stand it's a skinny wiseass."

"I'm not skinny," he said. "I'm buff. I'm ripped. Geeky guys are skinny."

There was a steady stream of guys coming up to Hooker, clapping him on the back, doing weird handshakes with him. "Hey, man," they'd say, "how's it going? What's happening?" And Hooker would say, "It's going good, man." Sometimes Hooker would say, "I'm looking for Wild Bill. Have you seen him?" And the answer was always the same. "Haven't seen him. What's up with that?"

A Miami Beach cop car parked at the curb across the street,

followed by two trucks and an RV. A bunch of people got out of the trucks and began off-loading equipment.

Hooker forked pancakes into his mouth. "Two possibilities," he said. "A movie with a volleyball scene, or else it's a fashion shoot. You can tell which it is when the girls come out of the RV. If they have big boobs, it's a volleyball scene."

"I seem to be the only one interested."

"At this time of year Ocean Drive is filled with this stuff. It gets old. Just like the club scene gets old."

"I can't believe you said that. NASCAR Guy thinks the club scene is boring. You keep that up and you'll ruin your image."

"I'll try to be extra shallow today to make up for it."

I finished my muffin, and I was working on a second cup of coffee when my cell phone rang. Hooker and I locked eyes at the first ring, both of us hoping it was Bill. I pulled the phone out of my bag and did a mental groan at the number on the screen. It was my mother.

"Where are you?" she wanted to know. "I've been calling your apartment, and there's never any answer. Then I called your work number, and they said you took a couple days off."

"I felt like I needed warm weather, so I flew down to Miami to visit Bill."

"You hate to fly."

"Yes, but I did it. And here I am. And it's warm."

"How is your brother? He never calls me."

"Bill isn't here. He's at sea, but he should be back any day now."

"When you see him, tell him his friend called yesterday looking for him."

"What friend is that?"

"He didn't leave a name, but he had a Hispanic accent. He said Bill was expecting his call. Something about a property dispute. Apparently Bill inadvertently took something that belongs to this man."

I talked to my mom for another minute, promised I'd be on guard for the roaches, and then I disconnected.

"You're going straight to hell," Hooker said. "You just lied to your mother, didn't you?"

"I don't want her to worry."

"Lying for a good cause. That's the worst kind of lying." He threw some money on the table and stood. "Let's go to the marina and see if my boat's drifted in."

I followed Hooker through the crowd to his Porsche. "Are you telling me you don't lie once in a while for a good cause?"

"I lie all the time. It's just that I'm going to hell for so many other reasons, lying doesn't hardly count."

"You didn't call my mother, did you?"

"No. Was I supposed to?"

"Someone with a Hispanic accent called and asked for Bill. They said it was regarding a property dispute."

Hooker parked at his condo building, and we walked up to the marina. The crime scene tape was still restricting entrance to the dockmaster's office, but it had been removed from the entrance to Pier E. We walked past Pier E to Hooker's pier. *Flex II* was tied up at the end of the dock. No one was on deck. The helicopter was still in place.

"How often does a boat like that cruise?" I asked Hooker.

"The corporate boats are out a lot when the weather's good. The executives use them to sweet talk clients and politicians. It's always nice to have a politician in your pocket."

We stopped at Hooker's slip. No boat.

"Shit," Hooker said. It was more a thought than an exclamation.

There was movement on board *Flex,* and we both turned to check it out. A couple crew members were setting out lunch at the back of the boat.

"Someone's on board," Hooker said.

Two pretty young women in bikini tops and wrap skirts came on deck. They were followed by two men who were in their late sixties, maybe early seventies. Moments later, they were joined by a man in a *Flex* uniform and a poster boy for the young, up-and-coming corporate executive.

"Do you recognize anyone?" I asked Hooker.

"The tall gray-haired guy in the uniform is the captain. I don't remember his name, but he's been around forever. He captained *Flex I* and then moved over to *Flex II* last year when the boat was launched."

"Is there still a *Flex I*?"

"No. It's been scrapped."

"Do you know anyone else?"

"The bald guy with a face like a bulldog. He's a state senator. The guy modeling for Tommy Bahama looks like corporate chum. I don't know who the women are. Entertainment probably."

"And what about the remaining man?"

"Don't know him."

The remaining man was average height and chunky. His thick, wavy hair was silver. His face was doughy. He was wearing tan slacks and a floral-print short-sleeve shirt. We were some distance from him, but something about his body language and the set to his mouth was repelling and sent my thoughts back to the giant flying cockroach.

"Want to share your thoughts?" Hooker asked.

"I was thinking about a cockroach."

"That would have been my second guess."

"He's probably a perfectly nice guy," I said.

Hooker was blatantly staring, hands in his pants pockets, back on his heels. "He looks like he kills people and eats them for breakfast."

The man looked our way and Hooker smiled and waved. "Hi," Hooker said.

The man watched us for a moment without expression and then turned his back on us and continued his conversation with the senator.

"Nice," I said to Hooker. "Now you've annoyed the professional killer."

"I was being friendly. For a minute there I thought we were bonding."

We turned away from *Flex* and walked back to the concrete path. There was a lot of activity around us. The weather was perfect, if you like hot and hotter. It was noon Friday, and by

Miami standards this seemed to constitute weekend. Hooker was wearing sandals, totally washed-out jeans with a lot of rips and holes in them, a bleach-stained black sleeveless T-shirt, sports sunglasses, and a ball cap that advertised tires. I had sunglasses but no hat and no sunblock. I felt like I could cook an egg on my scalp, and if I looked cross-eyed I swear, I could see my nose blistering.

A guy was walking toward us on the path. He had a schnauzer on a Burberry leash, and the dog was prancing along, head high, eyes vigilant under bushy schnauzer eyebrows. The guy caught my attention because he was everything Hooker wasn't. His brown hair was perfectly cut and styled. His face was clean shaved. His white three-button knit shirt was stain free and unwrinkled. His khaki shorts were crisply ironed and a perfect fit. He was maybe an inch shorter than Hooker, and he had only slightly less muscle. My best friend, Marjorie, says you can always tell if a guy is gay by the size of his pores. And, even from a distance I could see that this guy exfoliated.

The dog and his walker got even with Hooker and me, and the dog stopped and growled at Hooker.

"I am *so sorry*," the guy said. "He's just been in a mood today. I think he must need a bran muffin."

"No problem," Hooker said. "You've got a good grip on the leash, right?"

"Absolutely. *Down, Cujo*," the guy said to the dog.

"His name is Cujo?"

"No. Not really. His name is Brian."

I smiled at the dog walker. "Jude?"

"Yes?" He looked over at me, recognition slammed into him, and his eyes opened wide. "Barney? Omigod. I don't believe this!"

"This is Jude Corker. We went to grade school and high school together," I said to Hooker.

"Jude Corker, Sam Hooker. Sam Hooker, Jude Corker."

"Everyone calls me Judey now," he said, extending his hand to Hooker. "Barney and I were such good friends, and then we went off to college and completely lost touch."

"How long have you been down here?" I asked him.

"I went to school here and decided to stay. I met a lovely man my junior year and that was it. He had a thriving business here, so of course we couldn't move."

"And you're still a couple?"

"We broke up a year ago. Just one of those things. But I'm a Miamian now. What brings you here?"

"Bill lives here."

"No! I didn't know that. I haven't run across him." He looked back at Hooker. "And who is this person? Is this a love interest?"

"Associate."

"Nice body," Judey said. "But the hat has to go. Tires. Ick."

Hooker smiled at him. Friendly.

"I don't suppose you're gay?" Judey asked Hooker.

"Nope," Hooker said. "Not even a little."

"Too bad. The sleeveless tee is a good look for you."

Hooker kept smiling. NASCAR Guy wasn't threatened by Gay Guy.

"And so what does 'associate' mean?" Judey asked. "Because girlfriend, I don't see associate in his eyes. He's looking at you like you're lunch. And shame on you," Judey said, turning to Hooker. "You have her standing out here in the sun without a hat. Look at her little pink nose and her poor pink scalp. You're never going to get to first base if you let this pretty little blond sunburn."

Hooker took his hat off and put it on my head.

"Not *that* hat," Judey said. "That hat belongs in a garage. She's already been there done that. Go get her a nice hat."

Hooker blew out a sigh. "You're going to be here when I get back, right?" he said to me.

"Where would I go?"

"God only knows," Hooker said. And he ambled off.

"He's gorgeous," Judey said. "In a brutish kind of way. Totally ripped."

"He drives NASCAR. And he's from Texas."

"Omigod. Say no more. He's an asshole, isn't he?"

I looked after Hooker. "Truth is, I've known worse. As far as assholes go, he isn't all that bad."

I told Judey about the phone call and the missing boat and the searched apartment. I told him about Puke Face, and I was on a description of the second search when Hooker returned. He took his hat off my head and replaced it with a pink hat that said SEXY in pasted-on rhinestones.

"Much better," Judey said. "Totally tasteless. Very trashy. It's perfect Miami."

"I don't suppose you know any of the *Flex* crew members?" Hooker asked him.

53

"Well, of course I do. I know a very nice young man named Todd. And since the boat is tied up at the dock and doesn't seem to be going anywhere, Todd is most likely on the beach."

Ten minutes later we were all crammed into Hooker's Porsche. Hooker had the top down, and Judey and Brian were scrunched into the tiny backseat.

"Park at Eleventh," Judey said. "Todd is always at Eleventh Street."

The beach was broad at Eleventh and stretched far in both directions. The sand was white and hard packed. Vendors parked on the beach, selling iced coffee and assorted stuff. And bodies seeking skin cancer were everywhere. The bodies were fat and thin and everything in between. Some of the women were topless. Thongs were the order of the day. And a lot of the thongs were sucked into more cheek than I ever wanted to see.

Traffic buzzed in the background, competing with cell phones and MP3 players and with the *shushhhh* of waves breaking far out and calmly rolling in, swirling around the people who ventured into the water to wade and splash. Freighters and tankers hung on the horizon. A prop plane flew overhead trailing a banner that advertised a club.

We walked into the crowd of greased-up abs and flabs with Judey leading the way and Brian straining at the leash, snapping and snarling at passing dogs.

"He's *so* alpha," Judey explained. "It's the German in him."

"There's so much on display here," I said to Hooker.

"Doesn't it ruin the romance? Would you want to date one of these topless, thonged women?"

Hooker looked around. "I want to date *all* of them. No wait a minute. Not that fat one with the hair on her chin."

"That's a man."

"I don't want to date him."

"Jeepers," Judey said. "I don't want to date him either."

"It's like being in a bakery," Hooker said. "You look at the doughnuts and you want to eat them. Admit it, you walk into a bakery and you get hungry, right?"

"It's not the same."

"It is to a man. This beach is just one big bakery."

"You are so eloquent!" Judey said to Hooker.

"That's because I'm NASCAR Guy," Hooker said. He slung an arm around my shoulders and dragged me close to him. "This conversation isn't doing much to improve my chances of scoring with you, is it?"

"There he is," Judey said. "That's Todd. He's the luscious thing on the blue beach towel. And he's wearing his red thong. Don't you love it? He's such a Mr. Pickle Pants!"

Todd was stretched on a beach towel, broiling himself on the sand, halfway to the water's edge. He looked like he was probably in his early twenties. And Judey was right . . . Todd was luscious. He stood when he saw us, so we could better appreciate his lusciousness. His body was toned and golden, and the red thong showed off a terrific ass and a bunch of lumpy things in the front. I was trying to think positive about the bakery concept, but the bagels in his bathing suit weren't doing a lot for me.

Todd bent over to pet Brian, and I made an instant mental note to *never* bend over in a thong. Brian didn't share my perspective and thought it was all just fine. In fact, Brian was beside himself, wagging his tail, vibrating with happiness.

Judey introduced us to Todd and told him Bill was missing.

"Missing," Todd said. "What do you mean?"

"Gone. Poof. Disappeared," Judey said.

"We were told he quit."

"Yes. But then he disappeared. And his apartment has been searched. Twice!" Judey said.

"I don't know what to say. He didn't seem to be into anything weird. One minute he was there, and then he was gone. I was sorry to see him take off. He was a good guy."

Brian was dancing around, wanting to be petted some more. He was kicking sand up with his schnauzer toenails, and the sand was sticking to Todd's oiled, perfectly waxed legs.

"Did you work with him on the last trip?" I asked Todd, trying hard not to stare at the lumpy banana sling.

"Yeah. We were out for five days."

"Anything unusual happen?"

"No. It was a routine run, except it was cut short. We were supposed to be out for a full week. A Calflex vice president and a Calflex security guy were on board. A couple South Beach ladies. And four executives from some software company."

"Do you know why it was cut short?"

"No, but it happens. Usually it's because Calflex needs the boat to entertain someone more important. The drill is that the resident Calflex company man says he's sick, and we head back to port. We off-load the cargo, pick up the new VIP, and head back out again. This was a little strange because we were told we were sailing the following day, but then it was cancelled. And the boat's been sitting at the dock ever since. Not that I mind. I'm getting paid for beach time."

Brian wasn't getting any attention with the dancing around so he added some barking. *Arf, arf, arf.*

Judey gave a tug on the Burberry leash. "Stop it!" Judey said to Brian. "Behave yourself."

Arf, arf, arf, arf, arf.

"I got him in the property settlement when we split," Judey said. "I should have taken the Boxster."

Todd looked down at his legs. "I'm going to have to wash this sand off. It's going to ruin my tan."

We walked to the water's edge and waited while Todd plunged into the surf. A roller came in and caught him midthigh.

"Eeeeee. *Cold!*" he shrieked, jumping around, flapping his arms, splashing back to us, doodles bouncing in the silky red pouch.

Brian was at the end of his leash, panting, choking himself, trying to get to Todd. Judey was busy trying to control Brian. And Hooker and I were mesmerized. The bouncing doodles were hypnotic.

"Holy crap," Hooker said.

"You see my problem with the bakery theory."

"Yeah, but just so you know, my 'boys' would look better."

"Let me guess. You've got NASCAR 'boys.'"

"You betcha."

Todd stopped jumping around, and we all pulled ourselves together.

"There were some people on board *Flex* for lunch today," I said to Todd. "One of them was a state senator."

"Bulger. He's around a lot. Doesn't usually sail with us. Just comes to socialize. He pals around with Luis Salzar. Salzar was probably there, too."

We were back at the beach towel, and Todd stood air-drying his legs before reapplying oil.

"Is Salzar a chunky guy with a lot of silver gray hair? Looks like a professional killer?" I asked him.

"Yeah. That's Salzar. I hate when he's on board. The ship always gets locked down."

"Locked down?"

"The main deck is off limits to everyone but Salzar's personal crew. He's got his own steward, two bodyguards, and two-man helicopter crew. Plus the captain and the purser are company men, so they have access. And sometimes Salzar brings one or two members of his family. And I don't necessarily mean relatives when I say family. It's like cruising with Al Capone. Always lots of guns. Conversations that stop when a nonfamily member enters a room. It's pretty darn creepy."

"Salzar's a Cuban businessman," Judey said to Hooker and me. "Got his finger in a lot of pies. He lives in Miami, but the rumors go that he's mucho friendly with Fidel."

"Yeah," Todd said. "We fly Salzar to Cuba on poker night."

We all looked at Todd.

"Not really for poker night," Todd said. "That's just the joke on the boat. When Salzar sails with us we tie up at Shell Island Resort in the Bahamas. And in the dark of night, the helicopter mysteriously takes off and returns with the first light of dawn the following morning."

"You think it takes Salzar to Cuba? Isn't that illegal?" I asked.

Todd shrugged. "Lots of people go to Cuba these days. Not Americans, but everyone else."

"I thought we monitored flights."

"We monitor for drug flights and boat people. Anyway, I imagine a helicopter could go in low, under radar. This is all just conjecture, anyway. Like I said, the second deck is off limits when Salzar's in residence. Junior crew members, like me, don't have access to flight plans. In fact, sometimes we're not even sure where we are. If you want to keep your job on this boat, you do a lot of smiling, you don't ask questions, and you don't stick your nose in where it doesn't belong."

"That doesn't sound like Bill," I said.

Todd grinned. "No. Bill wasn't a total fit. Bill was like Brian. Into everything, tail wagging, kicking up sand."

"Was Salzar on the last trip?"

"Salzar hasn't sailed with us for a while. Maybe two or three weeks. I'd say on an average he goes out once a month. Sometimes his crew goes out without him. Sometimes the second deck gets locked down for just the Salzar people." Todd turned to Hooker. "You're a couple slips down from *Flex*, right? The name of your boat is *Happy Hooker*?"

"Yeah, the boat disappeared with Wild Bill."

"That's a good-size boat. Bill would have a hard time taking it in and out by himself."

"We think he had a girl with him," Hooker said. "You have any idea who it might be?"

"I could probably narrow it down to two or three hundred women."

"No one special?" I asked.

"They were all special," Todd said. "Last I talked to Bill, he was going clubbing. He probably brought someone home with him."

"Someone who could handle a boat," Hooker said.

"Someone who didn't mind a quickie," Judey said. "If they left the club at one, and they were stealing the boat an hour later, they didn't have a lot of foreplay time."

"Maybe Bill ran off with someone's wife and now the enraged husband is after him," Todd said.

A perfectly logical assumption, but the boat part of it bothered me. "I don't get the boat-stealing part," I said. "Bill's running from someone. Let's say it's the husband. Why does Bill take a boat? If you wanted a fast getaway you'd use a car. If you were going any distance you'd take a plane. A boat seems so limiting. And snatching the boat seems extreme. And what about the apartment trashing?" Not to mention Puke Face and the fear speech.

No one had an answer.

"Maybe it was that the boat was the fastest way out," Hooker finally said. "Or maybe it was the only way out. Maybe Bill didn't go home to his apartment. He was supposed to sail in the morning. So maybe he went back to *Flex*, and something happened, and he had to take off."

"We were supposed to sail early. Almost everyone stayed on the boat," Todd said. "I went to dinner with some friends, and I was back on the boat by ten."

"I have twin diesels. Combined they give me fifteen hundred fifty horses," Hooker said. "Didn't you hear *Happy Hooker* leave?"

"You can't hear a whole lot in crew quarters. Mostly you hear the generator. I can ask around, though. Maybe one of the other guys knows something." Todd's eyes opened wide. "Hey, wait a minute. *Happy Hooker* wasn't in its usual slip. There was something wrong with the electrical hookup, so they had her at the end of Pier F. Bill moved her. He had your key. He was listed as captain with the dockmaster."

"I walked every square inch of this marina, and I didn't see my boat," Hooker said. "Why didn't the dockmaster tell me the boat was moved?"

"It was a real mess when they discovered the guard. Nobody was thinking about anything but the murder. And then the office was a mess and the records were trashed. I guess it was a real bloody struggle. Probably no one even remembered about your boat."

"One last thing," I said to Todd. "Have you ever run into a big guy with a scar on the right side of his face? Glass eye?"

"That sounds like Hugo. Don't know his last name. He's one of Salzar's henchmen. Sails with us sometimes."

• • •

Hooker swung the Porsche into the lot that serviced Monty's. It had only been a ten-minute drive, but it felt like a lifetime. It looked like Bill had snatched a woman who belonged to Salzar. I didn't know what to think. Was this woman a daughter? A girlfriend? Personal chef?

Hooker and I got out. I took Brian. And Hooker hauled Judey out of the Porsche's pretend backseat.

"What sort of business are you involved in?" I asked Judey.

"Interior design. And I'm much sought after. Calvin and I were making a nice living . . . until he dumped me. The jerk." Judey took Brian's leash from me. "How about you? What have you been up to?"

"I work for Salyer Insurance Group. Property damage. I'm the supervisor over six claims adjusters." Not the world's most glamorous job, but it paid the rent. And paying the rent was important, since I wasn't doing so good in the finding-a-husband department. Unfortunately, it also wasn't a very forgiving job. Salyer Insurance Group wasn't going to be happy if I didn't show up for work on Monday.

"You were always the brain," Judey said. He turned to Hooker. "When we were kids, Barney always won the spelling contests in school. I was a complete loser, but Barney always got a perfect report card."

"You were smart," I said to Judey. "You just had a concentration problem."

"I was conflicted. I was having an identity crisis," Judey said.

"Right now I'm having a hunger crisis," I said. "I need lunch."

"There's a wonderful deli next to Monty's," Judey said. "They have spice cookies that Brian adores."

Brian's ears perked up at the mention of spice cookies.

"Isn't he the clever one," Judey said. "He knows 'spice cookies.'"

Hooker looked doubtful, and I was guessing Hooker wasn't a schnauzer person. Hooker looked more like an English bulldog sort of person. Hooker looked like the sort of guy who'd feed his dog beer. I could see Hooker sitting in front of his television, in his underwear, getting wasted with his bulldog.

"You're smiling," Hooker said to me. "What's that about?"

I didn't think it was a good idea to tell Hooker I was smiling about him in his underwear, so I popped out a lie. "It's Brian," I said. "Don't you think he's cute?"

"That's not a cute-dog smile," Hooker said. "I know a cute-dog smile when I see it, and that's not it."

"Are you calling me a liar?"

"Yeah."

"Uh-oh," Judey said. "Are we having a lovers' quarrel?"

"We're not lovers," I said to Judey.

Hooker steered me in the direction of the deli. "Not yet," he said.

FOUR

The deli was on the second level on the street side, and leaned more toward Williams-Sonoma than 7-Eleven. An overhead blackboard advertised large chilled shrimp and fresh grilled vegetables. A couple small round tables with chairs had been stuck between polished chrome racks holding gourmet staples.

I cruised past the glass and stainless display cases filled with salads and pasta, hand-rolled cigars, fresh baked bread, soups, chips, the shrimp, fruits, and fancy tapenades. I considered the Häagen-Dazs, cheesecake, and snack packs of Oreos. And then I settled on a turkey roll-up and a bottle of water. Judey got the same, plus an oatmeal raisin cookie for himself and a spice cookie for Brian. Hooker got a roast beef with cheese and coleslaw on a sub roll, a bag of chips, a Pepsi, and three giant chocolate chip cookies.

We sat outside at one of the scrolled concrete and blue tile picnic tables and ate our lunch. When we were done we followed Hooker up and down the piers, looking for his boat.

There were a lot of piers and a lot of boats but none of the boats was Hooker's. Hooker looked like he was thinking dark thoughts. Judey didn't look like he was thinking any thoughts. And all I could think about was Brian's spice cookie, and how I wished I had one. Finally, I gave up the fight, and I left the guys sitting in the sun while I ran back to the deli. I got a cookie and, on impulse, a newspaper, hoping there might be more information about the marina murder.

I joined Hooker and Judey and paged through the paper while I ate my cookie. Nothing new about the murder. I checked out the movie section and read the comics.

I was about to set the paper aside when a photo and headline caught my attention. The photo was of a pretty young woman with lots of wavy dark hair and dark eyes with long dark lashes. She was smiling at the camera, looking a little mysterious. The headline said she was missing. Maria Raffles, age twenty-seven, disappeared Monday evening. She'd been clubbing with her roommate but decided to leave early and went home alone. Foul play was feared. Her apartment had been broken into and violently searched. Maria had been born in Cuba but had managed to reach Florida four years ago. She was an accomplished diver and sailor. And she worked in a Miami cigar factory.

The article went on to explain the immigration service policy of allowing Cuban nationals to remain in this country if they touch U.S. soil, as opposed to being intercepted at sea.

I was holding the paper and my eyes were wide and my mouth was open.

"Let me guess," Hooker said. "Ben and Jerry came out with a new flavor."

I read the piece to Hooker and Judey.

"By God, Watson," Hooker said. "I think you've found something."

"Maybe not," Judey said. "This is Miami. Probably a lot of women disappear after clubbing."

"Don't rain on my parade," I told Judey. "I haven't got anything else. I'm at a dead end in the how-to-find-Bill idea department."

"Yes, but how would this woman relate to Salzar?"

"I don't know. They're both Cuban. There could be a connection."

"Maybe you should go to the police," Judey said. He followed up with a grimace. "I take that back. What was I thinking? This is Wild Bill we're talking about."

"In the past the police haven't totally shared Bill's relaxed attitude to the law," I explained to Hooker.

"Bill's a great guy," Judey said, "but he has a history of getting his brains caught in his zipper."

This had us both looking at Hooker, who we suspected suffered from the same dilemma.

"NASCAR Guy knows enough to wear button fly," Hooker said.

Judey and I smiled. NASCAR Guy was being a good sport.

"I think we move on this," Judey said. "The newspaper doesn't give Maria's address, so let's start with the cigar factory. There aren't that many of them. They're all in Little Havana, around Seventeenth and Calle Ocho."

•   •   •

Hooker took the Causeway Bridge out of Miami Beach into the city of Miami. He wound around some, crossed the Miami River, and found SW Eighth Street. We were now in a neighborhood where businesses advertised in both Spanish and English. *Sopa de pescado, camerones, congelados.* The street was wide and the buildings were low, with strip mall–style fronts. Stunted palm trees occasionally grew out of concrete sidewalks. The Porsche was common in South Beach. We were odd man out in Little Havana. This was the land of the family sedan. It was midafternoon and the air was hot and thick. It stuck on my face and caught in my hair. It was the McDonald's milk shake of air. You had to work to suck it in.

Hooker swung the Porsche onto Seventeenth and pulled to the curb. "Here we are," Hooker said. "Cigar factory number one."

I'm from Baltimore. Factories are big and noisy. They're in industrial parks. They're filled with guys in hard hats. They make machine parts, ceramic pipes, conduit wire, molded sheet metal. This left me completely unprepared for the cigar factory.

The cigar factory was half a block long, the inner workings visible behind large plate glass windows. One end of the factory was devoted to a small retail store. And at the other end, six women sat at individual tables. Barrels filled with tobacco leaves had been positioned beside the tables. A woman selected a leaf and then rolled it into a cigar. A man stood supervising. The man and all the women were smoking cigars. They looked up and smiled when they realized we were

67

watching. It was a silent invitation. Come in and buy a cigar.

"I'll wait here," Judey said. "Brian is very sensitive to smoke."

Hooker sauntered in and admired some tobacco leaves. He bought a cigar, and he asked one of the women about Maria Raffles.

No, she said solemnly. Maria didn't work there. It was a small community. They'd heard she was missing. The woman thought Maria worked at the National Cigar Factory on Fifteenth.

We climbed into the Porsche and Hooker drove to the National Cigar Factory. Again, there was a small retail store. And beside the store there were women rolling cigars in the window. There were six tables. But there were only five women.

I followed Hooker into the store and took a step back when one of the women jumped up and shrieked at Hooker.

"Omigod!" she yelled. "I know you. You're what's his name!"

"Sam Hooker?" he said.

"Yeah. That's it. You're Sam Hooker. I'm a huge fan. *Huge*. I saw you on television when you crashed at Loudin. I started crying. I was so worried."

"I got pushed into the wall," Hooker said.

"I saw that, too," I told him. "You were hotdogging and you deserved to crash."

"I thought you didn't watch NASCAR," Hooker said to me.

"My *family* watches NASCAR. I was at the house mooching dinner, and I was forced to watch." All right, so maybe sometimes I still enjoyed NASCAR.

"Who's she?" the woman wanted to know.

"I don't know," Hooker said. "She's been following me around all day."

I gave him a shot to the shoulder that knocked him back a couple inches.

Hooker said "*ow*," but he grinned when he said it.

"Alexandra Barnaby," I said extending my hand. "I'm looking for Maria Raffles."

"Rosa Florez," she said.

Rosa was my height, but more round. Fat round breasts. Round brown eyes. Flushed round cheeks. A round Jennifer Lopez bootie. A small, soft roll of fat circling her waist. She had pale Cuban skin, and she had a lot of wavy brown hair cut short. Hard to tell her age. In her forties, probably.

She was wearing a white V-neck knit shirt that showed a lot of cleavage, and jeans that were rolled at the ankle. If you stuck a quarter in Rosa's cleavage and turned her upside down the quarter wouldn't move. She was wearing clear plastic, open-toed four-inch heels that clacked when she walked. She was wearing minimum makeup and lots of flowery perfume.

"Maria isn't here," Rosa said. "She hasn't been here all week. I have to tell you, I'm real worried. It's not like her to miss work. Or not to call anyone. We were real good friends. She would have told me if she was going away."

"Were you at the club with her?"·

"No. I don't go to those clubs. I mostly stay in Miami. Maria didn't used to go to those clubs either. She's a Cuban girl, you know. She always stayed in the neighborhood. Then one day a couple months ago she decided she wanted to be by the marina in South Beach. When she was in Cuba she lived in a little town right on the water. She said she missed the diving and the boating since she's been here." Rosa lowered her voice. "I think she was looking to get out of the cigar factory, too. She thought maybe she could meet someone and maybe get a job on a boat. I think that's why she started clubbing. She was pretty. She could get in for free and look at the rich men with the boats. And she was crazy about the diving. Always looking at charts. Always talking about the diving."

"Did she ever mention Luis Salzar?"

"Not that I remember. Maybe just in conversation. Everyone in Little Havana knows of Salzar."

Rosa looked beyond us to the parked Porsche. "Is that your car?" she asked Hooker.

"Yep."

"It's a Porsche, right?"

"Yep."

"So what's the deal here?" Rosa asked. "Why are you looking for Maria?"

"My brother is missing, and we think Maria and Bill might be together."

"On my boat," Hooker said.

"What would they be doing on your boat?" Rosa wanted to know.

"They stole it," he said.

I pressed my lips together. "Borrowed it."

Rosa liked that. "No kidding?"

"The newspaper article didn't give her address," I said.

"I know her address!" Rosa said. "I could show you. I

could go with you in the Porsche. I always wanted to ride in a Porsche."

I looked over at the other women. They were older than Rosa and their roundness had turned blocky. They'd all stopped working and were openly staring, waiting to see what would happen next.

"What about your job?" I asked.

"It's almost the end of the day," Rosa said. "I could take off a half hour early."

"You take off a half hour early and you're fired," the lone male foreman said.

"Kiss my ass," Rosa said. "Kiss his ass. Kiss all their asses."

The women burst out laughing and made kissing sounds at the foreman.

"Rosa Louisa Francesca Florez, you're a bad influence," the man said.

"It's true," Rosa said to Hooker and me. "I'm a big *bitch*." She grabbed her purse off the table and shoved her cigar in her mouth. "Okay, let's go."

We all pushed through the door and stood on the sidewalk by the Porsche. Judey was already in the backseat, hugging Brian to his chest.

"News flash," Hooker said. "We're not going to fit."

"Who's the gay guy with the hairy rat?" Rosa asked.

"That's Judey," I told her. "How do you know he's gay?"

"Look at his complexion," Rosa said. "He exfoliates. I'd kill for skin like that. And he's got two eyebrows."

Hooker raised a hand to feel his eyebrows. "I have two eyebrows, don't I?"

"I'm not getting out," Judey said. "I was here first."

Rosa shoved past Hooker and me and climbed over the car, into the backseat. "Just move your skinny little gay ass over and we can both fit," she said to Judey.

"It's too small," Judey said. "You're going to squish my Brian."

"Your Brian?" Rosa asked.

"My dog!"

"Oh jeez," she said. "I thought you were talking about your thingy. You know how guys are always naming their thingy."

"I've never named my thingy," Hooker said. "I feel left out."

"It's important to get the right name," Rosa said, trying to maneuver her ass onto the seat. "They all have their own personality."

Judey was trying to make himself very small in the backseat. "It should have something to do with NASCAR."

I slid a look at Hooker. "Speedy?"

"Sometimes," Hooker said.

Rosa was wedged into the back with one leg hanging outside the car and one foot on the console. "I'm ready," she said. "Take me to South Beach."

Maria lived a couple blocks from Bill on Jefferson. The building was similar but larger. Tan stucco. Six floors. Small balconies opening off each apartment. A small front foyer with two elevators. Not totally decrepit, but it looked like it had the potential to be home to the cow-size cockroach. The ever-present lizards skittered away from us as we approached the foyer door.

"Maria has a roommate," Rosa said, punching the button for the second floor. "She's a waitress working the dinner shift, so she should be home now getting ready to go to work."

There were six apartments to the floor. Maria lived in 2B. Rosa rang the doorbell and the chain slid back on the inside and the door was opened.

Maria's roommate was young. Twenty, maybe. She had long straight blond hair and lips so pumped up with collagen I took a step back in case they exploded. She had a tiny waist, and a tiny nose, and big boobs with big nipples jutting out of a tiny white T-shirt. She was pretty in a painful, manufactured generic sort of way.

"Rosa!" she said. "Omigod, this isn't bad news, is it? Tell me they didn't find her dead. She's okay, right?"

"Nobody's heard from her," Rosa said.

"That's good. I mean, at least she's not dead or maimed. I mean, not that we know of."

"These are friends of mine," Rosa said. "We're all looking for her. And this is Barbie," Rosa said by way of introduction.

Barbie. Judey, Hooker, and I went momentarily speechless.

Barbie's eyes opened wide at the sight of Brian. "Look at the cute doggie. And *hello* handsome," she said to Hooker.

"I'm handsome," Judey said.

"Yes, but your complexion is flawless, you're perfectly shaved, and you have two eyebrows. Gay, gay, gay."

73

Hooker did another eyebrow feel. "I'm starting to really worry about this eyebrow thing."

"We were hoping you'd have some ideas about Maria," Rosa said to Barbie. "Were you clubbing with her the night she disappeared?"

"Yeah, sort of. We went together, but then we got separated. You know how that is. I'm breaking into modeling so I try to work a room."

"Do you think she hooked up with anyone?"

"Don't know. I lost sight of her. She called me on my cell and told me she was leaving. That was around twelve. We had only just gotten there."

"What about before that?" I asked. "Did she talk about going away? Was she upset? Was she scared? Was she excited?"

"No, no, no. And yeah, sort of. She was working on some project. Some dive thing. I don't know anything about diving. *Hello*. Don't care either. *Boring*. But Maria was into that stuff. She had a bunch of maps in her room. Water maps."

"Charts?" Hooker said.

"Yeah. Charts. But they got stolen. Or maybe she took them. Or maybe someone took Maria *and* the charts. The apartment was trashed the night she disappeared, and so far as I can see the only things missing are the charts from her room. And I know this is really weird but the apartment got broken into and trashed a second time two days later. How's that for shitty luck?"

"Do you mind if we look at her room?" I asked.

"Knock yourself out. I have to get ready for work. I'm waiting tables until I get my big break into modeling. Don't mind her room. I tried to put it back together the first time, but I haven't gotten to cleaning up the second time."

Barbie disappeared into her bedroom and we all trooped into Maria's room.

"This is a mess," Rosa said. "Maria would die if she saw this. She was real organized. That's why she was so good with the cigars. She was neat. And she had good fingers."

"You won't really get fired, will you?" I asked.

"Nah. They're already down Maria. And there's not many people can roll a cigar. Most young people don't want to learn. Rather work at Burger King. When my generation retires they'll probably close down the factories."

I was combing through the clutter, looking for anything interesting, anything that might tie Maria to Bill. Rosa was doing the same. Judey, Hooker, and Brian took the rest of the apartment.

Judey danced into the bedroom and waved a little leather book at me. "I found her address book," he said. "I am the master detective. I am the Magnum of South Beach." And he handed the book over to me with a flourish. "I also found bags of chips and boxes of crackers in the microwave. And you know what *that* means."

I had no idea. "What?" I asked.

"Cockroaches," Rosa said. "They got roaches as big as a barn cat in here. They keep the chips in the microwave so the roaches don't get them."

Damn. "Do they fly?"

"I've never seen them fly," Rosa said. "But I wouldn't be surprised. We're talking major mutant roaches."

Hooker ambled in. "What's up?"

"Judey found an address book. Rosa and I didn't find anything."

Hooker looked around, his attention focusing on the small desk. "She has a laptop. Let's see where she goes on the net." He turned the laptop on and studied the icons at the bottom of the screen. "No AOL. Looks like she uses Explorer as her browser of choice." He went to the top of the screen and clicked on the phone connection. When he had a connection he hit the Explorer icon and the home page came on. He had several choices at the side of the page. He hit *history* and a chronology of Maria's Internet use appeared.

"Wow," I said. "I'm impressed."

"Not that impressive," Hooker said. "I have a lot of downtime, and I kill time by surfing. I lucked out here. Maria uses the same browser I use, so I sort of know where to go." Hooker started working his way through the dates. "Okay, I'm getting a little freaked," he said. "She's pulling some nasty stuff up. She started out with Cuban history. To be more specific, the Kennedy Missile Crisis. From there she went to sites detailing Soviet munitions brought onto the island. She looks at nuclear warheads. And then she goes to sites detailing chemical agents."

"Maybe someone else used her computer," Rosa said. "Like her roommate."

We all stared at Rosa.

"You're right," she said. "What was I thinking?"

"She's also been reading up on gold," Hooker said. "Weights and measures stuff."

"Anything else?"

"Nothing interesting. As you can see, the rest is more typical. Mostly eBay and weather."

Hooker shut the computer off, and we all trooped out of Maria's bedroom. We called good-bye to Barbie and let ourselves out. We silently entered the elevator and dropped to the ground floor. No one said anything until we were out of the building, at curbside, standing next to the Porsche.

Judey had been holding Brian the whole time. He put Brian down and Brian lifted his leg and peed on the Porsche's right rear tire.

"What a good boy," Judey cooed to Brian. "He had to go pee, and he held it all that time."

"You know there are places where they *eat* dogs," Rosa said.

I thumbed through the address book. "Bill's name isn't in here," I said.

We were on a corner, and just for the hell of it, I took Bill's keys out of my purse and pointed the automatic lock gizmo down the street. Nothing. I turned and tried the cross street. A red-and-white Mini Cooper, two cars away, beeped at me.

"Do it again," Hooker said.

I pointed the gizmo at the Mini and got the same response. The Mini flashed its lights and beeped.

"I don't get it," Rosa said. "What's with the car?"

"It's Bill's," I said. Leave it to Bill to drive a Mini Cooper.

We walked over to the car and looked inside.

"No bloodstains," Hooker said.

"That is *so gross,*" Judey said.

Rosa made the sign of the cross.

"It looks like Bill and Maria were together the night they disappeared," I said.

"Maria was excited about a dive project and her charts are missing. Plus Hooker's boat is missing. So I'm guessing Wild Bill and Maria are off on a sunken treasure hunt," Judey said. "Mystery solved."

"It must be the mother of all treasure hunts," Hooker said. "They both walked out on their jobs. Two different groups of people are after them. And one of those groups includes Salzar. A night watchman was killed at the marina. They 'borrowed' my boat. And Maria's been researching gold and warheads."

"I don't know anything about a night watchman getting killed," Rosa said. "And why is Salzar involved?"

"I'm surprised you didn't read about the murder in the paper," Judey said. "It was splashed all over."

"I live in a neighborhood where murder isn't big news. Guess I overlooked the fancy pants marina murder that was in the paper. I was probably in a hurry to see what Snoopy was doing."

"Monday night my brother and Maria went clubbing and it looks like they left together, took Hooker's boat, and disappeared. That night the watchman at the marina was stabbed and killed outside the dockmaster's office. And one of Salzar's employees broke into Bill's apartment last night and tried to kidnap me."

Rosa gave a single shake to her head. "I don't like this. Maria is mixed up in something bad. Such a nice girl, too."

"I'd like to know about the dive project," I said. "Maria must have talked to someone about it."

"Maybe family," Rosa said. "She hasn't got a lot. Just a cousin. She's never seen her father. She doesn't talk about it, but I think maybe he was killed or maybe put in prison. She has a hatred of Castro. Her mother died four years ago. That was when Maria left Cuba."

"No sisters or brothers?"

"No. Her mama never remarried."

"Do you know the cousin?"

"Felicia Ibarra. She lives a couple blocks from me. I know her from Maria, and sometimes I see her at showers and things. She's probably at work now. The Ibarras own the fruit stand on Fourth."

"Oh my goodness," Judey said. "Look at the time. I have to go. I have a dinner date tonight. I hate to punk out on the investigation, but this guy I'm dating knows someone at Joe's Stone Crab. And you know how hard it is to get into Joe's."

"Do you need a ride home?" I asked him.

"No. I live one block from here." He took a card out of his wallet and scribbled a number on it. "This is my cell phone. And my home phone is on the card, too. Call me if you need help. I'll get Todd to sniff around on *Flex*."

I gave Judey my cell number. "It's been great seeing you again," I said.

Judey gave me a hug, and he and Brian left.

I opened the driver's side door on the Mini, and Hooker grabbed me by the back of my T-shirt.

"What do you think you're doing?" he asked.

"I'm going to the fruit stand on Fourth."

"By yourself?"

"Sure."

"I don't think so."

"Well, I was going to take Rosa."

"Remember me? I'm the guy who's been driving you around?"

"Yes, but I have a car now."

"And you were going to leave me standing here?"

"Yeah."

Hooker smiled. "You're teasing me. That's a sign of affection, you know."

Actually, I hadn't been teasing.

"Don't forget about me," Rosa said to Hooker. "I could *really* give you a sign of affection. I'm a divorced woman. I'm desperate."

"Everybody in," I said. "Let's see what this little guy can do."

I positioned myself behind the wheel and felt like I was in a sports car whose growth had been stunted in childhood. The Mini had black leather trim and black leather bucket seats. It was deceptively comfortable and had great visibility. I turned the key and stepped on the gas, and the car leaped forward.

When I'm at home I drive a Ford Escape. Compared to the Escape, the Mini had the feel of a turbocharged roller skate.

I rocketed to the corner and hung a left without braking.

Rosa had both hands braced on the dash. "Holy mother," she said.

Hooker slid off the backseat, righted himself, and reached for the shoulder harness.

"Corners like a dream," I told them.

"Yeah," Hooker said, "but you drive like a nightmare. I don't suppose you'd want to relinquish the reins on these horses to me?"

"No chance."

I took the Causeway Bridge into Miami, sailing through traffic, enjoying the feel of the car. The car handled like a hummingbird—hovering at a light, zipping ahead, cutting in and out of gridlock.

The reality of my life is that I love to drive, and I probably would have been happier driving a truck for a living than I am working for an insurance company. But you don't spend all that time and money on a college education so you can drive a truck, do you?

Little Havana was busy at this time of day. It was Friday afternoon, and people were on their way home from work, running errands, gearing up for the weekend. I followed Rosa's directions to the fruit stand and pulled into the lot. I parked the Mini and heard Hooker mumble from the backseat.

"What was that?" I asked.

"You're a maniac."

"You're not used to being a passenger."

"True," Hooker said, climbing out of the car. "But you're still a maniac."

And that was probably also true. By reputation, I was the sensible, smart sibling. But that was only by comparison.

The stand was packed with people buying produce, fried polenta, and pulled pork to go. Rosa found Maria's cousin and brought her over to Hooker and me.

Felicia Ibarra was from the same mold as Rosa. A little shorter. Just as round. Different shoes. Ibarra was wearing wood clogs. Probably in deference to the smushed fruit that littered the pavement around the fruit stand. Ibarra was older. Maybe in her early sixties. And Ibarra had a heavy Cuban accent. Clearly, not U.S. born.

"Rosa tells me you're looking for Maria Raffles," Felicia said. "I have to tell you, I'm worried. She has so much trouble behind her. And now she's missing. I worry that this is more trouble. Heaven help her." And Felicia Ibarra crossed herself.

"What kind of trouble?" I asked.

"Just trouble. Some families carry the trouble. It happens. They have a curse. Or an obsession. Or just bad luck."

"And Maria's family?"

Felicia shook her head. "They have Cubano trouble. Sometimes it can be bad on the island. And what I know are only things whispered. Not from Maria. She never says anything. But I hear from my cousin who hears from her sister, Maria's mother, rest in peace. I was told there was trouble with Maria's grandfather. Enrique Raffles. He was a fisherman. He fish from a little town to the west of Havana. Nuevo Cabo. He owned a boat and sometimes he would use the boat for other things. Sometimes a boat would come from Russia and the cargo would be best kept secret. Maria's grandfather was good at not seeing things, so he would go out to the big boat and let them put things in the hold of the little boat to be taken ashore. He would do this at night, when there was no moon. And he would also bring things from Cuba to the Russian sailors."

"Maria's grandfather was a smuggler?" Rosa asked.

"Yes. And he work with another man because the boat was too big for one man. But I don't know this other man.

"Then one night the men went out to get special cargo, and somehow the little fishing boat ran into a reef and went down. The one man got to shore, but Maria's grandfather did not.

"Maria's father, Juan, was fourteen years old when this happened. He took a vow to bury his father and he started diving, looking for the boat. Many people looked for the boat, but no one found it.

"Juan married, and still he kept diving, even when his wife was pregnant. It was the vow to bury his father. And then one night, a month before Maria was born, the police came and took Juan away. He was never seen again. When the relatives came to help with the birth of Maria they found a fresh grave in the little backyard and a cross with *E. R.* hand carved into it. And everyone knew Juan had found his father.

"Some say there was gold on the boat that night it went down. Gold that belonged to Castro. And that's why Juan was taken away. Because Castro wanted his gold. And there are other rumors too. Rumors about a very bad weapon. Something new the Russians were sending into Cuba.

"Maria's mother never remarried. She stayed in the little village, always hoping Juan would return. She died four years ago. That is when Maria escaped the island and illegally sailed her little boat here to Miami."

"Such a tragic history," Rosa said. "I had no idea."

"She was marked by her family history. Like a thumbprint on her forehead. How you say it in this country . . . destiny? She was called to dive. Like her father. Always looking for the shipwreck."

FIVE

I took Rosa home and then I took Hooker back to his car. I parked behind the Porsche, and we sat in silence for a couple minutes. Both of us thinking about Maria.

"Fuck," Hooker finally said on a sigh.

I nodded my head in agreement.

"Your brother is involved in some serious shit," Hooker said.

"We don't know for sure."

"You're worried."

"Yeah."

"Never fear," Hooker said. "NASCAR Guy is here to help you."

Hooker was a nice guy, I decided, but he wasn't James Bond. I needed James Bond.

Hooker looked at me, his eyes hidden behind his dark sunglasses. "Don't underestimate NASCAR Guy."

"Does NASCAR Guy have any ideas about where to go from here?"

"Yep. NASCAR Guy thinks we should go to Monty's. Get a sandwich. Have a beer. Hang out. NASCAR Guy has some other ideas, too, but he's going to wait until he gets a beer in you before he shares those ideas."

"Do you want to follow me over?"

"You follow me. We'll use the garage at my condo. It'll be impossible to get a parking place at Monty's at this time of night."

"Okay," I said. "I'll follow you."

Now here's the thing, this wasn't the first time I'd gotten a middle-of-the-night call from Bill. Usually he was stranded somewhere and needed a ride home. Usually there was a woman involved. Twice he needed me to bail him out of jail. Neither of those incidents was serious. When I couldn't reach Bill after this latest call I was concerned enough to get on a plane, but truth is, I wasn't a wreck over it. I'd suspected it was business as usual. I thought I'd find Bill, help him out of a messy situation, and go home. When I discovered his apartment had been ransacked, I was thinking irate husband or boyfriend. When there was a murder at the marina I was trying to convince myself it was a meaningless coincidence. Pukey showing up to kidnap me raised my level of alarm by about two hundred percent.

Now I was thinking Bill had finally done it. Bill had finally managed to get himself involved in something serious. He'd put his nose someplace it absolutely didn't belong. He'd stolen a boat and gone off with a woman who was diving for God-knows-what.

I had a gnawing ache in my stomach that wasn't going to be fixed with pizza. I was afraid I might not be able to clean up the mess this time. I was afraid it might be too big and I might be too late.

I looked at the Porsche, turning into the parking garage in front of me and admitted to myself that I was happy to have Hooker involved. It didn't have anything to do with Hooker being NASCAR Guy. In fact, gender wasn't the comforting factor. It was just nice not to be afraid and alone.

Hooker and I parked and walked over to Monty's. The sun was starting to drop in the sky, and another day was passing without word from Bill.

Hooker slung an arm around my shoulders. "You're not going to cry, are you?" he asked me.

"No," I said. "Are you?"

"NASCAR Guy doesn't cry."

"What are we looking to accomplish at Monty's?"

"We're going to eat. And while we're eating we can check out the boats. Who knows, maybe Bill will come cruising in."

We sat at the bar, and we looked at the boats. We watched the people. We looked down the pier at *Flex*. Not much happening. No Florida politician or Cuban businessman in sight. I ordered a Diet Pepsi and a turkey club. Hooker got a beer, a cheeseburger, fries, a side of potato salad, and cheese-cake for dessert. Plus he ate the chips that came with my club.

"Where does it go?" I asked him. "You eat enough food

for three people. If I ate all that food I'd weigh seven hundred pounds."

"It's about metabolism," Hooker said. "I work out, so I have muscle. Muscle burns calories."

"I have muscle."

"Do you work out?"

"I take the escalator to get to the nosebleed seats at the Orioles games and then I jump up and down and scream my lungs out once in a while when they score."

"Strenuous."

"Damn straight."

Maria's address book was lying on the table. I'd thumbed through the little book twice now and nothing significant had jumped out at me. Of course there'd have to be a notation that hit me over the head before a name seemed significant. It would have to read *Riccardo Mattes, Cuban mafia hit man* for me to figure it out. Because I didn't have anything better to do, I ran through the book again. *Delores Daily, Francine DeVincent, Divetown . . .*

The lightbulb went on in my head. "Here's something," I said. "Maria was obsessed with diving. Now Maria has disappeared. Her charts have disappeared. Your boat has disappeared. What else does she need?"

"Dive equipment," Hooker said.

"Did you have dive equipment on your boat?"

"No. I tried diving a couple years ago, but it wasn't my thing."

"The roommate didn't say anything about dive equipment.

And it's sort of bulky, right? The roommate would have seen it."

"I'm not an expert, but when I was diving I had a buoyancy compensator vest, some tanks, a regulator, flippers, a light, a compass, a bunch of gauges."

"So where's her dive equipment?"

Hooker pulled a folded sticky note out of his pocket and punched a number into his cell phone.

"What's that?" I asked.

"It's the roommate's phone number."

"You got her phone number?"

"Hey, she gave it to me. She *forced* it on me."

I did an eye roll.

"I can't help it. I'm a hunk of burning love," Hooker said. "Women like me. Most women, anyway. Except for you. I get a *lot* of phone numbers. Sometimes they write them on their underwear."

"Eeeuw."

"It's not that bad. It's a variation of the bakery thing," Hooker said.

He connected with the roommate, did some preliminary flirting, and asked about the dive equipment.

"Maria has dive equipment," Hooker said, putting his phone back in his pocket. "It's in a storage locker in the apartment building. And it's still there. The roommate keeps her bike in the locker. She used the bike this morning, and she remembers seeing the dive equipment."

"So maybe this isn't about diving."

"Or maybe Maria and Bill knew someone was after them, and they only had time to get the charts. You can always buy more dive equipment."

I saw Hooker's eyes focus beyond my shoulder, and I turned to find a man smiling at us. He was nicely dressed in a black shirt and black slacks. His hair was slicked back. His face was perfectly tanned. His teeth were shockingly white and precisely even. Full veneers I was guessing. I was pretty sure it was the guy from the diner and the club. And maybe he was the guy Melvin saw coming out of Bill's apartment.

"Sam Hooker," he said. "I'm a fan. This is a real pleasure."

"Nice to see you," Hooker said.

"And this is Miss Barnaby, if I'm not mistaken?"

Hotshot NASCAR drivers are recognized all the time. Claims adjusters are rarely recognized. Actually, we're *never* recognized. And I was okay-looking, but I wasn't Julia Roberts. So being approached by a total stranger who knew my name (and maybe had been following me) was disconcerting.

"Do I know you?" I asked.

"No," he said. "And my name isn't important. What's important is that you pay attention, because I like watching Hooker drive, and I'd hate to see that end."

"And?" Hooker asked.

"And I'm going to have to takes steps if you continue to look for Maria Raffles. My employer is also looking for her, and you're muddying the water."

"My brother—"

"Your brother made a bad decision, and there's nothing

90

you can do now to help him. Go home. Go back to your job. Forget your brother."

"Who's your employer?" Hooker asked.

The guy in black dismissed the question with a small humorless smile. "I'm the one you need to worry about. I'm the one who will pull the trigger."

"Or hold the knife?" Hooker said.

He gave his head a slight shake. "That wasn't my work. That was clumsy. Ordinarily I wouldn't give a warning like this, but like I said, I enjoy watching you drive. Take my advice. Both of you. Go home."

And he turned and left.

Hooker and I watched him walk away, past the pool, disappearing into the dark shadows of the taproom and beyond.

"He was a little creepy," Hooker said.

"I *told* you I was being followed by some guy with slicked-back hair who dressed in black! Maybe we should turn this over to the police."

"I thought you were worried about your brother's involvement."

"That was before someone threatened to shoot us."

Bob Balfour met us at Bill's apartment. Balfour was plain-clothes Miami PD. He was in his early thirties, and he reminded me of a golden retriever. He had brown retriever eyes, and sandy blond retriever hair and a pleasant retriever personality. He was easy to talk to, and easy to look at, but if I'd had a choice I would have preferred a cop who reminded me of a Doberman. When I called the police I'd hoped to get a cop who could corner a rat and snatch it out of its hiding place.

Balfour looked around Bill's apartment and wrote in his little cop notebook. He listened carefully when I told him about the guy in black. He looked slightly disbelieving when I told him about Puke Face. He took down Bill's neighbor's name for possible future interrogation.

I told him about Maria surfing bomb sites. He included this in his notes. He asked if I thought she was a terrorist. I said no.

He said Bill would be added to Missing Persons. He said I should call him if I was threatened again. He suggested I follow the hit man's advice and go home. He asked Hooker what he thought about the restrictor plates NASCAR was imposing on the cars. And he left.

"Sort of unsatisfying," I said.

"Cops are like that. They have their own way of working."

"Mysterious."

"Yeah. Are you going home?"

"No. I'm going to keep bumbling along, looking for Bill. Let's check out some dive shops."

We drove back to Hooker's building and stood in front of the bank of elevators. Hooker pushed the up button, and I refused to crack my knuckles or faint or burst into tears. It's just a stupid elevator, for crying out loud, I told myself.

Hooker looked at me and grinned. "You really do hate elevators. You didn't blink when that guy threatened to kill us, but you're breaking into a sweat over this elevator."

The doors opened, Hooker stepped in and held the door, waiting for me.

I was thinking, get in the elevator, but my feet weren't moving.

Hooker reached out and grabbed me and pulled me into the elevator. He hit the button for the thirty-second floor, and I inadvertently whimpered. The doors closed, and he pulled me to him and kissed me. His tongue touched mine, and I think I whimpered again. And then the elevator doors opened.

"Do you want to go up and down a couple more times?" Hooker asked.

"No!" I jumped out of the elevator.

He slung an arm around my shoulders and steered me toward his condo. "Do you have any more irrational fears? Snakes? Spiders? Monkeys? Fear of eating pizza? Fear of making love to NASCAR drivers?"

"The NASCAR fear and the monkey fear might be redundant," I said.

Hooker unlocked his door, stepped in, and looked around. "Everything looks okay," he said. "I was worried I was going to find it had been destroyed. Every place we go into lately has been searched at least twice." He got a phone book and turned to the dive shop advertisements. "You're going to call," he said. "People are more willing to give information out to women. And besides, you're getting good at lying."

"What am I supposed to say?"

"Tell them your roommate called and asked you to pick up a regulator, but you don't know anything about diving, and she didn't say what kind of regulator. Ask if they know her, and they remember what she bought."

There were two dive shops in South Beach, a couple in Miami and one in Coral Gables. I called all of them. The store that was listed in Maria's book, Divetown, remembered her but hadn't seen her in weeks. The others had no knowledge of her.

"Maybe we're looking too close," Hooker said. "If they were running from someone, they might have stopped under way. Like in the Keys."

I got a hit on the second try. Scuba Dooba in Key West. Maria and Bill had been in on Wednesday.

"Hold a regulator for me," I said. "I'll pick it up tomorrow."

Fifteen minutes later, we were in the garage, arguing over cars and driving.

"We should take the Mini," I said. "The shooter with the slicked-back hair probably knows your car."

"Fine," Hooker said, "but I'm driving."

"No way. It's my brother's car. *I'm* driving."

"Yeah, but I'm the man."

"What the heck does that have to do with anything?"

"I don't know. It was all I could come up with. Come on, give me a break and let me drive. I've never driven one of these little things. Besides, I know the roads."

Knowing the roads got him a couple points. "Okay," I said, "but don't expect to *always* drive."

Hooker took the bridge out of South Beach, and I kept my eyes on the road behind us, watching to see that we weren't followed. Hard to do while we were in the multilane tangle of roads going through the city. Easy to do once we got out of the greater Miami area and traffic thinned.

Florida is flat, flat, flat. As far as I can see, the highest point in Florida could very well be a sanitary landfill. You don't notice the flatness so much when you're in a city like Miami. The planted palms, the flashy buildings, the waterways, the beautiful people, the expensive cars, and international influences add interest to the cityscape. As you leave the city and Route 1 dips south to Florida City and Key Largo, the tedium of the landscape becomes painfully apparent. The natural vegetation is scrubby, and the towns of south Dade County are small and unmemorable, hardly noticed in the relentless stream of strip malls lining the road.

The Mini engine hummed in my head and the concrete moving toward me was hypnotic. Thank God Hooker was driving because I was barely able to keep my eyes open. It turns out Hooker is unflappable in traffic and tireless on the open road. Not much of a surprise since he is, after all, NASCAR Guy.

I became more alert when we got to the bridge to Key Largo. Florida has never held much interest for me . . . with the exception of the Keys. The Keys conjured images of Ernest Hemingway. And the ecosystem was unique and as foreign to downtown Baltimore as I could possibly get. I know all this because I watch the Travel Channel.

We passed through Largo and began skimming along on bridges that felt inches above the water, hopping key to key. Plantation Key, Islamorada, Fiesta Key. The sun was setting and the sky was washed in Day-Glo flamingo pink broken by magenta slashes of cloud. The roadsides were cluttered with fried-food shacks, real-estate offices, Froggy's Gym, some chain restaurants, gift shops specializing in trinkets made from shells imported from Taiwan, gas stations, and convenience stores tucked into small strip malls.

We motored through Marathon, over the Seven Mile Bridge, through Little Torch Key. It was dark when we got to Key West. It was a weekend, and Key West was packed with tourists. The tourists clogged the sidewalks and streets. Lots of overweight men in brown socks and sandals and baggy khaki shorts. Lots of overweight women wearing T-shirts that advertised bars, bait shops, their status as grandmothers, ice cream, motorcycles, Key West, and beer. Restaurants were lit, their tables spilling onto sidewalks. Shops were open selling local art and Jimmy Buffet everything. Vendors hawked T-shirts. Ernest Hemingway look-alikes offered themselves up on street corners. Ten dollars and you can have your picture taken with Ernest Hemingway.

"I thought it would be a little more . . . island," I said.

"Honey, this *is* island. If Ernest was alive today, he'd be living in South Beach doing the clubs."

"I don't see a lot of hotels. Are we going to be able to get a room?"

"I know a guy, Richard Vana, who has a house here. We can crash there overnight."

Hooker turned down a side street, away from the crush of tourists. He drove two blocks and pulled into a driveway. We were in a pocket of small elaborate Victorian houses and plantation-shuttered island bungalows that were lost in shadow, tucked back from the narrow street behind tiny yards filled with exotic flowering bushes and trees.

I took my bag and followed Hooker to the house. It was a single-story bungalow. Hard to see the color in the dark, but it looked like it might be yellow with white trim. The air was heavy with the scent of night-blooming jasmine and roses. No lights on inside the house.

"It looks like your friend isn't home," I said to Hooker.

"He's never here. A couple weeks out of the year. I called before we left Miami and asked if we could use his house." Hooker ran his hand above the doorjamb and came up with a key. "One of the advantages to driving NASCAR. You meet a lot of interesting people. This guy has a boat I can borrow, too . . . if we need a boat." Hooker opened the door and switched on the foyer light.

The house wasn't big, but it was comfy. Furniture was rattan and overstuffed. Colors were crimson, yellow, and white. Floors were cherry.

"There are two guest bedrooms down the hall to the right," Hooker said. "Take whichever one you want. They're both pretty much the same." He dropped his bag, wandered into the kitchen, and stuck his head in the refrigerator. "We've got Corona and Cristal champagne and diet cola. I'm going for the Corona. What would you like?"

"Corona. Looks like you know your way around the house."

"Yeah. I probably spend more time here than Rich. I like the Keys."

"Do you like it better here than South Beach?"

He took a long pull on his Corona. "Not better. I guess it depends on my mood. If I had a house here it wouldn't be Key West. It would be on one of the quieter Keys to the north. I like the fishing. I'm not crazy about the hordes of tourists. There are a lot of NASCAR fans here, and once I get recognized on the street I have to worry about a mob scene. I don't get much attention in South Beach. I'm low on the celebrity watch list there."

"Richard Vana sounds familiar."

Hooker slouched onto the couch in front of the television and remoted it on. "He's a baseball player. Houston."

My cell phone chirped, and I had a moment of terror, debating answering, worried it was my mother. But then I thought it could also be Bill, and I wouldn't want to miss that call.

It turned out it wasn't my mother, and it wasn't Bill. It was Rosa.

"Where are you?" Rosa asked. "I have to see you. I went back to talk to Felicia. And we asked around the neighborhood. Does anybody know anything? And they tell us to go to crazy Armond. Armond came to this country when they opened the prisons in Cuba and sent those people here to Miami. Armond says he was in the prison with Maria's father, and Armond says Juan would sometimes talk about the diving. And then he showed me on a map where Juan would like to dive."

"Can you tell me?"

"I have no names. The names aren't the same. But I have this little map Armond drew for us. I need to give you the map."

"Hooker and I are in Key West."

"What are you doing in Key West? Never mind. We'll bring you the map. We'll leave here early in the morning. Make sure you have your phone on. I'll call you when we get there." And Rosa hung up.

I rolled out of bed and followed my nose to the kitchen where Hooker had coffee brewing. He was dressed in wrinkled board shorts and a T-shirt that advertised motor oil. His hair was uncombed and his feet were bare. He looked very island, and I hated to admit it, but he also looked sexy . . . in an unkempt, fashion-disaster slob kind of way.

"We have coffee and creamer," Hooker said. "The only other food in the house is some microwave popcorn. Usually I have wasabi peas and beer nuts for breakfast when I stay here, but we ate them last night."

I poured myself a mug of coffee and added two packets of creamer. "Do you think that guy with the slicked-back hair was for real yesterday?"

"Yeah. I think he was for real. I think the night watchman was really dead. I think Maria Raffles is really screwed up. And I think your brother is an even bigger moron than I am when it comes to women."

"Anything else?"

"I think Maria and your brother are trying to bring something up from Cuban waters."

"Don't say that out loud. I don't want to hear that! Americans aren't supposed to go to Cuba. Cuba is closed to American citizens."

JANET EVANOVICH

"There are a lot of people who think we'll resume relations with Cuba in the near future, and it'll create economic havoc for south Florida. The island is only one hundred and sixty-five miles from Miami. Ninety miles from Key West. It could steal away a lot of tourism and manufacturing dollars. I know a guy who's brokering a land deal for future development."

"Isn't that risky?"

"Sure, but I guess you weigh the risk against the potential payoff."

"I'd think it was impossible for an American to make that sort of deal."

"Apparently there are ways if you know the right people."

I took my coffee into the shower with me, and a half hour later Hooker and I were ready to roll. The streets were much less crowded. It wasn't quite 8 AM and the shops were closed. A few bars were open, serving breakfast. We got breakfast burritos to go and ate them as we made our way to the docks. A giant cruise ship sat offshore. In a couple hours it would dump thousands of people into Key West, and Key West would be like the old lady in the shoe who had so many children she didn't know what to do. Personally, I didn't think it would be such a bad thing to divert some of the cruise ships to Cuba.

"I guess this isn't much of a vacation for you," I said to Hooker.

"It's not that bad," Hooker said. "I'm in Key West with a pretty girl. So far you haven't put out, but I still have hopes. Someone's threatening to kill me. I'm on sort of a treasure hunt. And the breakfast burrito was first-class."

100

"My fantasy is that we'll walk along these docks and stumble across your boat, complete with Bill and Maria."

"That's a decent fantasy. Want to hear mine?"

"*No.*"

"It involves wild gorilla sex."

"Gee, that's a surprise."

Hooker grinned. "I didn't want to disappoint you."

We walked the entire marina, but we didn't see Hooker's boat. We showed Bill's picture to a couple people, but no one recognized him. We stopped in at the dockmaster's office and got a hit. The boat came in on Tuesday and stayed one night. Bill paid for the space with a credit card Hooker had left on board.

Hooker called his credit card company to see if there'd been any further charges or cash withdrawals. There hadn't.

"Now what?" I asked.

"Now we hope Rosa's map is worth something."

We were at the edge of the marina parking lot, debating a latte and a bag of doughnuts when my phone rang.

"We're here," Rosa said. "We just crossed the bridge onto the island."

"Tell her we'll meet her in the marina parking lot," Hooker said. "Uh-oh."

"What uh-oh?"

"You see that family, by the trolley stop? I don't like the way they're looking at me."

"They're probably thinking you need a fashion makeover. Or maybe they're looking at me. Maybe they think I'm adorable in my pink hat."

"You don't know what it's like. It can get damn scary. Before you know it there are people running at you from all over the place. I don't have any security here."

"Don't worry. I'll protect you."

Hooker was still in the motor oil T-shirt and wrinkled shorts. He was wearing sunglasses, ratty sneakers without socks, and the hat advertising tires. He turned his back to the family and kept his head down. "Tell me when they're gone. I like my fans. I swear, I really do, but sometimes they scare the crap out of me."

"They aren't going away," I told him. "They're slowly creeping toward us. They look like a nice family. A couple little boys. And the mother and father are nicely dressed."

"They're all nice. It's just when you put them together and they turn into a mob."

"Well maybe if you weren't wearing a hat advertising tires and a T-shirt advertising motor oil . . ."

"My sponsors give this shit to me. I'm supposed to wear it. And anyway, I've got a billion of these T-shirts and hats. What am I supposed to do with them if I don't wear them?"

"It's *him*," the mother screamed. "It's Sam Hooker!"

The two kids ran up to Hooker. Hooker turned and smiled at them. Mr. Nice NASCAR Guy.

"Hey, how's it going?' Hooker said to the kids. "Do you guys like cars?"

The mother had a pen and the father had his hat in his hand. "Would you sign my hat?" he asked Hooker.

A couple more people trotted over. Hooker was smiling at them all, signing whatever was handed to him.

"See," I said to Hooker, "isn't this fun? Look how happy you're making these people."

"You're not doing your bodyguard thing," he said. "You have to keep them back a little so they don't crush into me. I can't sign if I've got my arms pinned against my chest."

I looked around. He was right. They were crushing into him, pushed by the people at the back. He was right about the numbers, too. There were suddenly *a lot* of people trying to get close to Hooker. They were waving hats and napkins and T-shirts and they were yelling at him. "Hooker. Hey Hooker, sign this. Sign this!"

I'd been standing next to him, but somehow I got elbowed aside and shoved to the rear. In a moment's time I was pushed so far back I couldn't see Hooker at all. I was looking for an opening to get back in when Rosa and Felicia showed up.

"What's all the excitement about?" Rosa wanted to know.

"Hooker's up there, autographing stuff," I said. "I was supposed to be doing crowd control, but I got pitched out. I'm worried about Hooker. I just saw a woman run by with a piece of his shirt in her hand."

"We gotta get Hooker away from this mob or there'll be nothing left of him but a grease spot on the sidewalk," Rosa said. "There's people coming from all over."

"I don't know what to do," I said. "I tried yelling at them and they laughed at me."

Rosa hiked her purse up on her shoulder. "Get out of my way. I'll take care of this." She leaned forward and shouted at the crowd. "Omigod! It's Britney Spears! *Britney Spears.*"

The people at the outermost edge turned to look. A murmur rippled through the mob.

"Now they're vulnerable," Rosa said. "Now we gotta ram our way through."

Rosa went first with her head down. She knocked people out of her way, and she kept going. "Britney Spears is back there," she kept saying. "Did you see Britney?"

Felicia followed Rosa. And I followed Felicia.

By the time we reached Hooker he'd climbed onto the roof of a Subaru. He only had one sneaker, and his hat and his shirt were gone.

The Subaru was surrounded by fans trying to grab Hooker. They were still shoving things at him to get signed. The fans were all yelling things like: *This is for my son. He's dying. Brain cancer . . . It's his birthday . . . It's for my mother. She tried to kill herself when you lost at Taledega . . . It's for my daughter. She sold her trailer so she could come to Daytona to see you race, and now she's homeless. It would mean a lot to her if you'd sign my sock . . . I haven't got any paper. Could you sign my forehead? . . . Could you sign my right breast? Look I've got it out for you. Here's a pen.*

Rosa and Felicia and I climbed onto the Subaru with Hooker.

"Lady, you suck as a bodyguard," Hooker said to me. "Where were you when they ripped my shirt off?"

"These people are crazy!"

"They're just a little excited. I don't understand it, but this happens to me a lot."

Two cop cars pulled into the lot, lights flashing. A couple cops got out and waded through the crowd.

"Hey look," one of the cops said. "It really is Sam Hooker. Man, I love to watch you drive," the cop said to Hooker. "You're the best. I almost lost it when you took out the Bud car last year at Miami."

"Yeah," Hooker said. "That was a good one. I'm in sort of a bind here, guys. I'm turning into fan food."

One of the cops got knocked to the ground. "Call for backup," he yelled to his partner. "We need riot control."

A half hour later, the crowd was dispersed. The cops all had autographs. A property damage report had been filed for the Subaru. One of the cops had gotten Hooker's shoe back. The hat and the shirt were never to be seen again.

"Thanks guys," Hooker said to the cops. "Appreciate the help."

We all piled into Rosa's gray Nissan Sentra, and the cops escorted us out of the lot and waved us away.

SIX

Rosa, Felicia, and I sat on the crimson-and-yellow couch in Rich Vana's living room and waited while Hooker went off to get another motor oil T-shirt.

"So," Felicia said to me. "Are you sleeping with him?"

"No!"

"That's a good thing. He's hot-looking, but he's probably diseased. I read the magazines, and I watch the celebrity shows on television. These race car drivers have sex on the brain. They're like barnyard animals."

"It's not just race car drivers," Rosa said. "It's men. All men have sex on the brain. That's why they can't multitask. Their whole brain is taken up with sex."

"Not all men are diseased, though," Felicia said.

"Puleeze," Rosa said, eyes rolling, hands in the air. "*All* men are diseased. What about herpes and genital warts? Do you honestly think there's a man in Miami without one of those?"

"Well, no. But I wasn't counting those. Do you think they count for disease?"

Hooker strolled into the living room. He was wearing a new hat and a new T-shirt that were exact replicas of the ones he'd lost. "What counts for disease?"

"Herpes," I said.

"Not if it's on your lip," Hooker said. "If it's on your lip you can call it a cold sore. And everyone knows a cold isn't a disease."

"I rest my case," Rosa said. "All men are sex-crazy and diseased."

"Yeah," Hooker said. "But we're fun, right?" He turned to me. "Just for the record, I'm not diseased."

Felicia put two maps on the coffee table. One was a fold-up road map of Cuba, and the other was crazy Armond's map, drawn on a piece of lined paper. The road map was dog-eared and worn at the folds. It had a coffee cup stain over Havana and an arrow drawn in red Magic Marker pointing to Club Med Varadero.

"Here, you see, is Maria's little town, Nuevo Cabo," Felicia said. "It is a very good place to be a fisherman because the fish are not far offshore, and because there is a safe harbor. It is also a good place to smuggle things you would like kept secret because it is a little remote, but it is still close to Mariel. There were many Russian ships going into Mariel when Maria's grandfather was looking to make money. The first of the missiles came into the port of Mariel to be taken to the site at Guanajay.

"Remember, there was the blockade by the U.S. Navy, and

still Maria's grandfather went out that night. It was craziness. And it started the curse."

"There's no curse," Rosa said. "Just greed."

Felicia made the sign of the cross. "Greed is a curse," she said. "If you look on crazy Armond's map, you will see where he puts Nuevo Cabo and Mariel. It was always thought the fishing boat went down in the harbor of Mariel. Or maybe that it started to sail to Havana. Armond says Juan found his father far west of there. Juan told Armond he found his father's bones still with the wedding band on his finger and with a bullet hole in his skull. There are islands and underwater caves to the far side of the Bahia de Cabana, and this is where Armond says Juan found his father. Armond has drawn three islands. One he calls the boot. And another he calls the bird in flight. And he says it is here that Juan did his final diving."

Hooker took the piece of paper and studied it. "How reliable is crazy Armond?"

"He's crazy," Felicia said. "How reliable is crazy?"

"Great."

"Tell me again why you are doing all this looking," Felicia said.

"I want to find my boat," Hooker said.

"And I want to find my brother," I said.

"But won't they come home by themselves when they are ready?"

"We're not the only ones looking for them," I said. "I want to find them before the bad guys find them."

"Is that possible?"

"Anything's possible," Hooker said. He had his cell phone in his hand, and he was scrolling through his phone book. He found what he was looking for and pushed *send*.

"Hey," Hooker said when the connection was made. "It's Sam Hooker. What's up? Un hunh. Un hunh. Un hunh." There was some NASCAR talk. Then there was some talk about cigars. And then Hooker asked the guy on the other end if he wanted to buzz some islands off the coast of Cuba. There was some laughing after that. Hooker disconnected and stood. "I'm going to the airport," Hooker said. "Anyone going with me?"

Key West International Airport is on the easternmost part of the island. The terminal is single story white stucco with an orange tile roof, and it seems too pretty, too relaxed, and too small to belong to something calling itself an international airport. We parked in the lot, under a couple palms, and we all followed Hooker into the building.

"You seem to know what you're doing," I said to Hooker.

"I've flown out of here before on fishing and sightseeing trips. Other than that, it's an illusion. I have no idea what I'm doing."

We stood to one side of the entrance and looked around. A slim guy with a great tan trotted over to us. He was wearing sandals and shorts and a short-sleeve, open-necked shirt with a lot of red and green parrots printed on it. His hair was long, pulled back into a ponytail, his sport sunglasses were on a cord around his neck, his eyes were blue and crinkled at the corners, his smile was wide.

"Where the hell have you been?" he said to Hooker. "I haven't seen you in months."

"End of the season always gets nutty. And then I had to go back to Texas for the holidays."

"So what are you doing, shopping for Cuban real estate?"

"My boat's wandered off. I thought I'd go out looking for it. This is Barney, Rosa, and Felicia. Barney's going with us."

The ponytail guy nodded to us. "Chuck DeWolfe. A pleasure, ladies."

"Isn't it illegal to fly over Cuba?" I asked Chuck.

"Not for me," he said. "I'm a Canadian citizen."

"So, what have you got?" Rosa wanted to know. "Seaplane?"

"Helicopter," Chuck said.

Helicopter! I'd never been in a helicopter. Never wanted to try one out. I'd take an elevator to Mars before I'd go a hundred feet in a helicopter.

"Barney gets a little nervous over heights," Hooker said.

"No problemo," Chuck said to me. "We'll fly nice and low."

Felicia was crossing herself and saying the rosary in Spanish. "You'll crash and die," she said. "No one will ever find you. The sharks will eat you, and there'll be nothing left. I can see it all."

"Yeah, you have to be nuts to go in a helicopter," Rosa said. "Only men go in helicopters. Women know better." She shook her finger at me. "Don't you let him talk you into going up in that helicopter. Just because he's a hottie doesn't mean he has any brains."

"Cripes," Hooker said. "Cut me some slack here."

"Yeah, that's harsh," Chuck said. "On the other hand, dog, they think you're a hottie."

Hooker and Chuck did a complicated variation on the high five.

"Probably there's no need for all of us to go," I said. "Why don't I wait here?"

Hooker locked eyes with me for a couple beats. "You're going to be here when I get back, right?"

"Right."

"Promise."

"Don't push it," I said.

Rosa and Felicia and I watched the two men walk away, out to the helicopter.

"He might be worth a disease," Felicia said. "Nothing major. A little one."

"I'm gonna tell your husband," Rosa said. "You're thinking dirty thoughts about another man."

"Thinking doesn't count," Felicia said. "A woman's allowed to think. Even a good Catholic woman can think."

"Here's the plan," Rosa said. "First we eat, and then we shop."

We went back to Old Town, parked by the harbor, and walked up Duval Street. We sat outside at a tourist-trap café, and we ate fried fish sandwiches and key lime pie.

"I make better pie," Felicia said. "The trick is you use condensed milk."

A flash of black caught my attention. Not a lot of people wearing black in Key West. I looked up from my pie and locked eyes with the shooter with the slicked-back hair. He seemed as surprised to see me as I was to see him.

We stared at each other for maybe ten seconds, and then he turned and crossed the street and walked toward the corner. He stopped outside a store, and I realized the store was Scuba Dooba. A guy who looked like he was in the Rent-A-Thug training program came out of Scuba Dooba and stood talking to the shooter. The two men swiveled their heads to look at me. We all stared at one another for what seemed like two years. The shooter made a gun with his hand, index finger extended, aimed it at me, and pulled the trigger.

Rosa and Felicia had been watching.

"Hey!" Rosa said. "Shoot this." And she gave him an entirely different hand gesture, *middle* finger extended.

Felicia did the same. And I didn't want to be left out, so I gave him the finger, too.

The shooter smiled at us. He was half a block away, but I could see the smile went to his eyes. The shooter thought we were funny.

"What's with him?" Rosa asked.

"I think he wants to kill me," I said.

"He's smiling."

"Yeah," I said. "Men. Go figure."

Rosa leaned forward, across the table at me. "Any special reason why he wants to kill you? Because aside from that, he's not too bad to look at."

I told them about the conversation at Monty's.

"You got a lot of nerve to stay here like this," Rosa said to me. "I'd be on a plane going home."

"I can't do that. It's my brother."

"What about the police?"

"I went to the police, but I couldn't tell them everything. I'm afraid Bill might be doing something illegal."

"You're a good sister," Felicia said.

The shooter and his partner turned away from us and disappeared down a side street.

"This is like a movie," Rosa said. "One of those scary ones where everyone gets murdered. And John Travolta is the hit man."

Felicia was crossing herself again.

"I wish you'd go light on that crossing," Rosa said to Felicia. "It's freaking me out."

"What crossing?" Felicia asked. "Was I crossing? I didn't notice."

We paid our bill, and we wandered down the street, past Scuba Dooba, to the next block. We looked at T-shirts, jewelry, sandals, and cotton shirts with island prints. Not high fashion here. This was tourist town. Fine by me, because I couldn't afford high fashion. Felicia bought T-shirts for her grandchildren, and Rosa bought a Jimmy Buffet shot glass. I didn't buy anything. It was Saturday, and I was very possibly two days away from being unemployed.

"It's almost four," Rosa said. "We should be heading back. I don't want to be driving too late at night."

We did an about-face and walked back on Whitehead Street. Felicia turned around twice and looked behind us.

"I got one of those feelings," Felicia said. "Anybody else got a feeling?"

Rosa and I looked at each other. We didn't have any feelings.

"What kind of a feeling are you talking about?" Rosa asked.

"Creepy. Like we're being followed by a big black bird."

"That's friggin' weird," Rosa said.

Felicia turned around for the third time. "There's something back there. I *know* there's something . . . what do you call it? Stalking! There's something stalking."

Rosa and I looked all around, but we didn't see anything stalking.

"Okay, now you've *really* got me freaked out," Rosa said. "I'm not crazy about being stalked by a big black bird. I don't even like birds all that much. What kind of bird is it? Is it, like, a crow?"

We were on a cross street, heading for the Sentra. The street was for the most part residential. Single-family homes and small bed-and-breakfasts. Cars lined both sides of the street. We walked past a yellow Hummer and the Rent-A-Thug stepped from between two parked cars and stood in front of us. He was followed by the shooter with the slicked-back hair.

"Excuse me, ladies," the shooter said. "I'd like to speak to Miss Barnaby, alone."

"No way," Rosa said, moving between me and the shooter. "She don't want to talk to you."

"I think she does want to talk to me," the shooter said to Rosa. "Please step aside."

"Take a hike," Rosa said. "I'm not stepping anywhere."

The shooter flicked a glance at the Rent-A-Thug. The Rent-A-Thug reached for Rosa, and Rosa bitch slapped him away.

"Watch it," Rosa said. "No touching."

The Rent-A-Thug pulled a gun out of his jacket pocket. Rosa screamed. I ducked behind a car. And Felicia whipped a gun out of her handbag and shot the Rent-A-Thug in the foot, and winged the shooter. The Rent-A-Thug went down to the ground like a sack of wet sand.

"Fuck," the Rent-A-Thug said. "The old lady shot me!"

The shooter stood in speechless astonishment, watching blood seep into the sleeve of his black shirt.

"Run!" Rosa yelled to us. "Run!"

We took off down the street, partially dragging Felicia. Felicia could shoot, it turned out, but she wasn't much good at running. We reached the Sentra, jumped in, and Rosa pulled away from the curb and floored it.

"I told you we were being stalked!" Felicia said.

"You said it was a bird," Rosa said. "I was looking for a bird."

I was in the backseat, and my heart was racing, and my lips felt numb. I'd never seen anyone shot before. In the movies and on television, but never in person. And I'd never had anyone pull a gun on me. Hard to believe, since I was born and raised in Baltimore. One time Andy Kulharchek chased me around the garage with a tire iron, but he was drunk off his ass and he kept falling down.

"I can't believe you shot them," I said to Felicia.

"It was one of those reactions."

"You don't look like someone who'd carry a gun."

"I always carry a gun. Do you know how many times the fruit stand has been robbed? I can't count that high. Now when someone tries to rob me I shoot them."

"You go, girl," Rosa said.

My heart was still skipping around. I could still hear the gunshots echoing in my ears. In my mind's eye I could see the two men getting shot.

Felicia pulled the visor down and looked at herself in the mirror. "He called me an old lady. Did you hear that? I don't think I look so old."

"He deserved to get shot," Rosa said. "He had no tact."

"I've been using this new cream from Olay," Felicia said. "It's supposed to make your skin luminous."

"I should get some of that," Rosa said. "You can never be too luminous."

I couldn't believe they were having this conversation. Felicia just shot two men! And they were talking about skin cream.

"We have to go home," Rosa said. "Do you have someplace safe where you can wait for Hooker?"

"You can take me back to Vana's house. I'll be okay there," I said.

"Just in case, you should take the gun," Felicia said, handing the gun to me. "It's a revolver. Easy to use. Still got four shots left."

"No! I couldn't take your gun." Don't want to. Won't use it! Terrified to touch it!

"It's okay. I always get rid of them after I shoot somebody," Felicia said. "It's simpler that way. When you're done with it, just throw it in the ocean. Make sure it's someplace deep. When I'm in Miami I throw them in the Miami River. Probably if the police dive down they find the Miami River filled with guns. Probably so many guns in the Miami River it raises the high-water line."

"I don't know anything about guns," I said.

"I thought you were from Baltimore," Rosa said. "Doesn't everyone in Baltimore have a gun?"

"Not me."

"Well, now you have a gun," Felicia said. "Now you just like everyone else from Baltimore and Miami."

"It won't go off all by itself, will it?"

"No," Felicia said. "You got to pull the hammer back and then squeeze the trigger. If you don't pull the hammer back the gun won't go *bang*."

Five minutes later we were idling in front of Vana's house.

"You be careful," Rosa said. "You call us if you need help."

"And don't go out of the house until Hooker gets back," Felicia said. "Maybe I should have killed those two guys, but I would have to say a lot of Hail Mary for that."

They waited until I got in the house and waved at them through the window that I was okay, and then they cruised off.

I had Felicia's gun in my handbag, and there was no way the shooter could know my location. None of this stopped me from mentally cracking my knuckles every ten seconds. I made sure the curtains were all drawn, and then I sat myself down in front of the television. I put the sound on low, so I could hear suspicious noises on the porch or in the bushes under the windows. And I waited for Hooker.

A little after eight a car pulled into the driveway and idled behind the Mini. I peeked from behind a curtain and saw that it was Hooker getting dropped off by his pilot friend.

I opened the front door, Hooker swaggered in, grabbed me by the front of my shirt, and kissed me.

"I'm home," he said. "And I'm hungry."

"For dinner?"

"Yeah, that too. I don't suppose food has magically appeared in the kitchen?"

"Must be the food fairy's day off."

"That's okay. I know a place where we can get sauce up to our elbows eating ribs."

"Probably that's not a good idea. We might want to order in." And I told him about the shooter and his partner.

Hooker had a full-on smile. Lots of perfect white teeth showing. Crinkles around his eyes. "Let me make sure I got this right. Felicia shot the guy in black? And she also shot his Rent-A-Thug."

I had to smile with him. Now that I had some distance it was sort of funny, in a surreal kind of way. "Yep. She shot them. One in the foot. One in the arm."

"And then you all ran away, they dropped you off here, and they left."

"Yeah. And Felicia gave me her gun."

"I'm jealous. You had a better day than I did."

"Did you find your boat?"

"Maybe. We found the islands. They're about ten miles offshore and a good distance from Nuevo Cabo. We couldn't see any sign of habitation. The vegetation is thick. And there are places where a boat could go up an arm of the sea and not easily be seen. Apparently some of these waterways are deep. We saw light reflecting from something on one of those cross-island arms. No way to know if it was off the *Happy Hooker*. We were afraid to spend too much time there or to go too low. I didn't want to chase Bill into a different hiding place."

"Now what?"

"Now we get some pizza delivered, and tomorrow we take Rich's boat and go look for Bill."

I'd left my cell phone on the coffee table, and it started to buzz and dance around.

"Hey girlfriend," Judey said when I answered. "I've got news. I just got a phoner from Todd. He was called back to *Flex*. They're leaving first thing in the morning. And Salzar is on board with a diver."

I dragged myself out of bed at 4 AM, took a shower to try to wake up, brushed my teeth, and gave my hair a blast with the dryer. I stumbled into the kitchen and found Hooker drinking coffee and eating cold leftover pizza.

"Good morning," Hooker said.

"This isn't morning. Morning has sun. Do you see sun?"

"We don't want sun. We want to board the boat and get under way without being seen. I know where there's an all-night convenience store. We'll clean them out of water and granola bars, and then I'll stash you and the food on the boat. I'll park the Mini somewhere and walk back. I don't want to leave Bill's car in the marina lot."

"You know all about boats, right?"

"I know enough to get us to the island and back . . . if there are no problems. We're supposed to have good weather. Calm water. No storms predicted. Rich has a sixty-foot Sunseeker Predator Powerboat. It can cruise at thirty-two knots. And it can carry enough fuel to take us where we want to go. You'll have to help me get away from the dock. Once we're under way the computer takes over."

"How long do you think we'll be gone?"

"I don't know. A couple days, I'm hoping. I haven't got a lot of time. I'm supposed to start doing promotions at the end of the month."

I grew up in Baltimore, on the harbor, but I know nothing about boats. I can tell the difference between a powerboat and a sailboat, and that's where my expertise ends. So it looked to me that Rich Vana had a boat with a big nose. The boat was sparkling white with a wide navy stripe running along the side. The place where you drive was at the back of the boat and was enclosed and cozy. When you went down a set of stairs, the inside of the boat was all high-gloss wood and luxuriously upholstered couches and chairs. It had a state-of-the-art kitchen, two bedrooms, two bathrooms with showers, and a small living room with a dining area.

Hooker dropped me off with the groceries and immediately left to park the Mini. I stashed the bread and peanut butter, cereal, milk, beer, bags of cookies, sealed packets of bologna, sliced ham, cheese, pretzels, granola bars, and cans of SpaghettiOs. And then before Hooker returned, I took a quick peek at the engines. I don't know boats, but I *do* know engines. And these were big boys. Two twin Manning diesels.

Okay, so I was more excited about the engines than the kitchen. Not that the kitchen wasn't great. A side-by-side Sub-Zero refrigerator and freezer, a microwave plus convection oven, a built-in coffeemaker, dishwasher, and a Sub-Zero wine cooler. Nice appliances but hardly in the same league as the diesels. Plus there was a 20kw generator, ten 24 V batteries, two 12 V batteries and chargers.

I scrambled back to the kitchen when I heard Hooker on deck. In an instant, he was down the ladder, moving around me, checking the mechanicals. He looked around and I guess everything was okay. He went up to the pilothouse and started the generator. He unplugged and stored the shore power electrical cord. He flipped breaker switches for the main engine start. He turned on the VHF radio, autopilot, radar, GPS receiver, depth sounder, and boat computer. He entered the GPS course from Key West to Cuba into the boat's computer. He did a test of the bow thruster.

All the while he was telling me what he was doing, and I was trying to remember in case I had to do this myself. You never know, right? He could get washed overboard. He could have a heart attack. He could get drunk and pass out!

"Vocabulary," Hooker said. "The ropes are called lines. The bumper things are called fenders. Right is starboard. Left is port. Front is the bow. Back is the stern. The steering wheel area is the helm. The kitchen is the galley. The crapper is the head. I don't know why any of these things have their own names. It makes no sense to me. Except maybe for the head."

Hooker handed me a walkie-talkie. "As soon as the engines are warmed up we're pulling out, and you're going to have to help me. I'm going to give you directions on the walkie-talkie. Ordinarily I'd have someone on the dock to help untie the lines, but we're trying to sneak off this morning, so we're going to have to manage without help. I'm going to hold the boat against the dock and you're going to untie the lines and throw them onto the boat. You're going to start at the bow and work your way back."

I was ready. First Mate Barney, at your command. I climbed over the rail that ran around the bow, and I scrambled onto the dock. I was wearing shorts and sneakers and my pink ball cap. I didn't need sunglasses because the sun was still struggling to rise out of the water. I had the walkie-talkie in my hand. And I was pretty darned excited.

Hooker was standing at the wheel, and I saw him put the walkie-talkie to his mouth. "I've got her steady," he said. "Start throwing the lines. Do the bow line first."

"Okay," I said. "Doing the bow line."

I reached for the bow line, the walkie-talkie slid from my hand, bounced off the dock, splashed into the water, and disappeared from sight. I looked up at Hooker, and his expression was a lot like the expression on the shooter's face when he watched his blood seep into his shirt.

"Sorry," I said to Hooker, knowing full well he couldn't hear me.

Hooker gave his head a small shake. He was saddled with a moron for a first mate.

"Give me a break here," I yelled at him. "I'm new at this."

Hooker smiled at me. Either he was a very forgiving kind of guy, or else I looked really sexy in my pink hat.

I threw the rest of the lines onto the boat and climbed on board. Hooker crept the boat back, inching away from the dock. He got clear of the dock and he reversed his direction and swung the boat around to leave the marina.

"We need to stay at idle speed, five knots, until we leave the marina," he said. "Once we get into open water I can increase the throttle to bring us to cruising speed."

I had no relationship to knots. I was strictly a miles-per-hour kind of person. And on my salary, which was going to be zero as of tomorrow, I didn't think I had to worry about cruising at thirty-two knots much beyond this trip. Still . . .

"I don't know what the hell a knot is," I said to Hooker.

"One knot equals 1.15 miles per hour."

The sun was finally above the horizon and the water in front of us looked like glass. We plowed through some small swells at the mouth of the harbor and then we were in the open water. I stored the lines and the fenders away as best I could. When I had everything tidy Hooker took the boat up to speed, and engaged the autopilot.

"The autopilot interfaces with the GPS chart plotter," Hooker said. "And it's a lot smarter than I am."

"Can you just walk away from it now?"

"In theory, but I wouldn't walk far. Especially not on this cruise. I need to keep my eyes open."

"Worried about pirates?"

"I don't know who I'm worried about."

SEVEN

After two hours of ocean cruising, the whole boat thing started to get old. There's not a lot to look at when you're in the middle of the ocean. The boat was noisy, making conversation a pain, and I got nauseated when I went below while we were under way.

After three and a half hours, I was looking for land.

"Cuba is off the port bow," Hooker said. "We're about fifteen miles offshore, and I don't want to get closer. The islands we're looking for are about ten miles out."

"You're pretty good at this boat stuff," I said.

"If the computer punks out, I'm a dead man."

I couldn't eyeball the island, but I could see the island approaching on the GPS screen. It was possible that Bill was just miles away. An unnerving thought. Chances were good that he wouldn't be happy to see Hooker and me. And chances were *very* good that *I* wouldn't be happy after hearing his story.

"You look tense," Hooker said.

"How confident are you that the boat you saw in the river was yours?"

"Not confident at all. In fact, I'm not even sure it was a boat."

Suddenly there were three dots on the horizon.

"The island we're after is in the middle," Hooker said.

My heart skipped a beat.

"Are you carrying Felicia's gun?" Hooker asked.

"Yes."

"Do you know how to use it?"

"Sure." In theory.

I had my eyes fixed on the island. It looked relatively flat and heavily vegetated with the exception of a narrow strip of sugar sand beach. "Pretty beach," I said.

"This island alternates between beach and mangrove. The back of the island is all mangrove."

Hooker disconnected the autopilot and eased back on the throttle. "We're going to have to watch the depth finder and make sure we've got enough water under us. My boat displaces a lot more than Rich's, so we should be okay . . . if it's my boat in there."

Hooker brought us into the cove at idle speed and we looked around. No sign of activity. No traces of civilization. No cute little beach shacks, no docks, no Burger King signs. There were seagulls and long-legged shorebirds among the mangroves, and the occasional fish jumped in front of the boat. The water was calm. Very little breeze. Nothing moved on the palms.

We'd seen other boats when we got within fifteen miles of Havana, but they were always far away. Planes occasionally passed overhead. Not a threat since no one knew to look for Vana's boat. Hooker and I were out of sight, at the helm, under a hardtop.

A helicopter came out of nowhere and buzzed the boat. Hooker and I held our breath. The helicopter disappeared over the treetops, and we both expelled a *whoosh* of air.

"It wasn't military," Hooker said. "Probably just some rich tourist seeing the sights."

"Are we going up the waterway?"

"I'm going to try. I'd feel more comfortable if we had a smaller boat. I'm probably going to have to back out. I'd like to back in, in case we have to leave fast, but I'm afraid to go in propellers first."

So here's the thing about a NASCAR guy. He might be an asshole, but at least he knows how to drive. And he's got *cojones*. Not even ordinary *cojones*. We're talking big brass ones.

Hooker approached the estuary and began creeping forward.

"Go to the bow," he said, "and watch for problems. Floating debris, narrowing of the water, signs that the water is getting too shallow. I've got a depth finder, but by the time it tells me I'm in trouble it could already be too late."

I carefully walked across the white fiberglass bow to the pointed prow. I dropped to hands and knees for better stability and leaned forward, studying the water ahead.

Hooker leaned around the windscreen and looked out at

me. "I know you're trying to be helpful," he said, "but I can't drag my eyes off you when you're in that position. Maybe you could try lying flat to the boat, or at least swinging your ass more to the side."

I turned slightly to look at him. "Deal with it," I said. And then I went back to watching the water. I was from Baltimore. I grew up in a garage. I had my own set of *cojones*. And there wasn't much a man could say that would surprise me.

The width narrowed, but the depth stayed constant. Trees from both banks formed a canopy over our heads, and the sun dappled the water through holes in the canopy. Hooker eased the boat around a bend, and a boat lay at anchor directly in front of us. The bow of the boat faced us, so no name was visible. I turned to look at Hooker, and he nodded yes. He brought the boat to a standstill, and I scrambled back to the pilothouse.

"Are you sure it's your boat?" I asked him.

"Yep."

It was slightly bigger than Vana's boat, and the proportions were different. I didn't know a lot about boats, but I knew Vana's boat was more speed boat. And Hooker's boat was for deep-sea fishing.

"Do you think they see us?"

"They could be below decks. Or they could be off exploring the island. I'd think they could hear the engine, no matter, even at idle. We aren't visible behind this tinted sunscreen, so most likely they're watching us from someplace, messing their pants, wondering who the hell we are."

"There's some satisfaction to that," I said.

Hooker smiled at me. "Sugar pie, you've got an evil streak in you. I think I'm getting turned on."

"Everything turns you on."

"Not everything."

"What doesn't turn you on?"

"Dennis Rodman in a wedding gown."

Hooker shifted to the side and leaned out the open window. "Hey Bill, you jerk-off," he yelled. "Get your ass out on deck where I can see you."

Bill popped into view. "Hooker?"

Hooker turned to me and kissed me. He was smiling when he broke away.

"I don't know," he said. "I just felt happy, and I wanted to kiss you."

Seemed to me that there was a lot of tongue in it for just a happy kiss, but hell, he was NASCAR Guy. What do I know? He probably kissed his mother like that. Not that I was complaining. Hooker was a terrific kisser.

Bill was on deck, squinting at us, hand shielding his eyes from the splotches of sun. "Hooker?" he asked again.

Hooker shoved his head back out the side window. "Yeah. I need to talk to you."

"Hey, I can explain about the boat."

"Just get your sorry ass over here. I have to talk to you."

"How's he going to get over here?" I asked.

"I carry a small rigid inflatable boat with an outboard motor. RIB for short. He's probably got it in the water, tied up behind the *Happy Hooker*."

Bill disappeared, and minutes later I heard an engine kick

in and Bill reappeared in the RIB. He maneuvered the inflatable to the dive platform at the back of the Sunseeker and tied up to us.

Bill has red hair that's cut short and is sort of Hollywood messy. He's got a little nose and blue eyes that smile 24/7. He's tanned and freckled. And he's five feet ten inches of solid Scottish-Irish muscle and bullshit. He was wearing Teva sandals and baggy flowery shorts that hit just above his knees. He climbed onto the dive platform and his cheeks went red under his tan when he saw me. "What the hell?" he said.

And I lost it. "You jerk!" I yelled at him. "You self-absorbed, inconsiderate miserable excuse for a brother. You irresponsible bag of monkey shit! How dare you make a phone call like that and then drop off the face of the earth. You scared the crap out of me. I'm going to lose my job because of you. My nose is peeling. My hair is a wreck. I've got seven messages from Mom on my cell phone that I'm afraid to access."

Bill smiled at me. "I'd almost forgotten how much fun you could be."

"Fun?"

I was right up there, in his face. I was so angry the roots of my hair felt like they were on fire. I gave Bill a shot to the shoulder that knocked him off balance and pitched him into the water.

Hooker gave a bark of laughter behind me. I whirled around and caught him with a kick to the back of the knee that doubled him over and rolled him off the edge of the dive platform, into the water with Bill.

Both men surfaced still smiling.

"Feel better?" Hooker asked.

"Yes. Sorry about the kick. I got carried away."

He pulled himself onto the platform and peeled his shirt off. "You're lying again. You're not sorry about the kick."

"I might be a *little* sorry."

Bill followed Hooker onto the platform. "You don't want to mess with her. She's always been a dirty fighter. And she used to be engaged to a kickboxer." Bill grabbed me and gave me a bear hug, leaving me almost as wet as he was. "I've missed you," he said. "God, it's good to see you."

Hooker raised his eyebrows at me. "Engaged?"

"She's been engaged three times," Bill said. "First there was the kickboxer. Then there was the photographer. And then the bartender. Barney's hell on men. I hope you haven't got any ideas."

I gave Bill the squinty eye. "You keep talking and I'm going to knock you into the water again."

"What should I do about anchoring this boat?" Hooker asked Bill.

"Who owns it?"

"Rich Vana."

"Anyone know you and Barney are on it?"

"No," Hooker said.

"We can probably chance dropping anchor in the cove. There's not enough room for both of us back here." Bill went to the helm. "Make sure the RIB is secure, and I'll start pushing her back."

A half hour later we were anchored in the cove.

"I can't believe you found me," Bill said. "I didn't think I left a trail."

"We're not the only ones looking for you," I said to Bill.

"Yeah, it was scary in the beginning, but I thought we were safe tucked away upstream. So what's going on with you two?"

"We're looking for *you*," I said.

"Well, here I am. And as you can see, I'm fine. And I've got a girl back there. So, probably I should be getting back."

"Excuse me," Hooker said. "That's *my* boat you're getting back to."

"I know," Bill said. "And I wouldn't have borrowed it if I wasn't really in a bind. If you could just give me a couple more days I'll have it back, tied up in South Beach, good as new. Swear to God."

"I want it back now," Hooker said.

"I can't give it back now. I'm involved in something here. It's important."

"I'm listening," Hooker said.

"I can't tell you about it."

"I know he's your brother," Hooker said to me, "but I think you should shoot him."

"My mother would hate that," I told Hooker. "And the gun's downstairs in my purse."

"Okay," Hooker said. "I'll get the gun. And I'll shoot him. *My* mother won't mind at all."

"Hey dog," Bill said. "It's just a boat."

"It's a three-million-dollar boat. I had to crash into a lot of walls to pay for that boat. And I was supposed to be out fishing this week. It's perfect weather."

"Maria's going to be pissed off if I tell you."

"We already know some of it," I said. "It's about her father and her grandfather, right?"

Bill grinned. "Actually it's about seventeen million, three hundred thousand dollars in gold bars."

"That's a lot of gold," Hooker said.

"A hundred bars, each weighing twenty-seven pounds."

"Is it on my boat?" Hooker asked.

"We're taking up the last load tonight."

"And then?"

"I'm taking it to Naples. I rented a house in Port Royal when we stopped in the Keys. It's on a canal. I just tie the boat up to the dock and off-load the gold."

Hooker grinned. "You're going in through Gordon Pass?" He turned to me. "Naples is a pretty little town on the Gulf. It's built around canals and filled with multi-million-dollar houses. It's the most respectable place in Florida. Not as much flash as Miami Beach or Palm Beach. Just tons of money. Very safe. And the Port Royal neighborhood is the richest. A three-million-dollar house in Port Royal is considered a tear-down."

"What are you going to do with these gold bars?" I asked Bill.

"I'm not doing anything with them. They belong to Maria."

Hooker and I exchanged glances.

"We need to have a conversation with Maria," Hooker said.

The rigid inflatable was about twelve feet long with an outboard. We all piled in. Bill took the wheel and motored us upstream to Hooker's boat. At this lower level, the tropical forest was beautiful but claustrophobic. Ground vegetation was dense and dark. The second tier was wrapped in flowering vines and occasionally dotted with roosting waterbirds. The air was liquid, soaking into my hair and shirt, sitting like dew on my forearms, trickling down the sides of my face. It was South Beach air magnified, and the cloying scent of flowers and damp earth and plant rot mixed with the brine from the sea.

We tied up to the small dive platform at the back of *Happy Hooker* and climbed on board. Everything was shiny white fiberglass, which I assumed was for easy cleanup when fishing. A fighting chair was bolted to the cockpit deck. A door and large windows looked into the salon from the cockpit, but the glass was darkly tinted and it was impossible to see inside.

Bill opened the salon door and we all trooped in. Maria stood in the middle of the salon with a gun in her hand. She was maybe five three with a lot of wavy dark brown hair that swirled around her tanned face and brushed the tops of her shoulders. Her features were delicate, her mouth naturally pouty, her eyes were the color of melted chocolate. She was slim with large breasts that swayed under her white cotton T-shirt when she moved.

"I'm understanding everything now," Hooker said to me.

I gave him raised eyebrows.

"Probably you don't want to shoot this guy," Bill said to Maria, "since he owns this boat."

"All the more reason," Maria said.

"Yeah, you're right," Bill said. "But don't shoot Barney. She's my sister."

Maria went off in Spanish, waving her hands, yelling at Bill. I looked to Hooker.

"She's unhappy," Hooker said.

I didn't need a translator to figure that out.

"And she's calling him some names I've only heard in Texas stockyards. She's going so fast I can't get it all, but there's something about the size of his privates with the size of his brain and neither of them are looking good." He cut his eyes to me. "Just so you know, I've never had any problems with size in the privates department. The size of my brain has sometimes been questionable."

"Gee, I'm glad you shared that with me," I said.

"I thought you might want to know."

Now Bill was shouting back at Maria. He was shouting in English, but it was hard to tell what he was saying, since the two of them were nose to nose, both yelling at the same time.

"*Hey!*" Hooker said. "*Chill.*"

Maria and Bill turned and looked at Hooker.

"You've got bigger problems than us," Hooker said. "You should be worrying about the guys who trashed your apartments, twice. And the guy who threatened to kill us. And probably you should be worrying about whoever it is that actually owns the gold. Not to mention the Cuban government."

"I own the gold," Maria said. "It was on my grandfather's boat."

"I'm guessing not everyone shares that point of view," Hooker said.

Bill locked eyes with Maria. "The truth is," he said to her, "we could use some help."

Maria looked at Hooker and me, and then she looked back at Bill. "And you trust them?"

"Hooker, yes. Barney, I'm not so sure of."

"You'd better watch your step," I said to Bill. "You'll be in big trouble if I tell Mom you stole a boat."

Bill gave me another bear hug.

Maria put the gun on the black granite galley counter. "I guess it's okay. You start to tell them the story."

"I met Maria at a club a couple weeks ago. We talked but we never got together. Then I saw her Monday night. Again, it was just hello. She left real early."

"I met a guy the night before," Maria said. "I didn't like him, and when I saw he was at the club again I decided to leave. I wasn't in a club mood anyway. I walked home, and I was about to go into my apartment building when a man stepped out of the shadows and put a gun to my head. There were two more men waiting in a car at the curb, and they drove me to the marina. When we got to the boat I asked them what this was about and they said I was going back to Cuba. They said I was going to take a helicopter trip to Cuba. That was when I started to struggle."

"I decided to leave the club early too," Bill said. "We were supposed to go back out first thing Tuesday morning, and I

136

didn't want to get wasted. I was in the marina lot, heading for *Flex*, when the car pulled in with Maria. I saw them help her out of the car and walk her down the pier. I recognized the car and the men as Salzar's. He's brought women on board before, so I didn't think much about it. It wasn't until she started struggling at the end of the pier that I realized she was being forced onto the boat. Probably I should have called the police, but all I could think of was to get her off *Flex*.

"I waited for about ten minutes and then I boarded. Everything was quiet. The rest of the crew was asleep. There was a light on in the pilothouse, but that was it. I crept around, trying doors, and found her bound and gagged in one of the VIP staterooms on the second deck."

"Wasn't the door locked?"

"Yeah, but I accidentally came into possession of a master key the first week I worked on *Flex*. You never know when you might need a master key, right?"

Yessir, this was my brother.

"Anyway," Bill said, "I cut Maria loose, and we hauled ass out of there. Maria didn't want to call the police. She just wanted to get some stuff out of her apartment."

"I knew when they discovered I was gone they would go to my apartment and search for my charts," Maria said. "Before this night, I didn't realize anyone knew about me. I didn't bother to hide my charts. I thought the shipwreck had been forgotten. Gone with my father."

"So you think Salzar wants either you or the charts so he can salvage the wreck?"

"My father discovered gold when he went diving for my

grandfather. He came back with my grandfather's remains, and he told my mother. My mother told me on her deathbed. She always said to everyone that she didn't know where my father went to dive, but she always knew. And she knew about the gold."

A small prop plane buzzed the treetops, and we all went still until it passed.

"I can tell you what I think," Maria said. "I think the gold was for Castro. My grandfather was lost at sea two days after President Kennedy put the blockade up. I think one of the big Russian ships had gold for Castro. The ship couldn't get to port, so perhaps they sent my grandfather out to get the gold. It was always a rumor in my village. I never believed it until my mother told me."

"And?"

"And something happened. My grandfather's boat hit a reef and never arrived at Mariel. There were two men on the boat. The one man was rescued at sea in a lifeboat. He said my grandfather's boat was damaged and taking on water, but my grandfather wouldn't leave the boat. For years the man who survived looked for the boat, but he always looked in the shoals around Mariel. Everyone thought he was looking for my grandfather, but now I think he was looking for the gold."

"Oh boy," Hooker said. "I have Castro's gold on my boat."

Maria cut her eyes to him. "It's *my* gold on your boat."

"How did your father know where to look for the shipwreck?"

"He heard that a fisherman from Playa el Morrillo was catching fish off a wreck in this harbor. When my father heard of a wreck he would go to investigate. It didn't matter how far."

Hooker went to the refrigerator and got a beer. "Anyone?" he asked.

Bill took a beer. Maria and I declined.

"If I brought the gold up while I lived in Cuba it would do me no good," Maria said. "The government would come and take it. And they might throw me in prison like my father. So I came to Miami and I looked for someone to help me."

"That would be me," Bill said.

Maria smiled at Bill. "An unlikely hero."

Bill slid a protective arm around Maria, and she leaned into him. It was a simple gesture, but it was surprisingly tender.

"I'm in love," Bill announced to Hooker and me.

I smiled at Bill and Maria, and I mentally wished them well, but I'd heard this *a lot.* Bill fell in love easily. And often. Bill was four years old the first time he made this announcement. Carol Lazar had allowed him to take a peek at her panties and Bill was in love. And Bill has been peeking at girls' panties and falling in love ever since. I think it would be nice if Bill could find the right woman and commit, but in the meantime, at least his sex life wasn't without love.

Hooker smiled at Bill, too. Hard to tell if Hooker's smile was cynical or wistful.

"To love," Hooker said. And he took a pull on his beer.

"What was the scream about at the end of your phone call to me?" I asked Bill.

"We were casting off and the night watchman showed up with a gun. I guess he thought we were stealing the boat."

"Imagine that," Hooker said.

"The night watchman is dead," I said to Bill. "Knifed an hour after you took off. Both of your apartments have been searched, twice. Once by two Cuban guys. And once by two Caucasians. One of the Caucasians always wears black and has slicked-back hair. The slicked-back-hair guy threatened to kill me and Hooker if we kept looking for you. I was attacked by a mutant named Hugo, who I prefer to call Puke Face. Puke Face tried to kidnap me with hopes of trading up to you. Puke Face works for Salzar. And Puke Face's message was that you were in possession of Salzar's property. I imagine he was talking about Maria. Oh yeah, and they called Mom and left a message for you. Those are pretty much the high points."

"And then there's your computer," Hooker said to Maria. "With the gold and the warhead research. The gold I get. Maybe you should tell us about the warhead."

"It was part of the rumor. That besides the gold, there was some new weapon on board my grandfather's ship. My mother said my father was afraid it was true. My father told her there was a canister not far from the gold. He said it looked like it might be a bomb. He didn't want Castro gaining control of this weapon, so he wouldn't talk. When they came to take him away, he told my mother he would never reveal the wreck. My mother told me some of the markings on the canister, and I tried to identify it on the Internet, but I couldn't find anything."

"You've been diving," Hooker said. "Is the canister down there?"

Maria nodded. Solemn. "Yes."

"Do we know the connection between Salzar and Calflex?" I asked Bill.

"There was a rumor a while back that Salzar was brokering a Cuban land deal for Calflex. Not sure if it's true."

"A better question," I said. "How does Salzar know about the wreck?"

"He's originally from Cuba, no?" Maria said. "He's of an age where he might have heard the rumors."

"Seems like he's investing a lot of energy in a rumor," Hooker said. "I can be a pretty aggressive guy, but I don't think I'd kidnap someone on the basis of a rumor."

"There could be others who would know the ship's cargo," Maria said. "My grandfather's partner would know. My mother spoke of him sometimes. His name was Roberto Ruiz. And he could have told people. The men on the Russian ship might know. Someone had to put the gold and the canister on board the fishing boat. And Castro would know. Maybe some of his aides."

"Salzar could be working for Castro," Bill said. "They're supposed to be buddies."

"Why is Salzar going after you now?" I asked. "Why did he wait so long? You've been in Miami for four years."

"I don't know. Maybe he just found out. Not long ago, there was an article in the newspaper about the cigar factory with my picture and my name in it. The newspaper man spoke to me because I am the youngest of all the women who roll the cigars."

Another plane flew overhead.

"You're reflecting light through the trees," Hooker said to Bill.

"I know. I was hoping it wasn't too bad. If this had been planned out I would have gotten a tarp. We only need one more night, and we'll be out of here. We've been diving at night, so we wouldn't be seen. The harbor is deep in the middle. Sixty feet. And that's where the boat went down. Maria brings the gold up using lift bags, and we ferry it back to the boat in the RIB. Tonight we'll bring the boat out and take off when we get the last of the gold . . . if it's okay with you."

"Sure," Hooker said. "I wouldn't want to see Castro's gold go to waste."

The birds had stopped chattering and had settled in for the night. The water was still. No trace of a breeze. The sun was a fireball, sinking into the island palms. Hooker and I were on deck, waiting for Bill and Maria.

"That was nice of you to let him use your boat," I said to Hooker.

"I didn't see where I had much choice."

"You could have asked for some of the gold."

Hooker was slouched in a deck chair, bare legs outstretched, eyes closed, arms crossed over his moth-eaten T-shirt. "I don't need the gold." He opened his eyes and looked over at me.

"We've got a few minutes, in case you want to jump my bones."

"I've got your number."

"Oh yeah? What's my number?"

"Every time you do something nice you have to follow it up with some asshole remark. Just to keep the balance. To keep things at a safe distance."

"Think you're pretty smart, hunh? Maybe I meant what I said. Maybe I'd really like you to jump my bones. Maybe bones jumping is what Texas NASCAR drivers do best."

"There's no doubt in my mind that Texas NASCAR drivers are excellent bones jumpers. It was the unromantic announcement that guaranteed failure."

"Damn, I thought that was a good line. I thought I was being real classy. I didn't even say anything about what a great rack you have."

"You're doing it again!"

Hooker smiled and closed his eyes. "Just funnin' with you. We haven't got enough time. When I finally let you jump my bones it's going to go on for hours. And sugar pie, you won't even see it coming."

And the horrible part was . . . I believed him.

EIGHT

I heard the boat engine turn over upstream. Bill was moving out before he was in total darkness.

"He's good at this, isn't he?" I asked Hooker.

Hooker sat up. "At working the boat? Or at looting gold?"

"Working the boat."

"He's very good at working the boat. He's one of the few people I'd trust to captain her. The *Happy Hooker* is a big boat with a deep draft. I'd need a whole crew to get me out of that estuary if I was at the helm. Even then I'd probably run into a bank."

"But you think Bill and Maria can do it?"

"Yep. He couldn't do it alone, but it sounds like Maria's been around boats all her life. She's probably a good mate. Bill would have asked if he needed my help. He doesn't take chances with boats."

The engine noise drew closer, and the boat appeared and

stopped before moving into the more open water of the cove. Bill went to the prow, attached the remote to the windlass, and dropped anchor.

A half hour later, in total darkness, I heard the hoist swing out and set the RIB on the water. The sky was black and moonless. We knew the course of the RIB more by sound than by sight. A low-level hum. It was moving toward the middle of the small harbor. Then the outboard cut off. Snatches of muted conversation carried over to us. There was a soft splash and all was quiet.

"She's diving to sixty feet," Hooker said. "It'll take her two minutes to get down and a minute to get up. And she's probably got a little over an hour work time. She's using lift bags to bring the gold up, so you'll know she's coming up when you see the white bags."

Forty minutes later, the lift bags bubbled to the surface like giant marshmallows, and a light appeared at the side of the RIB.

Hooker had taken a walkie-talkie from the *Happy Hooker,* and the talkie came to life.

"She has to go down again," Bill said. "If you bring Vana's boat around to the far side of the lift bags we can load onto your dive platform. I'll talk you through it. Keep your running lights off."

Hooker cranked the boat over and we raised anchor.

Bill was back on the talkie. "Follow my light beam," he said. "I'm going to bring you around to the far side of the RIB."

When we were in position I resumed breathing.

Hooker looked over at me and grinned. "You look like you're about ready to pass out."

"I was worried we were going to run them over. Our boat is so big, and the RIB is so small."

"Barney girl, you need to learn to trust people. Your brother's a good guy. He's kind of a horn dog, but he knows what he's doing when he's on a boat. It's like when I'm racing, and I've got spotters telling me I can make it through a wall of smoke and fire. You figure out who you can trust and then you go with it."

"So you weren't scared just now?"

"Almost messed my pants twice. Don't tell your brother."

Maria was sitting on the side of the RIB. She adjusted her mask and mouthpiece. She touched hands with Bill. And she went over, into the black water, and disappeared. I followed Hooker to the dive platform, and we started working with Bill, hauling the gold out of the water, onto the platform, being careful not to damage the bricks.

"This is a lot easier than trying to get the gold into the RIB," Bill said. "I didn't want to bring the *Happy Hooker* out until I was ready to make a run for it. I know the *Flex* chopper is doing airtime looking for us."

"You've never cared that much for money," I said to Bill. "I'm surprised you're risking your life for this."

"I'm risking my life for Maria," Bill said. "This is her gold, not mine. She thinks her father might still be alive in prison. She's hoping she can buy him out with the gold."

"Oh shit," Hooker said. "We're doing this for a good cause. How crappy is that?"

The lift bags bobbed to the surface for the second time. Maria followed them up, and we tugged the bags over to the dive platform. Bill helped Maria come on board and get out of her equipment.

"This is it," she said. "This is everything that was down there. At least everything I could find." She slipped back into the water to guide the last bag while Hooker and Bill hauled it onto the boat.

We opened the bag, and we all stood back, looking at the contents. A single metal canister, approximately a foot and a half wide by three feet long. Very heavy. Maybe eighty pounds. Russian writing barely visible running along one side. The end cap had been painted red. And there were two thin green-and-black bands painted onto the rear of the canister.

Hooker toed the canister. "Anyone read Russian?"

Nope. No one read Russian.

"It *does* sort of look like a bomb," Bill said.

"Probably we shouldn't open it," I said.

Hooker squatted beside it for a better look. "Probably we *can't* open it. At least not without an acetylene torch and a crowbar. This baby is *sealed*."

If this came off a Russian ship that was stopped by the blockade, I didn't even want to speculate on its purpose. "I keep going back to what Puke Face said about fear," I told Hooker. "He said this was about fear and what it can do for you."

"And maybe this is something to fear? Not a good thought. I don't want to go there."

"I brought it up because I was worried it was no longer

safe to leave it in the cove. It should be turned over to the authorities," Maria said. "My father suffered to keep this out of Castro's hands. I don't want that suffering to have been in vain."

We heard the beat of a helicopter coming at us from the north. We scrambled to get the lift bags out of sight and ducked into the cabin. The copter did a flyby, sweeping the water with its light. The beam missed the boat, and the helicopter continued south.

The instant we could no longer hear the chopper, Bill and Maria were off the dive platform, into the inflatable.

"I'll bring *Happy Hooker* around, and we can use the hoist to load," Bill said.

A half hour later the boats were in position to transfer cargo, and Bill was on the talkie to Hooker.

"I've got a problem here. I can't get the boat out of idle."

"What do you mean, you can't get it out of idle?"

"If I try to increase speed it cuts out."

"So?"

"So that's not good."

"Can you fix it?"

"Not my thing, pardner. Send Barney over."

"Barney? Did I copy you . . . Barney?" Hooker asked.

"She's good with engines."

"You're kidding."

I was standing behind Hooker, listening to the conversation broadcast over the walkie-talkie, and I had a real strong urge to kick him in the knee again.

"Do you know anything about marine engines?" I asked Hooker.

"Not a damn thing," Hooker said. "I don't even know anything about car engines."

"How could you make a living driving cars and not know anything about engines?"

"I drive them. I don't repair them."

Truth is, I was itching to see his engines. I scrambled across to the Hatteras and followed Bill into the mechanical room.

"He's got twin CATs," Bill said. "Twice as big as the Sunseeker's Mannings. I took a quick look but nothing jumped out at me. I guess that doesn't mean much. I was never that interested in garage stuff."

"Holy Toledo," I said, eyeballing the CATs. "This is *way* over my head. I can take a car apart and put it back together again, but I don't know *anything* about *any* of this."

"Take a deep breath," Bill said. "They're just engines . . . only bigger."

Maria was at the helm on the walkie-talkie. "The helicopter's coming back," she said. "Kill the lights."

Hooker, Bill, and I stood in the darkness, waiting for Maria's all clear. My mind was racing and my heart was skipping around. I was in a broken boat that was filled with Castro's gold and something that looked like a bomb. And the bad guys were looking for us.

"All clear," Maria said.

Hooker flipped the lights back on. "How bad is this loss-of-power problem?"

"I don't know how bad it is," Bill said.

"Executive decision," Hooker said. "Let's use the hoist to transfer the gold over to the Sunseeker while Barney pokes around down here. It's probably better to have it in Rich's boat anyway. No one's looking for his boat. You guys can take off as soon as you're loaded up, and we'll follow when we can."

I found the service record and some manuals and I began walking my way through basic troubleshooting. At the very least I thought we could limp out of the harbor and get far enough out of Cuban waters to radio for help and not get arrested.

I was checking hoses and seals when I heard the Sunseeker's engines turn over. I looked at my watch. I'd been working for two hours. I stepped out of the mechanical room and went on deck. Bill was pulling away, moving toward open ocean. Maria was flat on the prow with a handheld halogen, periodically searching the water in front of them.

Major lump in the throat time.

"He'll be okay," Hooker said.

I nodded, sucking back tears, not wanting to go hormonal in front of Hooker.

"I think I found the problem," I told him. "You had water in the fuel, probably from condensation over a period of time. And it affects both engines. I was able to drain the water that collected in the fuel filters, and we should be good, unless they fill with water again. I don't know why they didn't catch this when the boat was last serviced. I have a few more things to check and then I'll be done."

"Take your time. Bill's a lot more skilled than I am when it comes to running this boat. I'd rather wait and get under way at dawn when I can see where I'm going."

"Do you think it's dangerous to wait?"

"Yes. Unfortunately, chances of us getting stranded on a sandbar are good if I try to go out in the dark. I got this boat with the idea in mind that I'd always have a captain. I've learned how to do the minimal, but I'm not a pro."

I went below deck to finish and Hooker followed me down with two glasses and a bottle of wine.

"Do you mind if I watch?" he asked.

"Nope."

"Do you mind if I talk?"

"Nope. I'm a multi-tasker."

"I thought you worked for an insurance company."

"Your use of the past tense is probably appropriate."

"So what's with the mechanic thing?"

"My dad owns a garage. I helped out."

"You must have more than helped out. Bill thinks you're a mechanical genius."

"Bill's my brother. He has to think things like that."

He handed me a glass of wine. "Not true. I have two sisters and I think they're both airheads. What did you study in college?"

"None of your business."

"Art? American history? Mechanical engineering?"

I sipped some wine. "Engineering, but I never did anything with it. By the time I graduated I was disenchanted with job prospects."

I finished my wine and my checklist at precisely the same time. "I think we're good to go," I told Hooker. "Start her up and check out the gauge."

Hooker came back two minutes later. "We have a problem," he said.

"The gauge?"

"The gauge isn't in the same league as this problem. There's a boat sitting at the mouth of the harbor. Not the Sunseeker. It's got its lights off, but I can see the white hull reflecting in the water."

"Could it be *Flex*?"

"No. It's not nearly that big."

Hooker and I went topside and looked at the boat.

"Maybe it's here for the fishing or snorkeling," I said. "Maybe it's just an innocent pleasure boat."

"Innocent pleasure boats don't arrive at two in the morning and turn off all their running lights. I'm worried that someone did a flyover and picked us up and motored out here. Calflex has a bunch of smaller boats. It could be one of those."

"Looks to me like they're blocking our way out. If they think Maria is on board, maybe they'll just send a couple henchmen out in the morning. Or maybe at this very moment, the henchmen are getting into scuba gear."

"I really hate that idea," Hooker said. "Especially since I gave Bill the gun. The RIB is tied up to the dive platform. Throw a couple bottles of water and some granola bars into it and get in. I'll be right behind you."

I grabbed the water and granola bars and ran to the RIB. And in the dark, I crashed into the canister.

"What the heck is this?" I said. "They didn't take the canister!"

Hooker came up behind me. "Shit, we were rushing to get the gold on board and forgot about this thing back here on the dive platform."

"What should we do with it?"

"We're going to have to take it with us. I don't know what it is, and I don't want to chance leaving it here."

We struggled to get the canister into the RIB, Hooker climbed in with a backpack, and we set off for the island interior. We were about fifty feet upstream when we saw the flash of a penlight on the double H deck.

"Fuck," Hooker said.

That pretty much summed up my feelings, too.

Hooker pulled the outboard up and went the rest of the way using oars. Not especially easy but quieter and safer, and we were able to get farther upstream, poling most of the way. It was so dark under the canopy I couldn't see the hand in front of my face. When we ran aground we got out and dragged the boat above the waterline. Then we got back into the boat and searched for a comfortable position to spend the night.

I was stumbling around, and I felt Hooker's hand grab hold of my leg.

"You're like a hound dog looking for the perfect spot," Hooker said. "Just sit down."

"I can't see anything. I don't know what I'm sitting on."

"You have no spirit of adventure," Hooker said. "Take a chance." He yanked me down and pulled me back against him. "Now you're sitting on me. Relax."

"You've got your hand on my breast."

"Oh. Sorry. It's dark. I didn't know."

"You didn't know you had your hand on my breast?"

"Okay, so I knew. Did you like it?"

"Good grief."

"I was hoping you liked it."

I was sitting between his legs with his arms around me and his chin against my temple.

"*I* liked it," he said. And he kissed me just in front of my ear.

I liked it too. And I liked the kiss. And I couldn't believe I was sitting between Hooker's legs, feeling randy when there were scuba guys combing the *Happy Hooker,* looking for the gold, probably hoping they'd get to kill someone.

"This isn't a good time," I told him.

"I know. No condoms. I don't suppose you picked up any of Bill's?"

"I was talking about the frogmen and the fact that they might want to kill us."

"I'd forgotten about the frogmen. Hell, if we're going to die, we don't have to worry about condoms."

"What time is it?"

"Three-thirty."

I closed my eyes, and I was instantly asleep. When I woke up the sun was shining through tiny pinpoints in the tree cover, and Hooker's hand was back on my breast.

"I can't believe this," I said. "You've got your hand back on my breast."

"It's not my fault. It goes there all by itself. I'm not responsible for what my hand does when I'm sleeping."

"You're not sleeping. You're wide awake."

"Good point." And he fondled me. "Are you sure you don't like it?"

"Maybe a little, but it doesn't matter. I need a shower. I need a toothbrush. I need to shave my legs. *Omigod!*"

"What?" Hooker was on his feet, looking around. "*What?*"

"There's no bathroom."

He had his hand to his heart. "You scared the bejeezus out of me."

"I need a bathroom."

Hooker's eyes strayed to the jungle.

"No way!"

"Don't wander too far," Hooker said. "It wouldn't be good to get lost. And watch where you step."

"This is all my brother's fault," I said. "Every mess I've ever been in has been his fault."

"The three engagements?"

"Men!" I said. And I huffed off, viciously kicking and slashing my way through the tangle of vines and bushes. I did what I had to do, and I followed the trail of smashed vegetation back to the stream.

Hooker was sitting on the side of the boat, eating a granola bar. He looked at me and his eyes got wide and his mouth dropped open.

"What?" I said. "All right, so I know I tinkled on my sneaker. It's not easy doing this when you're a girl."

He dropped the granola bar on the ground and reached for an oar. "Honey, I don't want you to panic, but you've got something in your hair."

I rolled my eyes up, trying to see through my skull, and reached for the top of my head.

"No! Don't touch it!" Hooker said. "Don't move. Stand perfectly still."

"What is it?"

"You don't want to know."

"What are you going to do with the oar?"

"I'm going to flick it off."

"Why don't you just use your hand?"

"What are you, nuts? That's the biggest fucking spider I've ever seen. That motherfucker is the size of a dinner plate. I don't know how it's even staying on your head."

"*Spider!*" And I started screaming and doing the yucky dance. "*GET IT OFF! GET IT OFF! GET IT OFF!*" Everything went cobwebby and I fainted.

When I came around, Hooker was bending over me looking worried.

"What happened?" I asked him.

"You fainted. You were screaming and then your eyes rolled back and went over like *CRASH*."

"I never faint. You probably hit me with the oar and knocked me out."

"Honey bunch, if I hit you with the oar you'd still have your eyes closed."

"Help me up. At least I got rid of the spider." I looked up at Hooker. "I *did* get rid of him, didn't I?"

He got me to my feet. "Yeah, you got rid of him."

I picked a long slim black thing off the front of my shirt. "What is this?"

"Spider leg," Hooker said. "You fell on him when you went down, and he's sort of smushed all over the back of you."

"Not even."

"The good news is . . . he's dead."

I started to cry. I know it was stupid to cry, but there it was. I'd held it back lots of times, and I couldn't hold it back anymore. I had spider guts on me, and I was crying.

"Listen, we can fix this," Hooker said. "We'll just wash you off in the stream. "Most of it fell out of your hair already, anyway. Well, *some* of it. But, we can get the rest out. Damn, I wish you'd stop crying. I really hate when you cry."

Okay, get a grip, I told myself. Get out of the spider guts clothes, wade into the water, and wash your hair. Simple.

"Here's the plan," I said to Hooker. "I'm going to get undressed, and you're not going to look. Then I'm going to wash off, and you're not going to look. And if you look, I'm going to cry."

"Anything! Just no more crying."

I walked to the edge of the stream, got undressed, and dropped the clothes with the spider guts attached into the water to soak. Then I waded out and dunked myself. I swished my hair around a lot, hoping that would do it in the absence of shampoo. I waded back to the bank and caught Hooker looking at me.

"You're really pretty," Hooker said.

157

"You're looking!"

"Of course, I'm looking. I'm a man. I have to look. I'd lose my union card if I didn't look. I'd have my testicles repossessed."

"You promised."

"Promises never count when naked women are involved. Everybody knows that. If it would make you feel better, I could get naked, too."

"Tempting, but no. Is my hair clean? I got all the spider guts out, right?"

Hooker looked at my hair. "Oh shit."

"Now what?"

"Leeches."

I started crying again.

"It's not that bad," Hooker said. "There are only a couple of them. Maybe three. Or four. And mostly they're not attached. Well okay, probably they're not *real* attached. Stay right there, and I'll get a stick."

"A *stick*?"

"To pry them off."

Now I was up to openmouthed sobbing.

"Oh man, I'm sorry you've got leeches. I'll pick them off. Look, I'm picking them off. Do you think you could stop crying?"

"I don't know why I'm crying," I said, tears streaming down my sunburned face, sliding past my peeling nose and blistered lips. "I never cry. I'm really brave. And I'm a good sport."

"Sure you are," Hooker said, flipping a leech into the

bushes. "Anybody could see how brave you are." He tossed another leech. "Yuk," he said. "Ick."

"I don't usually lose it like this. I'm always the sensible, dependable person. Okay, so I don't like heights and I don't like spiders, but I'm pretty good with snakes."

"I hate snakes. And I'm not too crazy about leeches. *Oh man,* this is a big one. Hold still."

I wiped my nose with the back of my hand. "Life sucks," I said.

"Life isn't so bad. You'll feel better about life now that the spider guts and the leeches are all gone." He took half a step backward and his gaze wandered south. "Maybe before you get dressed I should check out the rest of you for leeches. They seem to like ah, hairy places."

I started shrieking and Hooker clapped a hand over my mouth.

"Not so loud!" Hooker said. "The bad guys could still be out there."

I felt around and was relieved not to find any more leeches.

"Sorry," I said. "I got a little hysterical."

"Perfectly natural," Hooker said. "Even NASCAR Guy would get hysterical if he thought he had leeches on his stick shift. You just need to relax. You know what you need? Sex."

"Sex? You just finished picking leeches off my head and you want to have sex?"

"Yeah."

Men never cease to amaze me. I remembered reading somewhere a description of men and women in terms of boxes. The female box had a bunch of knobs and buttons and complicated instructions. And the male box had an *off/on* switch. That was it. Just a single switch. Hooker's switch was always turned to *on*.

"I'm not feeling really sexy right now," I said.

"I just thought since you were already naked it would be a good idea. This way we wouldn't have to go through that awkward getting undressed part."

"Speaking of clothes . . ."

"Seems like a shame to cover you up, but if that's what you want, NASCAR Guy is here to help." And he scooped my panties out of the boat and dangled them by one finger.

I took the panties and the bra that followed and put them on. Hooker waded into the stream, swished my shorts and shirt around, looked them over, and threw them into the jungle. "Not gonna happen, sweetie. Trust me, you don't want to *ever* wear those clothes."

"They're the only clothes I have!"

He took his shirt off and gave it to me. "Wear my shirt until we get back to the boat."

"Do you think we can go back to the boat?"

"I don't know. I'm going to walk back and take a look. Stay with the RIB. If you hear any noise at all, hide in the jungle."

An hour later, Hooker crashed through the brush behind me.

"The boat is still there," he said. "It looks like a Sea Ray. No sign of life on it. I watched the *Happy Hooker* for a while, and I didn't see any activity there either, but I think chances are good that someone's on board. It's what I would do. I'd sit and wait. I have a hoist, so it's obvious I have the ability to carry an inflatable. Since no one's come upstream, I can only assume they decided to wait for Bill and Maria to return."

"They're going to be disappointed when we show up."

"Yeah, they're going to torture us and make us tell them where to find Bill and Maria."

"I'd faint but I've already done that."

"We can stay here until we starve to death, or we can go back and rat on Bill and Maria. What do you think?"

"I think I'm tired of sitting here in my underpants."

We moved to get into the RIB, and we both stopped and stared at the canister.

"We don't want to take this with us," Hooker said. "If there's someone on the boat, we don't want to chance dropping this into their hands . . . whatever the hell it is."

"Don't expect me to help you carry it into the jungle. I've already done the spider-leech thing."

"We can drop it in the water. It's about fifteen feet deep at the first bend. No one will find it there."

We got into the RIB and Hooker motored us downstream. We dropped the canister and continued on to the harbor entrance, where we sat for a half hour, watching Hooker's boat. It was midday and the jungle was steaming. No breeze and a hundred percent humidity. The air was condensing on my forehead and running down the sides of my face, dripping off my chin.

"Do you have air-conditioning on that boat?" I asked Hooker.

"Yep."

"Take me to it."

We cruised over to the *Happy Hooker* and circled it. No sign of life.

"Do you think the bad guys are on board, waiting for us?" I asked Hooker.

"Yep."

"Do you think we could make Miami in the RIB?"

"What's your relationship with God?"

"It's shaky."

"Then I wouldn't count on making Miami in the RIB."

"I'm feeling a little vulnerable in my underwear."

Hooker gave his head a shake. "I'm sorry I didn't do a better job of protecting you. I should have been smarter."

"Not your fault. You were great. You picked leeches off my head with your bare hands."

"I almost threw up. Good thing I can drive, because I sure as hell couldn't wrangle leeches for a living."

We sat off the starboard side for another ten minutes. Neither of us said anything. We were listening. Finally I got restless.

"Let's get on with it," I said to Hooker. "I'm tired of waiting. Let's tie up to the dive platform."

"I'm not going to tie up," Hooker said. "Stay in the RIB and I'll look around. You know how to work this thing if you have to, right?"

"Yes."

Hooker looped the line once around to stabilize the RIB and climbed out. "If you have to take off, try to get to the mainland. It's all I can come up with."

I watched him cross the deck behind the fighting chair and open the cabin door. The door partially closed behind him. I heard him yell *"Barney, go!"* There was a gunshot. And Hooker reeled out of the cabin and collapsed onto the deck.

The guy with the slicked-back hair and his partner appeared in the doorway. The partner had his foot completely wrapped in a bandage. The guy with the slicked-back hair had his arm in a sling. Slick and Gimpy, I thought. They both had guns, and they didn't look happy to see me. No surprise there.

"Lucky me," Slick said. "My favorite person. I can't get rid of you. You're like a bad rash. Where's your brother?"

NINE

I couldn't believe they shot Hooker. He was facedown on the deck, and he wasn't moving. My heart was in my throat, and I was so enraged my vision was blurred.

"Get in the cabin," Slick said, motioning at me with his gun.

"Listen to me, you sack of slime," I yelled, coming out of the RIB wielding an oar. "I've had a really bad day. First the spider and then the leeches. My underwear's riding up my ass, and I hate this freaking humidity. I'm not going into the cabin. The only way you're going to get me into the cabin is to shoot me, like you shot Hooker."

"Lady, that's really tempting, but I need to get some answers from you."

"You're not getting *any* answers from me. And get off our boat."

Both guys blew out a sigh.

"Get her," Slick said to Gimpy.

Gimpy stepped over Hooker and reached for me. I spun around and caught him square in the stomach with the oar. *Thwack*. And Gimpy went down to the deck with the wind knocked out of him.

The move had been instinctual, the result of a bad engagement to a great kickboxer. Bruce Leskowitz didn't have a lot upstairs, and his Mr. Stupid had a tendency to roam. On the plus side, Leskowitz had a fabulous body, and he brought me up to a brown belt. Who would have thought I'd ever use the moves? God works in mysterious ways.

Slick leveled his gun at me. "Put the oar down."

"No."

"Don't make me shoot you."

"Go ahead, shoot me," I said to Slick. "If you don't shoot me, I'm going to kick your ass."

Okay, I admit it. I was a little nuts. I was rolling on adrenaline and desperation. The bad guy had a gun, and I had an oar. And the truth is, even though I knew some karate, I didn't have a lot of history behind me in the ass-kicking department. It just seemed like the thing to say. It's what The Rock would say, right?

Since I don't have entirely the same presence as The Rock, Slick started laughing. It was a perfectly appropriate response, but it's not something you want to do to a woman on the edge.

I lunged at him with the oar, and he stepped to the side. He didn't have a lot of room to maneuver away from me. I whirled and tagged him in the bad arm with the blade. He got off a wild shot. I shoved the oar at him, knocked him off balance, and he went sailing into space, off the side of the boat.

Gimpy was on hands and knees, sucking air. I grabbed the revolver that had fallen out of his hand when he went down, and I jumped back to a safe distance. I dropped the oar, and I two-handed the gun. Even with two hands, the gun was shaking.

Gimpy's eyes were on me, wide with terror. And I thought my eyes probably looked like that, too.

"Don't shoot me," he said. "Take it easy. Jesus, I never believed in gun control until I met you."

"Into the water," I said.

"What?"

"Jump!"

"I got a bad foot. I'll sink like a stone."

I sighted down the gun barrel, pulled the hammer back, and he jumped off the boat.

He bobbed to the surface beside Slick, and the two of them hung there, about fifteen feet off the starboard side.

"Swim!" I yelled at them.

Gimpy was floundering, taking in some water, and Slick wasn't doing much better.

"For Pete's sake," I said. "Take the RIB."

There was a lot of splashing and sputtering, but they weren't making much progress moving, so I grabbed the line to the RIB and dragged the RIB around to them. They hung on for a while, catching their breath, coughing up seawater. Then they dragged themselves into the RIB and lay there like a couple dead fish.

I gave the RIB a shove with the oar, and the RIB drifted off. When I turned back to Hooker he was sitting on the deck, knees bent, head down.

I knelt beside him. "Are you okay?"

"Give me a minute. I've got a real bad case of the whirlies."

I went back to looking at the guys in the RIB. They were just sitting there, letting the RIB drift. Not far enough away for me to feel safe. I fired off a shot that I knew would go far right of them. They looked at me like I was Demon Woman. Gimpy cranked the outboard over and headed for shore.

Hooker was beside me, holding on to the fighting chair. "They've got the RIB?"

"Yeah, they were going to drown."

"Isn't that a good thing? Dead bad guys?"

"I've never killed anyone."

"This would have been a great place to start."

Hooker leaned over the rail and threw up. When he was done throwing up he flopped back onto the deck and lay spread-eagle, eyes closed. "What happened?"

"They tranked you."

"Tranked me?"

"I know all about it because I watch *Wild Kingdom* reruns on television. I thought you were shot, but you aren't bleeding, and there's a dart stuck in your chest. Don't move."

I pulled the dart out and looked at it. I was having a hard time seeing it because my hands were still shaking, and the dart was surprisingly small.

"Lucky for you they weren't using the big-game dart

gun," I said. "This must be the dart they use to tranquilize rabbits."

"How'd you get them off the boat?"

"I asked them nicely."

Hooker smiled and rubbed his chest where the dart had gone in. "It stings," he said. "Want to kiss it and make it better?"

I bent and kissed him just to the side of the puncture.

"I'd kiss you back, but I just threw up," he said.

NASCAR Guy's sensitive side.

I stood and checked on the bad guys. They were pulling the RIB onto the shore. They looked okay.

"We should get out of here," I said to Hooker. "Can you help me get the anchor up?"

"No problemo." He crawled to the dive platform, leaned over, and stuck his head in the water. He dragged his head out of the water, crawled to the fighting chair, and pulled himself to his feet. "You really should have killed them," he said.

We hauled the anchor up, and we got under way with Slick and Gimpy watching us. They didn't wave good-bye.

Hooker inched his way over to the Sea Ray. "Throw out a couple fenders on the port side. Let's see if we can tie up to their boat and get you on board so you can *fix* their engines."

Ten minutes later I was climbing off the Sea Ray, back onto the *Happy Hooker*, bringing in the fenders. I'd sliced through fuel lines and sabotaged the electrical system. If Slick and Gimpy got back to the States, it wasn't going to be in the Sea Ray.

"Next stop, Florida," Hooker said. And he took the *Happy Hooker* up to cruising speed.

I played the binoculars across the water for a while, but

there wasn't anything else to see. Just azure sky and gently undulating ocean.

Hooker stayed in the chair, at the helm, and I stretched out on the banquette behind him. It was Monday, and I supposed I was unemployed. It didn't seem especially important anymore. I fell asleep, and when I woke up we were plowing through heavy seas.

"We're going into Key West," Hooker said. "The weather's changed, and I'm not feeling comfortable with waves this size. I need to refuel anyway. If I can use Vana's slip I'll stay in Key West. If I can't, I'll try to get a captain to take her to Miami with me."

Ten minutes later, Key West was in sight and Hooker was on the radio, calling the Key West dockmaster, arranging to use Vana's slip.

"I got the slip," Hooker said to me, "but this is going to be messy. This is way too much boat for me to dock by myself in these conditions."

We rode into the marina on whitecapped rollers, and Hooker cut to an idle. We found our spot, and Hooker sent me to the back of the boat with a walkie-talkie. There were two dockhands from the dockmaster's office already in place, waiting to help us tie up.

"Watch your footing back there," Hooker said to me. "I've got wind and tide pushing me, and I'm probably going to ram the pier. I don't want to dump you into the water."

When we were finally secure, Hooker thanked the dock hands, and then he turned and rapped his head on the control panel. *Thunk, thunk, thunk.*

"I need a drink," he said. "A big one."

"It wasn't so bad. You only rammed the pier twice. And you didn't do any damage when you drifted into that other boat. Well, not a *lot* of damage."

"On the bright side," Hooker said. "You did great. You didn't even drop the talkie."

We collected some food, grabbed our duffel bags, and walked three blocks to the Mini. Hooker drove around a little, making sure we weren't being followed, before parking at Vana's. We went inside and collapsed on the couch.

"I'm exhausted," Hooker said.

"You've had a full day. You wrangled leeches. You got tranked. You trashed a pier."

"I'd chase you around the house," Hooker said, "but I don't think I can get off the couch."

I took the food into the kitchen and made us sandwiches. I brought the sandwiches out to the living room with a bottle of vodka and a single glass.

"Not drinking?" Hooker asked, taking a plate from me.

"Maybe later. I have seventeen messages I have to answer, and I don't want to be drunk when I talk to my mother."

"Yeah, mothers hate that."

Ten minutes later, Hooker was asleep on the couch. I draped a blanket over him and tucked myself into a guest room. I slipped under the covers of Vana's comfy guest bed, but it was a while before I fell asleep. Too many things to worry about. Too many loose ends

•　　•　　•

Hooker was showered and dressed in fresh clothes, drinking coffee in the kitchen when I shuffled past him in a guest robe and poured out a mug of coffee.

"Morning," I said.

"Morning." He wrapped an arm around me and dropped a friendly kiss on the top of my head, like we were an old married couple.

"Nice," I told him.

"It's going to get nicer. Unfortunately, not immediately. I just got off the phone with Judey. Todd called him first thing this morning. Todd said *Flex* moved from Miami to Key West. We didn't see her because they're anchored on the other side of the island. Todd said the helicopter's been flying nonstop, and that everyone was told to take shore leave today. Todd went to the marina to have breakfast with a friend and saw the *Happy Hooker*. He thought maybe Bill was living on the boat."

"Good thing we're safe in this house."

"We're not that safe. If someone halfway tried, they'd come up with Vana's name and address, since the boat's in his slip."

"Are we scrambling to get out of town?"

"Darlin', we're scrambling big time."

I took a three-minute shower and threw some clothes on. We grabbed our bags, made sure the lights were out, locked up the house, and followed the stepping-stones to the Mini. The instant we were in the car, a black Town Car pulled in behind us, blocking our exit. Two men came out of nowhere, one on either side of the Mini. They had guns drawn.

"Stay cool," Hooker said to me.

The doors were wrenched open and we were walked back to the Town Car. One of the men got in the back with us and one got in next to the driver.

"Mr. Salzar would like to talk to you," the guy in the back said. "He's invited you onto *Flex*."

Flex was still anchored offshore. No place big enough for it in the marina, I guess. Or maybe they wanted to be far enough away so the tourists couldn't hear me screaming while I was being tortured. Whatever the reason, we were put in a large RIB and motored out to the boat. The RIB tied up at the stern and we were escorted to the second deck.

Even under these circumstances it was hard not to be impressed. There was a lot of high-gloss wood and polished brass. Fresh flowers in vases. The furniture was perfectly restored Biedermeier. Couches and comfy chairs were upholstered in the ship's colors of navy and gold.

Salzar was waiting for us in the salon. He was at a writing desk. A laptop and a mug of coffee sat to one side on the desk. Puke Face stood behind Salzar. There were two chairs in front of the desk.

"Be seated," Salzar said. As if this was some friendly little meeting. Like maybe he was a mortgage broker. Or a marriage counselor.

Hooker slouched into his chair and smiled at Salzar. "Nice boat."

"Thank you," Salzar said. "It's quite unique. Calflex is very proud of it."

"Nice of you to invite us on board," Hooker said.

This got a weird little cat-playing-with-the-mouse smile from Salzar. "You have something that I very much desire. I've been on your boat. The object that I desire isn't there. And I've just received a call from my associate. The object isn't in Richard Vana's house. And it isn't in the Mini Cooper. So I have to assume you've hidden this object."

"What object are we talking about?" Hooker asked him.

"A canister. Red cone. Black-and-green stripe. Sound familiar?"

"We turned that over to the navy when we arrived," Hooker said.

Salzar shifted his eyes to an aide by the door, and the aide left the room. "That would be unfortunate," Salzar said. "That would make me unhappy. And it would mean I'd have to torture you for no good purpose. Other than pleasure, of course."

"What's so special about this canister?" Hooker asked him.

"It's filled with fear," Salzar said, smiling again. "And fear is power, isn't it?"

The aide returned and shook his head, no.

"My source tells me the canister was never delivered to the navy," Salzar said. "You might want to rethink your answer."

"Your source is wrong," Hooker said.

Salzar hit a button on his laptop and a photo appeared on the screen. He turned the laptop so Hooker and I could see the photo. It was a picture of Maria. Her hair was lank and stuck to her face. She had a swollen lip and a bruise just under her left eye. She was looking into the camera, and she was spewing hatred.

"This picture was taken earlier this morning," Salzar said. "The chopper picked up the Sunseeker leaving the island. Infrared technology is so helpful. It allows you to see all sorts of things, like people and very dense cargo such as gold bricks. Bottom line is, we followed Bill and Maria to Port Royal and paid them a visit. My men found the gold, but unfortunately, not the canister. As you can see, we gave Maria an opportunity to share with us, but it turned out she didn't have much to share. Now you have a similar opportunity." He leaned forward on the desk. The line of his mouth compressed, and his pupils shrank to pinpoints. "I want that canister. I'll stop at nothing to get it. *Nothing.* Do you understand?"

Hooker and I didn't say anything.

"I have another picture you might enjoy," Salzar said. "The resolution isn't as good as I'd like . . . picture phone quality. Still, I think it's a compelling photo." He clicked on an icon and a second photo filled the screen. It was Bill, sprawled on a carpeted floor, bleeding. He'd been shot in the upper arm and chest. Hard to tell if he was dead or alive.

I heard someone sob. I guess it was me. And then Hooker reached over and grabbed my wrist and squeezed. And that was all I felt. Hooker at my wrist. No thoughts in my head. No emotion. Just Hooker squeezing my wrist. How's that for a defense mechanism? Can I do denial, or what?

There was absolute silence in the room. Time stood still for several moments. And then the silence was pierced by a siren. Everyone stood, me included. My first thought was *police siren,* but the siren was internal to the ship.

Salzar closed the laptop and handed it over to Puke Face.

The door to the salon was opened, and aides were running outside the salon. The siren stopped and the captain came on over the intercom.

"We have a fire below decks. All guests are advised to leave the ship."

Salzar moved from behind the desk. "Hugo, you come with me. Roger and Leo, take Ms. Barnaby and Mr. Hooker to shore and see that they're safely transported to the garage."

Smoke was beginning to seep into the salon, so we all migrated to the sundeck at the stern. Before we could get to the stairs, there was an explosion below decks and the lower deck was engulfed in flames. Salzar and Puke Face moved forward along the outside rail and were swallowed up in black billowing smoke. The smoke roiled around us, and the next thing I knew I was flying through the air. Hooker had picked me up and sailed me out over the rail like a Frisbee.

I splashed down and immediately kicked myself up to the surface. Hooker was a couple feet away.

"Swim for shore," he yelled at me.

I did a couple strokes and an RIB pulled up to me. It was Todd. He dragged Hooker and me into the RIB and took off. I was choking on smoke and seawater, holding on for dear life as the RIB bounced through the chop. There were a lot of boats in the area now. Emergency vehicles screaming in the distance. The shoreline was filling up with gawkers. Todd aimed for a small sand beach away from most of the traffic. He rammed the RIB aground, and we splashed to shore.

"I have the Mini parked close by," he yelled. And we ran after Todd.

Hooker took the wheel. I took the seat next to Hooker. And Todd crammed himself into the backseat. No one spoke. We just hunkered down, teeth chattering, and rocketed out of there. We got onto Route 1 and crossed the bridge to Cow Key.

Todd was the first to talk. "I guess I'm out of a job," he said.

"Holy fuck," Hooker said. "Saved by a fire. What are the chances?"

"Pretty good, since I set it," Todd said. "Judey called me back and filled me in. I was staying with a friend not far from Vana's house, so I walked over to see if I could help with anything. I saw them load you into the car and take off. Another car immediately showed up and did a fast search of the house and the Mini. When they left I borrowed the Mini. Lucky the keys were still in the ignition. I parked at Wickers Beach and saw them ferrying you out to *Flex*. So, I ran and got a RIB. No one noticed me tie up to *Flex*. The only people left on the boat were Salzar's people, and they were all in the main deck salon and in the pilothouse. I knew you were in trouble, so I thought I'd set the fire alarm off. I was down in the engine room, holding my lighter up to a sensor, and I don't know what happened, but I heard something go *pop* and then there was fire everywhere. I ran out and got back into the RIB. I didn't know what else to do. And then all of a sudden Barney came flying through the air!"

"Do you know anything about Bill?" Hooker asked Todd.

"No. What about Bill?"

Hooker took his cell phone out of his pocket. He shook the phone and water sloshed out. "Do you have a cell phone on you?" he asked Todd.

"Yep."

"Salzar had a picture of Bill bleeding," Hooker said. "It looked like he'd been shot. I know Bill was in Naples, so let's start there. Call the hospital in Naples and see if Bill's been brought in."

Todd got connected to the hospital and asked about Bill. There was a lot of un hunh, un hunh, un hunh. And Todd disconnected.

"Okay," Todd said when he got off the phone. "There's good news and there's bad news. The bad news is Bill has been shot. The good news is he's in stable condition. They said he was in the recovery room. That he was out of surgery. And he was stable."

I leaned back and closed my eyes and took a deep breath. "I don't like when Bill's hurt. I know he's all grown up, well, sort of grown up . . . but he's still my little brother."

"Bill's going to be okay," Hooker said, his hand back at my wrist with a reassuring squeeze. "We'll try calling in an hour. Maybe you can talk to him."

We passed through the lower Keys and then we were on the Seven Mile Bridge. The water was choppy below us and the Mini was buffeted by wind, but she held the road. We came up to Marathon Plaza and Hooker slowed for two guys fixing a flat on the shoulder. The car was a white Ford Taurus. We got closer and Hooker shook his head. Disbelieving. It was Slick and Gimpy.

"I'd really like to run them over," Hooker said, "but I don't think I could get away with it this close to the Plaza."

"Too bad we threw Gimpy's gun way. We could shoot them."

"God knows how many people that gun has killed," Hooker said. "It wouldn't have been smart to get caught in possession of that gun."

Slick looked up just as we blew by them, and I saw the shock of recognition register.

"I think we got busted," I said to Hooker.

He looked in the rearview mirror. "They still have to get the tire on. Maybe we can get off the Keys before they catch us. Once we pass Largo I have more road choices."

A half hour later, just when I was beginning to feel comfortable, Todd saw the car behind us.

"Your friends have caught up to us," Todd said. "This is turning into *one of those days,* isn't it?"

It was midmorning, midweek and there weren't a lot of cars on the road. Three rolled by going south. The road behind them was empty. No cars behind Slick and Gimpy.

"Here's where they'll make their move," Hooker said. "This is going to be fun. Slick's going to force us to pull over."

The white Taurus swung out to pass, and Hooker smiled and watched his side-view mirror.

"Gimpy's got a gun sighted on us," I said. "I don't think it's a dart gun."

"I see it," Hooker said.

Todd ducked down below window level. *"Criminy!"*

They were directly abreast of us, and Gimpy was motioning with the gun to pull over. Hooker nodded acknowledgment and dropped the Mini back a couple inches.

"It's all in the timing and placement," Hooker said. "Hang on." Then he jerked the car to the left and slammed into the Taurus.

"Omigod," Todd said, head still down. "What are you doing? This isn't a demolition derby!"

The Taurus careened across the road, caught air going off a small embankment, rolled once, and came to a smoking stop, tires up, in a strip of mangrove.

"Amateurs," Hooker said, back in his lane, his foot still steady on the accelerator.

Todd popped up in time to see the roll. "Ouch."

"It was a good hit, but it seems pretty lame compared to blowing up a billion-dollar ship," Hooker said.

"I didn't do that," Todd said. "I was never there."

"Do you think we should go back to see if they're okay?" I asked.

"Darlin', they just pointed a gun at you," Hooker said. "If we go back for anything it'll be to set fire to their car."

"I've still got my lighter," Todd said.

We passed Largo and stayed on Route 1. Hooker pulled into a strip mall when we got to Florida City, so we could stretch and check the damage to the car.

I was out, but Hooker couldn't get his door open and his window wouldn't slide down.

"Sit tight," I said. "I'm good at this."

I poked through the junk in the cargo area and came up with a big ass screwdriver. I shoved the screwdriver between the door and the frame and pried the door open.

"Lesson number one from my father," I told Hooker. "Never go anywhere without a Maglight and a screwdriver. The bigger the better."

"Lesson number one from my father had to do with opening a beer bottle," Hooker said. He got out and looked at the Mini. "This is a tough little car. Considering how small it is, it really stood up. The side needs some body work. Well, okay, Bill probably needs a whole left side."

"Nothing structural," I said, on my back, under the car. "At first look, I don't see any damage to the frame or wheel wells."

We all went into a convenience store, got some cold sodas, and came back to the car.

"I'm cutting north here to the Tamiami Trail," Hooker said to Todd. "I'm taking Barney to Naples, so we can check on Bill. I have some of my crew in Homestead. Some sort of schmooze thing going on at the track. I can get one of them to pick you up here and take you back to Miami Beach, or wherever. Since you just destroyed *Flex* you might not want to go home for a while. Not until we get this straightened out."

"Thanks. That would be great. I have someone I can stay with in North Miami."

Hooker used Todd's phone again, and ten minutes later he swung the Mini out of the lot and back to Route 1.

"I'm taking the Trail instead of going all the way up to Alligator Alley. It's a slower road, but the distance is shorter. We should make Naples in two hours," Hooker said.

The Tamiami Trail cuts across the bottom tip of Florida, running through mile after mile of flat swampland, the tedium occasionally broken by signs advertising Indian-guided airboat rides. For the most part, it's a two-lane road used by people who aren't in a hurry. Hooker didn't fall into the *not in a hurry* category. Hooker was doing ninety, weaving in and out of traffic like this was just another day at the job. If anyone other than Hooker had been driving, I would have had my feet braced on the dash, ready to escape the car at the first opportunity.

"What's this schmooze thing going on in Homestead?" I asked him.

"Some kind of a preseason sponsor event. They wanted me to participate, but I refused. The season is long and hard, and I never shirk my corporate responsibilities, but this is my time, and I'm not giving it up. I told them to send a car instead. We have a couple cars that roll around in a transporter and are used for this stuff. They look like my car, but they can be used to give rides to the fans. They're cars we've raced and retired so they're pretty authentic."

Hooker dropped to the speed limit as we approached Naples, the scenery suddenly changing from swamp to civilization.

Movie theaters, shopping malls, golf course communities, high-end furniture stores, and car dealerships lined the Trail. I'd called ahead and gotten an address for the hospital. I'd been told Bill was in his room but sedated and not able to talk.

By the time we got to the hospital Bill was more or less awake. He was hooked up to an I.V. and a respiration monitor. I'd learned from a nurse that no vital organs had been damaged, but he'd lost some blood.

"I know my eyes are open," Bill said, his words soft and slurred. "But I'm feeling a little slow."

"We aren't going anywhere," I told him. "Take a nap. We'll be here when you wake up."

It was early evening when Bill opened his eyes again. "Hi," he said. His voice was stronger, and his pupils were no longer dilated to the size of quarters. "How did you know I was here?"

"That's a long story," I said. "We might want to save it for another time."

"Yeah, and parts of it are too good to waste on you in your drugged-up condition," Hooker said.

I was standing at bedside, and I could feel Hooker pressed into my back with his hand lightly resting at the base of my neck. Probably worried I'd faint. I was pretty sure his fear was ungrounded, but it was still nice to have the support.

"They found us," Bill said. "I don't know how. The helicopter probably. It did a couple flyovers when we were in the Gulf. I didn't think they saw me go into Gordon Pass, but hell . . ."

He was white again and his breaths were shallow.

"Are you okay?" I asked. "Are you in pain?"

"Pain that you can't fix, Barney. They've got Maria, don't they? We were in the house I rented, in bed, sleeping, when they came in," Bill said. "Two Cuban guys. They grabbed Maria. She was screaming and crying, and I tried to get to her, and they shot me. That's the last I remember."

"There's a cop outside, waiting to talk to you. He said you were shot in your driveway."

"I guess I dragged myself out there."

Good thing, too. The cop in the hall told us Bill was found by a passing motorist who saw him lying on the driveway. If Bill had stayed in the house, no one would have found him. He most likely would have bled to death.

"I'm going to tell the cop about the Cubans and Maria, but not about the gold," Bill said. "You need to go to the house and see if the gold is still there. I left it on the boat. The boat is tied to the dock directly behind the house." His eyes filled. "I love her, Barney. I really love her. It's going to work out okay, isn't it?"

"Yeah, it's going to work out okay."

"We'll get her back, right?" Bill asked.

I nodded, barely able to speak. "We'll get her back."

TEN

I talked to Bill's doctor while the cop talked to Bill. If Bill's signs stayed stable he'd be allowed to go home tomorrow. He had a flesh wound in his upper arm, and the bullet in his chest had cracked a rib but missed everything else. Bill had been lucky . . . if you can call getting shot twice lucky.

The cop was expressionless when he left Bill. I don't imagine he was all that happy. He had a kidnapping and shooting without motive. It didn't take a genius to figure out there were holes in the story.

I could have told the cop I'd been kidnapped and threatened by Salzar. I could have told him Salzar had photos of Bill and Maria. Problem was I didn't have the photos in my possession. And the kidnapping was Salzar's word against mine and Hooker's. And our only witness was a guy who blew up a billion-dollar boat.

So, I didn't especially want to talk to the cop. Not to mention, my cop experience to date wasn't impressive. What I really wanted to do was scoop Bill up and take him someplace where he'd be safe. And then figure out a plan to defuse everything.

We stayed until nine. Bill was sedated and drifted off to sleep. Hooker and I dragged ourselves out of the hospital, into the parking lot.

"I'm adding this to my list of really shitty days," Hooker said. "I've had a bunch of them. Not a lot of people get shot in NASCAR, but people get hurt and people die. It's always awful."

"Why do you drive?"

"I don't know. I guess it's just what I do. It's what I'm good at. I used to think it was for the fame, but it turns out the fame is a pain in the ass. I suppose it could be for the money, but the truth is I've got enough. And I still keep racing. Crazy, hunh?"

"You like it."

Hooker grinned. Boyish. Caught by the simple truth. "Yeah, I like it."

"You're a good driver."

"I thought you didn't follow NASCAR."

"I was at Richmond last year. You were brilliant."

"Damn. I'm all flummoxed. I'm not used to you being nice to me."

"You have a short memory. I kissed your dart wound."

"I figured that was a pity kiss. I was pathetic."

"Well yeah, but I was still being nice to you."

We got into the battered Mini, and Hooker drove south toward town.

"I haven't spent a lot of time in Naples, but I think I can find my way to the house," Hooker said. "Bill gave me directions."

Hooker turned right at Fifth Avenue and drove past blocks of restaurants and shops. People were eating at outdoor tables and strolling into art galleries. The pace was slower than South Beach. The dress was more conservative. Palm trees were wound in twinkle lights. Cars were expensive.

We took a left onto Gordon Drive and watched the houses get larger as we drove south. No more restaurants or shops. No high-rise condos. Just block after block of expensive houses and professionally landscaped yards. And beyond the houses to our right was the Gulf of Mexico.

When we reached the Port Royal Beach Club, Hooker turned left into a neighborhood of curving streets that we knew followed a series of man-made canals. Half the houses were 1970s ranches and half the houses were new mega McMansions. The McMansions filled their lots and were hidden behind wrought iron gates that opened to brick drive courts and lush gardens. I suspected there were some older residents of Naples who might roll their eyes at the McMansions. *I* thought the McMansions were glorious. For that matter, I thought the ranches weren't bad either.

In my mind I imagined movie stars living behind the wrought iron gates, or possibly *Fortune* 500 CEOs. The reality was probably much less fun. Probably these houses were all owned by realtors who'd made a killing in the grossly inflated housing market.

Bill had rented one of the ranches. It was easily recognized by the yellow crime scene tape stretched across the front of the property, preventing people from using the circular drive.

Hooker parked at the side of the road, and we ducked under the tape and walked to the front door. Even in the dark it was possible to see the bloodstains on the yellow brick drive and concrete front porch.

"Maybe you should go back to the car," Hooker said. "It's not necessary for both of us to do this. I'm just going to collect Bill's things and check out the boat."

"Thanks," I said, "but I'm okay."

In the absence of fake dog poop, Bill had hidden the key under a flowerpot on the front porch. Hooker found the key and opened the door. We stepped inside, and Hooker hit the light switch. The foyer was white marble and beyond that beige wall-to-wall carpet. There was a grisly trail of blood through the foyer to the carpet. The blood was smeared where Bill had fallen and dragged himself up. In the middle of the foyer was a perfect bloody handprint. Bill's handprint. Drops splattered out in an arc.

I felt my stomach sicken, and I went down hard on my knees. I was on all fours, fighting back nausea, shaking with the effort.

Hooker scooped me up and carried me into the powder room off the foyer. He sat me on the toilet seat, shoved my head between my legs, and draped a soaking wet hand towel over my head and neck.

"Breathe," he said. His hand was on the towel at the back of my neck. "Push against my hand. *Push.*"

"I guess I wasn't okay," I said.

"No one should ever be okay when they see something

like that." He replaced the towel with a fresh one, and water ran down my neck and soaked into my shirt and my shorts. "I'm going to leave you here while I get Bill's things. You have to promise me you won't move an inch."

"I promise."

Ten minutes later, he came back for me. "I have Bill's and Maria's things in the back of the Mini. Can you stand?"

"Yes. I'm horrified and disgusted and angry, but I'm not sick. And I'm not going to turn to mush when I see the blood on the way out. It caught me by surprise."

Hooker took my hand and led me past the blood in the foyer and out the door. He turned the lights off, locked the door, and pocketed the key.

"I want to show you something out back," he said. "Take a walk with me."

We followed a footpath around the side of the house, past trees filled with oranges and grapefruits and flowers that were still fragrant in the warm night air. A pool stretched the width of the yard, and beyond the pool was a swath of manicured lawn and beyond the lawn was a dock and beyond the dock was the canal. A full moon hung in the lower sky, reflecting light that shimmered across the black water.

"It's pretty, isn't it?" Hooker said.

It was more than pretty. It was calming. Standing there, looking out at the canal, it was hard to imagine anything bad had happened in the house behind us.

"No Sunseeker," I said.

"No. But then we already knew they had the gold."

We returned to the car and left Port Royal. Hooker retraced his route and got back onto the Trail, heading north. This part of the road was clogged with traffic. Professional buildings, strip malls, furniture stores, and chain hotels lined both sides of the highway. Hooker pulled into the first hotel he came across and parked in the unloading zone.

"I'll run in and see if I can get a room," he said. "I don't suppose you'd want to sleep with me?"

It was said with such little boy hopeful hopelessness that I laughed out loud. "I'm not ready for that," I told him.

He curled his fingers into my T-shirt, pulled me close to him, and kissed me. His fingers were pressed into my breasts, his tongue slid over mine, and I felt my engine turn over and hum.

"Let me know when you're ready," he said. "Because I've been ready since the first day I met you."

Okay, so maybe I wanted to rethink the little boy part. I wasn't seeing any evidence of a little boy here. In fact, I was thinking Hooker showed the same single-mindedness of purpose when he focused on a woman that he showed on the track. Hooker kept his eye on the prize.

Hooker gave the battered door a good hard shot with his fist to get it to open. He angled himself out of the Mini and jogged to the hotel's revolving front door. He came back ten minutes later and got our bags out of the trunk.

"Darlin', we're in business," he said. "We've got rooms without bad guys."

•　　•　　•

The next morning, Bill's doctor assured me that Bill's signs were all good and he was strong enough to leave the hospital. You wouldn't know by looking. Bill was still pale. His arm was bandaged and in a sling. His chest was wrapped and double wrapped. He had blood caked under his fingernails and a bump on his forehead the size of a walnut. I had him dressed in khaki shorts and an orange-and-blue flowered shirt, hoping it would cheer him. It turned out Bill didn't need anything to cheer him because Bill was shot up with painkillers and happy juice for the ride home.

The hospital and police had assumed Bill was returning to the rental house. Hooker and I hadn't said anything to change their minds, but we had other plans. We loaded Bill into the front seat of the Mini, and we took off for Miami Beach.

It was noon when we rolled across the Causeway Bridge and into South Beach. It was a brilliant blue-sky day with temperatures in the low eighties and not a breath of air stirring. Hooker turned onto Alton Avenue and drove straight to Judey's condo building.

"We're leaving you with Jude," I said to Bill. "Do you remember Jude?"

"Ju-u-u-de," Bill said.

Bill was wasted.

"I don't know what they gave him," Hooker said. "But I wouldn't mind having some."

Hooker parked in the condo garage, we maneuvered Bill out of the car, and we locked arms around his back and steered him to the elevator.

Hooker hit the button for the twenty-seventh floor and

looked over at me. "Are you going to be okay?"

"Sure. Twenty-seven. Piece of cake." I was just grateful it wasn't thirty-two.

We shuffled Bill out of the elevator, down the short hall, and rang Judey's bell.

"Oh my goodness," Judey said, throwing the door wide open to us. "Just look at this poor little sad sack."

"He's a lot higher than the twenty-seventh floor," I told Judey. "They gave him some painkillers for the ride home."

"Lucky duck," Judey said. "I have my guest room all ready. We'll just tuck Wild Bill in, and I'll take good care of him. I'm very nurturing. And I won't leave him alone for a minute. Nothing bad is going to happen to him while I'm on the job."

Judey's condo was decorated in bold warm colors. Tangerine walls and hot red couches. A zebra skin coffee table ottoman. Black granite counters in the kitchen. It was striking, but it was a little like looking through your eyelids when you have a hangover.

We walked Bill into the guest room and put him to bed.

"Everything's red," he said. "Am I in hell?"

"No," I told him. "You're in Judey's guest room."

"J-u-u-deeee."

I handed the bag containing Bill's antibiotic and pain medication over to Judey. "Instructions are on the labels," I said. "There's also a sheet with instructions for changing the dressings and for doctor's visits."

"Never fear. Judey's here." Judey cut his eyes to Hooker. "And you take good care of Barney."

"I'm trying," Hooker said.

We left Judey and Bill, and we walked the short distance to the elevator. The doors opened, we stepped in, and Hooker hit the lobby button.

"If you're afraid of the elevator, big brave NASCAR Guy would be willing to hold you close and make you feel safe," Hooker said.

"Thanks, but I'm too numb to be afraid."

"Could you pretend?"

When we were kids Bill was always bringing stray animals into the house. Dogs, cats, birds with broken wings, baby bunnies. My parents didn't have the heart to turn the strays away, but the rule was that the animals were only allowed in the yard and in Bill's room. Of course, eventually the blind dog and the cat with half an ear chewed off found their way into the living room. The birds were healed and set free but refused to leave. The bunnies grew up and migrated throughout the house, eating the wires and gnawing on the baseboards. And we loved them all. The point to this is that Bill loves easily and immediately. And the rest of my family, me included, loves more slowly.

Against my better judgment, Hooker was growing on me like one of Bill's adopted animals. The smart part of me was saying *are you kidding?* The soft squishy part of me that let the one-eared cat sleep on my chest all night long, almost smothering me for five years, was finding Hooker endearing. And the sex part of me was thinking the bakery theory was one of those male things I'd never fully understand. My way was to develop a craving for a particular pastry, to obsess about it, to dream about it, to desire it. And finally to lose control and buy it and eat it.

And now Hooker was looking tasty. Scary, hunh?

We took the elevator to the parking garage and found our way back to the Mini. Hooker and I had new cell phones. Mine rang just as I was about to buckle up.

"Barney," my mother said. "Where are you? Is everything all right?"

"Everything is fine. I'm still in Miami."

"Are you with Bill?"

"I just left him."

"He never answers his phone. His message machine is filled. I can't leave any more messages."

"I'll tell him to call you. Maybe tomorrow."

"When are you coming home? Should I go over to your apartment and water your plants?"

"I don't have any plants."

"What do you mean you don't have plants? Everybody has plants."

"Mine are plastic."

"I never noticed."

I hung up and Hooker smiled at me. "Do you really have plastic plants?"

"So sue me, I'm not a gardener."

My phone rang again. It was my boss.

"Family emergency," I told her. "I left you a message on your voice mail. Yes, I know this is inconvenient. Actually, I'm not sure when I'll be back, but I think it'll be soon."

"Did that work out okay?" Hooker asked when I hung up.

"Yep. Everything's great." I was fired, but what the hell, I didn't like the job anyway.

I had two more phone calls. One from my friend Lola. And the other from a woman who worked with me at the insurance company. I told both of them I was fine and I'd call them back.

Finally a call came in from Rosa. It was the call I'd been waiting for. I'd asked Rosa to do some research for me.

"I got it," Rosa said. "I got a list of all the properties Salzar owns in Miami. Felicia helped me. She has a cousin who works in the tax office. We even got his girlfriend's address."

I disconnected and turned to Hooker. "Rosa's got the list."

Hooker found a parking space half a block from the cigar factory. We had sodas and burgers from a drive-thru, and we took a couple minutes to finish eating. Hooker's cell phone rang. He looked at the readout and shut his phone off. He drank some soda and saw that I was watching him.

"My publicist," he said. "That's the fourth call today. This guy never gives up."

"This is about the schmooze thing in Homestead?"

"Yeah. I talked to him earlier. The transporter's there with the PR car. He's still trying to talk me into making an appearance."

"Maybe you should go."

"Don't want to go. And who'll protect you if I go?"

"In the beginning you were following me around because you didn't trust me."

"Yes, but all that's changed. That was only partly true, any-way. I was mostly following you around because of the little pink skirt and your long pink legs."

A blue Crown Vic parked on the opposite side of the street at the far end of the block, and Slick and Gimpy got out.

"I don't believe this," Hooker said. "What are the chances?"

Slick still had his arm in the sling, plus he had a huge Band-Aid across his nose, and both his eyes were black and blue. Gimpy was wearing a neck brace and a knee brace. His foot was still bandaged and wrapped in a thing that looked like a Velcro sandal, and he had a single crutch to help him walk.

Neither of the men saw us. They crossed the street and walked into the cigar factory.

"Maybe we should call the police," Hooker said.

"The police won't get here in time. We should go in to see if we can help Rosa."

We were half out of the Mini when the door to the cigar factory crashed open and the crutch flew out, followed by Slick and Gimpy. They went to the ground, stumbled up, and scrambled for the Crown Vic.

The entire factory emptied onto the sidewalk, yelling in Spanish. Rosa and two other women had guns. *Pow!* Rosa squeezed off a shot that ripped into the rear quarter panel of the Crown Vic. *Pow, pow.* The other women fired.

Slick cranked the Crown Vic over and laid a quarter of an inch of rubber on takeoff.

"Silly butthole," one of the old women yelled at the flee-ing car.

We walked over to the group.

"What happened?" I asked.

"Some losers came in and tried to take Rosa away, can you imagine?"

"It was those two guys from Key West," Rosa said. "They say they want to talk to me outside. I say to them I don't think so. I tell them they can talk to me *inside*. Then they start to get smart mouth, threatening me if I don't go outside."

A chunky old woman with short gray hair and a cigar in her mouth elbowed Rosa. "We show them, hunh? You don't get smart mouth in this shop. We kick their asses good. We get all over them."

"You wait here," Rosa said to Hooker and me. "I'll get the list."

The crutch was still in the middle of the road.

A dusty pickup truck with gardening equipment in the back rattled up to the crutch and stopped. A man got out, walked to the crutch, and examined it. Then he threw the crutch into the back of the truck and took off.

"You never know when you're going to need a crutch," Hooker said.

Rosa swung out of the cigar factory with her big straw bag over her arm and a piece of paper in her hand. She was wearing clear plastic open-toed shoes with four-inch spike heels, blue cotton pants that came to midcalf, and a red T-shirt that advertised a crab house.

"All right," Rosa said. "I'm ready to go. All we have to do is pick up Felicia."

Hooker grinned at me. "And to think I was going to waste my time on a fishing trip."

We stopped at the fruit stand and Felicia crammed herself in next to Rosa.

"You know those two guys you shot?" Rosa said to Felicia. "They stopped by the cigar factory just now and tried to get me to go with them."

"They did not."

"They did!"

"What'd you say to them?"

"I said they should eat some lead."

"Maybe they going to stop here next, and I'll miss them. That would be disappointing," Felicia said.

"If they want to talk to you bad enough, they'll be back," Rosa said. "In the meantime, maybe your husband will shoot them." Rosa leaned forward. "Turn right at the next corner," she told Hooker. "And then go two blocks. The first property will be on the right. It's an apartment building."

The apartment building was four stories tall, and the ground-level wall was covered with gang graffiti. The front door was missing. Just some hinges left on the jamb. Inside there was a small dark foyer with four mailboxes built into the one wall and a scary-looking stairwell to the right. We all squeezed into the foyer and read the names on the mailboxes.

"I don't know none of these people," Felicia said. "They must be foreign. Some of those South Americans."

The foyer didn't smell great. And the stairwell smelled even worse.

"No point to all of us trooping up the stairs," Hooker said. "I'll go, and you three wait here."

"Be careful," Felicia said. "Watch for the big cockroaches."

Hooker went upstairs, and Rosa, Felicia, and I stepped out of the foyer, onto the sidewalk.

"This building could use some bleach," Rosa said. "That's the best thing to clean up a building like this."

"Be better if it had a fire," Felicia said. "Urban renewal. Start over."

Ten minutes later I was looking up at the windows, worrying about Hooker.

"He should be down by now," I said.

"No gunshots," Rosa said.

"Yeah, and no screaming," Felicia said. "We give him some more time."

A couple minutes and Hooker appeared at the bottom of the stairs, followed by a bunch of smiling people.

One man had *Hooker* written on his forehead.

"Good-bye, Sam Hooker," they were saying.

"Thank you for autographing my hat."

"Thank you for calling my sister."

A woman came running with a camera, and the group posed for a picture with Hooker smiling in the middle of it all.

We got into the Mini and pulled away.

"Race fans," Hooker said. "Maria wasn't in there."

We searched two more apartment buildings with similar results. The fourth property on the list was a warehouse. We all thought this had some potential, since a truck filled with gold could be hidden in the warehouse.

The warehouse was three stories tall and took up half of a city block. There were three garage bays and a standard door. All were closed and locked. Windows were dark above the doors. Second-floor windows were broken. We drove down a refuse-strewn alley that intersected the block and backed up to the rear of the warehouse. There were a couple Dumpsters back there, and there was a rear door, also locked. Ground-floor windows were painted black and secured with iron bars.

"Get on the Dumpster," Felicia said to Hooker. "Then you can go in through the window above it."

Hooker looked at the Dumpster and the window. "Wouldn't that be breaking and entering?"

"Yeah, so?"

"What if someone's in there?"

"Then we run like hell. Unless they're race fans, and then you can stay to sign autographs."

"I guess I'd look like a hero if I found Maria. And since I'm doing this for your brother, you'd be real grateful," Hooker said to me.

Felicia shook her finger at him. "Shame on you. I know what you're thinking."

"I'd be grateful," Rosa said.

"Something to remember," Hooker said.

Hooker dragged a crate over to the Dumpster and used it as a step. He stood on the Dumpster and tried the window.

"It's locked," he said. "And it's too high. I can't see in."

"And?" Felicia said.

"And I can't get in."

"Break it."

"I'm not going to break it! You can't just go around breaking windows."

Rosa climbed onto the crate and then onto the Dumpster.

"Hand me the crate," she said to Felicia.

Felicia passed the crate up to Rosa, Rosa swung the crate in an arc and smashed the window. There weren't any alarms. No one came running.

"I'm gonna look in," Rosa said to Hooker. "Give me a boost."

And Rosa started climbing up Hooker. She had her heel on his thigh and her big boobs in his face. Hooker had a grip on her leg. Rosa got her foot on Hooker's shoulder and Hooker got his hand under her ass and pushed her up to the window.

"What do you see?" Felicia asked.

"Nothing. It's just a big empty warehouse. There's nothing in it. It's three stories high, but it's all space. There's no other doors in it, so it doesn't even have a bathroom." She looked at Hooker. "You can put me down now."

Hooker was braced against the building. "Be careful where you put the heels."

Rosa had one heel snagged into Hooker's waistband and her other leg crooked around his neck. She grabbed his shirt and swung her leg free, and Hooker lost his balance.

"Oh shit!" Hooker said. He was flailing his arms, looking for a handhold, and Rosa was hanging on for all she was worth, wrapped on him monkey style.

Hooker hit the Dumpster flat on his back with Rosa on top of him.

"This isn't so bad," Rosa said.

"Call 911," Hooker said.

I was on tiptoes, peeking over the Dumpster at Hooker. "Are you hurt?"

"No. I'm going to kill Rosa."

ELEVEN

We got Hooker and Rosa off the Dumpster and back into the Mini.

"There's two more warehouses," Felicia said. "One down the street and one on the next block."

We drove to both warehouses and found the garage doors open on both of them. Rosa volunteered to go in and look around while she asked directions. "We're lost," she'd say. "We're looking for Flagler Terrace. And what do you guys do here, anyway? And do you have a ladies' room?"

Both warehouses came up zero.

We checked out a parking lot, a Laundromat, several deli marts, and two more slum apartment buildings. We skipped Salzar's house and his girlfriend's condo.

"The only thing left is an office building on Calle Ocho," Felicia said. "That is where Salzar has his offices."

We all did a silent groan. None of us wanted to run into Salzar.

"He don't know me," Felicia said. "I'll go in and ask around."

"I'll go with you," Rosa said. "He don't know me either."

There was a small, unattended parking lot adjacent to the office building. The lot was full so Hooker pulled the Mini into the lot and idled in an exit lane while Rosa and Felicia went into the building. Hooker and I sat in the car, facing Calle Ocho. We watched the rush hour traffic and we kept an eye on the building's front door.

A black Lincoln Town Car dropped out of the traffic and parked at the curb. Puke Face exited the building and held the front door open. Salzar strode through the door, crossed the wide sidewalk, and paused at the Town Car. He turned and glanced at the lot where we were parked. His face showed no expression but his eyes locked onto the Mini.

Hooker did a little finger wave. "Hi," Hooker said, smiling. "Nice to see you survived the fire."

Salzar turned from us, disappeared into the backseat of the Town Car, and the car eased from the curb and rolled down the street.

I looked over at Hooker.

"What?" he said.

"I can't believe you did that."

"He was looking at us. I was being friendly."

"Give me a break. That was announcing your dick was bigger than his."

"You're right," Hooker said. "He brings out the NASCAR in me."

Hooker put the Mini into gear and drove out of the lot and

circled the block. Rosa and Felicia were waiting for us when we returned.

"We didn't find anything," Rosa said. "But Salzar has a fancy ass office. We didn't go in. We just looked through the big glass door."

"I could smell brimstone," Felicia said. "Good thing I'm wearing my cross."

We took Felicia back to the fruit stand, and we dropped Rosa off at her apartment.

"Now what?" I asked Hooker.

"I don't know. I'm a race car driver. I'm not a detective. I'm just stumbling along here."

"What about Columbo, James Bond, Charlie's Angels? What would they do?"

"I know what James Bond would do."

"Forget James Bond. James Bond probably isn't a great role model for you."

"Okay, how about this. Let's find a convenience store and get a load of junk and park and eat."

We got the bag of junk, which consisted of soda, nachos, Twizzlers, a box of cookies, a couple shrink-wrapped sandwiches, and a big bag of chips, but we couldn't find a place to eat.

"It has to be someplace romantic so I can make a move on you," Hooker said. "Hey, look here, we can park in this alley. There's some space just past those garbage cans."

"Garbage cans aren't romantic."

"See, that's the difference between a man and a woman," Hooker said, jockeying into a parking space. "A man has imagination when it comes to romance. A man is willing to overlook a few things in the interest of romance." He pushed his seat back and handed me a sandwich. "This isn't so bad. It's nice and private. Here we are in this little car. Just the two of us."

Okay, I have to admit, it was cozy. And I *had* been thinking Hooker had nice legs. Tan and muscular, the hair on them sun bleached. And I *had* been wondering what it would feel like to lay my hand flat against his washboard stomach. That didn't mean I wanted to have car sex in an alley next to some garbage cans. Been there, done that.

"We're in a public alley," I said. "You're not really thinking of doing anything dumb, are you?"

"You mean like having my way with you? Yeah, I was thinking about it. It's what James Bond would do."

"I should never have mentioned James Bond. James Bond had a sex addiction."

"Hey, if you're going to have an addiction, pick a good one. Why waste time on smoking and cocaine when you can have a sex addiction."

"Would you like some cookies? How about more chips? There are some chips left."

"No good, darlin', I'm in James Bond mode now."

"James Bond didn't call women *darlin'*."

He leaned close and slid his arm around my shoulders. "I'm a Texas James Bond."

"Get away from me."

"You don't mean that. Women always put out for James Bond."

"*Put out?* You expect me to *put out?*"

"I guess that was an unfortunate choice of phrase. Probably you don't think that's romantic, eh? What I meant was . . . oh hell."

And he kissed me. A lot. And after a couple minutes of this I was thinking the alley was pretty private, and I could hardly smell the garbage cans, and maybe car sex would work after all. His hands were under my shirt, and his tongue was sliding over mine, and somehow I'd gotten onto my back in the Mini. I had my ass half on the gearshift between the two front seats and a leg draped around the steering column. I had my head pressed into the side door and suddenly I couldn't move. My hair was tangled in the door handle.

"Help," I whispered to Hooker.

"Don't worry, darlin'. I know what I'm doing."

"I don't think so."

"Just give me some direction. I'm good at taking direction."

"It's my hair."

"I love your hair. You have great hair."

"Thank you. The problem is . . ."

"The problem is we're talking about your *other* hair, right? I've already seen it, darlin'. I know you're not a natural blond. It's okay by me. Shit, I wouldn't care if you were bald."

"Hooker, my hair's *caught!*"

"Caught? Caught in what? Caught in your zipper?"

"Caught in the door handle."

"How could that be . . . you don't even have your pants off. *Oh! CRAP!*"

He got his knee on the floor and examined my hair.

"Is it bad?" I asked him.

"No. It's just a little tangled. I've seen worse. I'll have you back in action in a minute. I'll just unwrap a few of these little hairs. . . . Actually, we've got more than a few hairs involved in this. Well, okay, we're talking about major hair involvement. Jesus, how did you do this? All right, don't panic."

"I'm *not panicked*."

"That's good. No reason for *both* of us to be panicked. Maybe if I just . . ."

"*Yow!* You're pulling my hair out."

"I wish it was that simple."

I rolled my eyes up and saw a cop looking down, in the window at me.

"Excuse me," he said. "You're going to have to leave."

"Back off," Hooker said. "I'm having a problem here."

The cop smiled at me. "Jeez, lady, you must have needed it real bad to end up on your back in a little car like this."

"It was my boyish charm," Hooker said.

"Gets them every time," the cop said.

"I just . . . slipped," I said.

A second cop arrived and looked down at me. "What's the delay?"

"He was diddlin' her, and she slipped, and she got her hair caught in the door handle."

"He was *not* diddling me!" Unfortunately.

Hooker looked up at them. "I don't suppose either of you guys would have scissors on you?"

"Scissors?" I said, my voice up an octave. "No! *No cutting.*"

"I got a knife," the first cop said. "You want a knife?"

"No!" I said.

"Yeah," Hooker said.

I narrowed my eyes at Hooker. "You touch a single hair with that knife, and I'll make sure you sing soprano for the rest of your life."

"Wow, she's scary," the first cop said to Hooker. "You might want to think about this relationship."

"Are you kidding?" Hooker said. "Look how cute she is with her hair all wrapped around the door handle. Well, maybe not with the hair wrapped around the door handle . . . but usually."

"All I know is, you gotta get out of here. This is a public alley. Hey, are you Sam Hooker?"

Oh great.

"Yep, that's me," Hooker said. "In the flesh."

"I saw you win at Daytona. That was the best day of my life."

"*Hello,*" I said. "Remember me? How about someone untangling my goddamn hair!"

Hooker blew out a sigh. "Darlin', unless you want to be a Mini Cooper accessory for the rest of your life, you're going to have to get cut free."

"Can't you just drive me to a hair salon?"

Hooker looked out at the two cops. "Do you guys know of any all-night hair salons around here?"

They mumbled something about me being a nut and shook their heads.

"Fine. *Great.* Cut me free," I said. "What am I worried about? I haven't had a good hair day since I've been in this state. It's a swamp for crying out loud."

"That's real negative," the first cop said. "It's hard to live with a woman who's negative. Maybe she's not the one, you know what I mean? You're a NASCAR guy. You can probably have anyone you want."

Hooker sawed at my hair with the knife. "Just a little bit more . . . *oops.*"

"What *oops*?" I asked. "I don't like *oops.*"

"Did I say *oops*? I didn't mean *oops.* I meant thank goodness you're untangled." He handed the knife back to the cop "Now all we have to do is get you to sit up."

"My leg is caught on the steering wheel and my foot is asleep."

The first cop ran around to the other side of the car to help get my leg free. And the second cop opened the passenger-side door, grabbed me under my armpits, and pulled me out.

"This is a little embarrassing," I said to the two cops, "but thanks for the help."

I got back into the car, buckled my shoulder harness, and gave Hooker a death look. "This is all your fault."

Hooker gave the Mini some gas and motored out of the alley, down the street. "My fault?"

"You started it all with that kiss."

Hooker smiled. "It was a pretty decent kiss."

"Sure, easy for you to think that. You didn't get *your* hair caught."

"Seems like it's a good idea to be on top when you're having car sex."

"Do you have a lot of car sex?"

"Yeah, but I'm usually alone."

"I'm afraid to look in the mirror. How bad is my hair? It looks like there's an awful lot of it stuck in the handle."

Hooker cut his eyes to me and ran off the road onto a lawn. He made a fast correction and was back on the road. "It's not bad."

"You just ran off the road."

"I was . . . distracted."

I reached for the mirror on the sun visor and Hooker knocked my hand away.

"Don't do that. You don't want to look," he said. He grabbed the visor and gave it a twist and snapped it off at the pivot point. He powered his window down and threw the visor out the window.

My eyes were wide. "You just broke my brother's car!"

"Darlin', your brother's car is a wreck. He'll never notice the missing visor."

I put my hands up to feel my hair.

"I'm telling you it's not so bad," Hooker said. "Well, okay, it's pretty bad, but I'm really sorry. I'll make it up to you. I'll buy you another hat. A nicer one. Hell, I'll buy you a car. Would you like a car? And you're still cute. I swear, you're still cute. If you put your little pink skirt on, no one's gonna notice your hair."

I just stared at him. I could feel that my mouth was open, but there weren't any words coming out of it. I was all out of words.

"Oh boy," Hooker said. "You're upset, aren't you? I really hate when you're upset. You're not going to cry again, are you? I'll do anything. Honest to God, I'll do anything. What would you like? A vacation? A good seat for Daytona? Marriage? Do you want to get married?"

"You'd marry me?"

"No, not me. But I could find someone."

I sucked in some air.

"Only foolin' with you," Hooker said. "Of course I'd marry you. I mean, it isn't like your hair won't grow back, right? Any man would be lucky to get married to you."

"And you'd marry me, why?"

"Because I just feel so sorry for you. No, wait a minute that's not it. That's a bad answer, isn't it? Because . . . I don't know why. I was trying to make you happy. You know, take your mind off your hair. Women always want to get married."

"I appreciate the effort, but I don't want to get married."

"Really?"

"Not now, anyway. And not to you."

"What's wrong with me?"

"For starters, I hardly know you."

"I could fix that."

"No! I can't afford to lose any more hair."

I put my pink hat on, settled back in my seat, and called Judey to check on Bill.

"He's sleeping like a little lamb," Judey said. "I'm keeping him comfy. Don't worry about a thing."

Hooker had a country western station on the radio. Some woman was singing about her man dying and her heart breaking. And if that wasn't bad enough it sounded like she didn't have a home and then her dog ran off.

"See," Hooker said. "You don't have it so bad. You could

be like that poor woman singing. Her boyfriend died and left her all alone. And you just lost a patch of hair."

"Do you like country western music?"

"I hate it. Depresses the shit out of me. I just get sucked into it every now and then. One of those Texas things."

I searched for a rock station, didn't have a lot of luck, and finally settled on Latin dance music.

"Unless you have a better idea, I'm taking us back to my condo," Hooker said. "I don't know where else to go, I could use some new clothes, and I wouldn't mind trading this car for my Porsche."

"Don't you think that might be dangerous? We're the only ones who know where the canister is located. Suppose the bad guys are waiting for you to go home?"

"I'll deal with it. I need a place to think."

Hooker drove down Alton Road and turned left onto First Street and then onto Washington. "I'm still hungry," he said. "I'm going to run into Joe's and get some take-out stone crabs."

He double-parked and ran into the restaurant. A parking place opened up in front of me, so I scooted over behind the wheel and parked the Mini. Ten minutes later, Hooker came out with a bag of food and slid in next to me.

I returned to Alton Road and entered the parking garage. Hooker had two numbered spaces. His Porsche was in one. I pulled the Mini into the other, beside the Porsche. I caught a flash of movement in my rearview mirror. I looked up and saw Slick move toward us, his white sling standing out in the dim light.

I threw the Mini into reverse and gave it gas. The car jumped back, there was a shriek and a thud, and Gimpy tumbled off to the side. Slick jumped in front of the Mini, arms wide in a *stop* gesture. I shifted into drive, stomped on the accelerator, and bounced Slick off the hood. I swung the car around and headed for the exit. Gunshots echoed in the cavernous space. I gritted my teeth, put my head down, and sped out of the garage.

I cut across a couple streets, hit Collins, and drove north. Hooker was slumped in his seat, looking dazed, clutching the food bag.

"Are you okay?" I asked him.

"Hunh?"

There was a fine line of blood trickling down the side of his face. I slid to a stop under a streetlight. The blood was oozing from a gash in Hooker's forehead. It wasn't a gunshot wound, and it didn't seem to be deep. The area around it was red and swollen. I shifted my attention to the windshield and saw the point of impact. Hooker'd released his shoulder harness and hadn't rebuckled in time. At some point in the garage fiasco I'd pitched him into the windshield.

"Good thing you're such a tough guy," I said to Hooker.

"Yeah," he said. "And I'm going to protect you, too. Both of you. You're going to have to hold still, though. I can't protect you when you keep spinning like that."

"Hang on. I'm going to take you to the emergency room."

"That's nice," Hooker said. "I like going places with you."

• • •

I called Judey and got directions to South Shore Hospital. It was a weeknight, and Hooker and I arrived after the hospital'd had a flurry of rush-hour road-rage victims and before the hospital got into the late-night parade of drug- and alcohol-induced disasters. Since we were between peak hours Hooker was seen almost immediately. His head was examined and a Band-Aid applied. Some tests were taken. He was diagnosed as having a moderate concussion. I was given a sheet with instructions regarding his care for the next twenty-four hours. And we were dismissed.

I had Hooker by the elbow, guiding him down the hall to the exit. A gurney rolled toward us, pushed by a male nurse. A man was on the gurney, most of him covered by a sheet. His chart had been placed on his stomach. I passed close by the gurney and made eye contact with the man. It was Gimpy.

Gimpy gave a startled gasp. "*You!*" he yelled, suddenly sitting up, clawing out at me, sending the chart clattering to the floor.

I jumped away, and the nurse gave the gurney a quick shove ahead.

"You didn't hit him hard enough," Hooker whispered to me. "It's like he's the living dead. You can't kill him."

Good to know Hooker was feeling better.

I helped him get into the Mini, which now had one side entirely crumpled, a missing visor, and a scattering of bullet holes in the lower part of the hatchback.

I crossed South Beach and drove north on Collins. I didn't

want to chance going back to Hooker's, or Bill's, or Judey's. For that matter, I didn't want to chance staying in South Beach.

Hooker had his eyes closed and his hand to his head. "I have a massive headache," he said. "I have the mother of all headaches."

"Don't fall asleep. You're not supposed to sleep."

"Barney, I'd have to be dead to fall asleep with this headache."

"I thought I'd drive north of town and look for a hotel."

"There are lots of hotels on Collins. Once you get north of the Fontainebleau we should be safe."

I tried four hotels, including the Fontainebleau, and none had a vacancy. This was high season in Florida. The fifth hotel had a single room. Fine by me. I was afraid to leave Hooker alone anyway.

I moved us in, and I called Judey to tell him everything was okay. The room was clean and comfortable. The hotel was on the beach, but our room faced Collins.

Hooker stretched out on the king-size bed, and I crept into the bathroom to check my hair. I stood in front of the mirror, held my breath, and whipped the hat off.

Shit.

I blew out a sigh and put the hat back on. It'll grow back, I told myself. And it's just one chunk. And it's not like I'm bald. I must have at least an inch or two of hair left where he chopped it.

I returned to the bedroom, and I sat in an armchair and watched Hooker. He opened one eye and looked at me.

"You're not going to sit there and watch me all night, are you? It's creepy."

"I'm following the instruction sheet they gave me at the hospital."

"Those instructions were for a *bad* concussion. I've only got a moderate concussion. They gave you the wrong instructions. Your instructions should read that you go to bed with the concussed."

"I don't think so."

"You can't sit in that chair all night. You'll be tired in the morning. You won't be able to outsmart the bad guys."

He had a point.

I lay down next to him. "We'll leave the lights on so I can check on you. And you have to behave yourself."

"I'll be fine as long as you don't fondle me when I'm sleeping."

"I'm not going to fondle you! And you're not supposed to be sleeping."

I closed my eyes and instantly fell asleep. When I woke up the lights were off and the room was dark. I reached over to check on Hooker.

"I knew you couldn't help yourself," Hooker said.

"That wasn't a fondle. That was a bed check. You were supposed to leave the lights on."

"I couldn't sleep with the lights on."

"You aren't supposed to sleep."

"I can nap. Anyway, it's impossible to sleep with the sound effects."

And that's when I heard it. *Thump, thump, thump, thump.*

It was the bed in the next room hitting the wall. "Omigod."

"Wait. It'll get better. She's a moaner and a screamer."

"Not even."

"Swear to God. Wait until you hear her. If it wasn't for the headache I'd have a woody."

"I don't hear anything but thumping."

"You have to be quiet."

We lay there together in the dark, listening. There was some muffled moaning and then some mumbled talking.

"I can't hear what they're saying," I said to Hooker.

"Shhh!"

The thumping resumed and some more moaning. The moaning got louder.

"Here it comes," Hooker whispered.

"Yes," came through the wall. "Oh yes. Oh God. Oh God. Oh God."

Thump, thump, thump, thump. BANG, BANG, BANG.

I was afraid the picture hanging over our headboard was going to get knocked off the wall and crash down on us.

"*OH GOD!*"

And then it was quiet.

"Well," Hooker said. "That was fun."

"She faked it."

"It didn't sound fake to me."

"Give me a break. No woman sounds like that unless she's faking it."

"That's a disturbing piece of information."

•　　•　　•

Hooker was feeling better in the morning. He had dark circles under his eyes, and he had a lump on his head, but his headache was gone, and he wasn't seeing double.

We ordered room service breakfast, and halfway through breakfast my phone rang.

"He's *gone!*" Judey wailed.

"Who?"

"Bill! Wild Bill is gone. I took a shower and when I came out he was gone. I don't understand it. We were having such a good time. He was feeling so much better this morning. He came out and sat at the table for breakfast. I made him pancakes. How could he leave after I made him pancakes?"

"Did he say anything about leaving? Did you hear anything? Did it look like someone broke in and took him?"

"No, no, and no. The little shit just left. He got dressed in *my* clothes. And he left."

"Did he leave a note?"

"A note," Judey said. "I was so upset, I didn't look for a note."

I sat with my lips pressed tight together, listening while Judey searched.

"I found it!" Judey said. "It was on the kitchen counter. It says he went to get Maria back. That's all. I'm so sorry. This is terrible. I was supposed to be watching him."

"It's not your fault. This is why we call him Wild Bill. Call me if you hear from him."

Hooker pushed back from his breakfast. "That didn't sound good."

"Bill went to get Maria."

217

"Unless he knows something we don't know, he'll be sniffing around Salzar. How do you think he'll do that? From what I've seen, Salzar's never alone. He's always got a couple big guys with him."

"Bill's not known for his cunning. Bill just goes after whatever it is he wants. I wouldn't be surprised if he walked up to Salzar and put a gun to his head."

TWELVE

It was a little after ten when I drove past Salzar's office building on Calle Ocho. It was a perfectly nice-looking building, in a nice neighborhood. And this would have been a perfectly nice day, if only things were different. I must have been doing a lot of unconscious sighing because Hooker reached over and put his hand at the nape of my neck.

It seemed to me we were always taking one step forward and two steps backward. And with each step, no matter that it was forward or backward, Hooker and I got dragged deeper into the mess, Bill's future got increasingly precarious, and I didn't know what to think about Maria. I hoped she still *had* a future.

Until a week ago, my life had been so easy. No major illnesses, no big disasters. Nothing to make me uncomfortable. Okay, I had a couple aborted romances that caused me some pain. And sometimes I felt like I was aimlessly drifting, marking time. But I'd never had to fear for my life or for the premature death of someone I loved. Until a week ago, I'd never looked down the barrel of a gun.

Now I know what it's like to live with real fear . . . and I'm not crazy about it. I'd get on a plane and go home, but that wouldn't make it all go away. I suspect the bad guys would track me down, no matter where I ran. And I couldn't live with myself if I bailed on Bill. Sometimes his brain isn't fully engaged, but his heart's always in the right spot.

And then there's this other thing that I'm struggling over. The canister. The truth is, I'm a person who pretty much lives day to day. I haven't got a lot of large heroic ambitions. I'd like a better job, but up to this point I was always working too hard to pay the rent to take a chance on a move. And even with a better job, I guess my aspirations are small. It's not like I want to be a movie star or an astronaut or the queen of England. I'd just like to find something that's a little more fun. Not that it has to be fun all the time . . . but some of the time would be a good thing. And God knows, I never wanted to save the world. So I'm a little unprepared for the current responsibility of knowing where a canister (that could possibly be a warhead) is hidden. And I'm a *lot* unprepared for the almost violent resolve I have that it won't fall into the wrong hands.

"We need help," I said to Hooker. "This isn't like the time Bill stole the keg. This is serious, and it's not going away. We need to get some sort of law enforcement involved here."

"I agree," Hooker said. "What kind of help should we get?"

"I don't know. Who would be in charge of possible bomb disposal?"

"I'm a little stumped on that one. I can drive, and I can dance, and I can even scramble an egg, but I don't know a whole lot about possible bombs. I guess we could start with the FBI."

I drove around the block three times. Finally a space opened up a half block from Salzar's building, and I maneuvered the Mini into it.

"Do you want to get in touch with authorities now?" Hooker asked. "Or do you want to try to head Bill off first?"

"Bill first. If possible."

There was a decent amount of traffic on Calle Ocho at this time of day. Cars would slow when they came up to the Mini, the occupants eyes would widen, and then the cars would speed up.

Hooker slouched in his seat. "You'd think this was the first time anybody ever saw a car riddled with bullet holes."

We let a half hour go by. No Bill in sight. I couldn't call him. He didn't have his cell phone. I called Judey. Judey hadn't heard from him.

"We should go in and ask around," Hooker said. "See if he went past the front desk."

I did an inadvertent grimace.

"Hey, it could be fun," Hooker said.

"You're not worried?"

"You want the truth? My boys got the creepy crawlies. When this is done you're gonna owe me large."

We got out of the car and walked the half block to the building entrance. We pushed through the glass doors, crossed the lobby, and went to the front desk.

"I was supposed to meet my brother here," I told the guy behind the counter.

"Bill Barnaby?"

My stomach went into free fall. "Yes."

"He's with Mr. Salzar. They're expecting you."

Great. I turned to Hooker. "They're expecting us."

Hooker had his hand back at my neck. "No need for both of us to go up. Why don't you wait here? I know you need to use the ladies' room."

I bobbed my head at the desk guy. "Ladies' room?"

"Take the corridor to the side of the elevators. It's on the right."

Hooker and I walked to the elevators together.

"Get out of here," Hooker said. "Make it look like you're going to the ladies' room and find a way out. I'll call your cell when Bill and I are out of the building. If you don't hear from me in the next ten minutes, go to the police."

I walked down the corridor to the ladies' room and looked around. Security camera at the end of the hall. I went into the ladies' room and took a couple deep breaths. I was the only one in the ladies room. It was on the ground floor. There was a window next to the sink. Frosted glass. I unlocked the window and opened it. The window backed up to a service driveway. I climbed out the window and dropped to the ground. I looked for security cameras. One at the far end of the building over the rear entrance. I walked in the opposite direction.

I cut through another service driveway and circled the block. I didn't want to go to the Mini. Hooker had been in the building for ten minutes now and he hadn't called. Time to call the police. I was back on Calle Ocho. I was standing in a doorway one building down from Salzar's building. From where I stood I could see Salzar's small parking lot and the front entrance.

A man left the building and went to one of two Lincoln Town Cars parked in the lot. He got into the car and drove out of the lot. I ran to the corner and saw the car make its way down the cross street and turn into the service road. I ran to the service road and stood on the corner and watched. The car stopped at Salzar's rear entrance. After a moment the door opened and Bill and Hooker were marched out and loaded into the Town Car. There were three other men with them. Two of the men got into the car, and the car drove off.

There was a slim chance that I could follow the Town Car if I could get a ride fast enough. No time to run back to the Mini. I was afraid to go back to it anyway. I jogged down the cross street, looking in car windows for keys left in the ignition. I found one almost immediately. Honda Civic with the door open and the keys dangling. It was parked in front of a hole-in-the-wall restaurant advertising fast food and takeout. Someone had been in a hurry and was way too trusting.

I slid behind the wheel, turned the key in the ignition, and took off. I got to the corner, and the Town Car cruised by, going west on Seventh Street. I was several cars back by the time I was able to make the turn, but I had the Town Car in sight. Traffic was slow on Seventh. We inched along. The Town Car turned north on Seventeenth.

After three blocks, I caught a flash of lights in my rearview mirror. Cop car. Damn. Take another deep breath, I told myself. Don't panic. Pretend they're an escort. This could be a good thing, right? Just have them follow and help to get Bill and Hooker out of the Town Car.

Three more blocks. The cop car was still behind me, lights flashing. I could be wrong, but it looked like a second cop car was behind the first one. I saw the Lincoln sail across First Street. I approached the intersection and a third cop car came from First, angled in front of me, and stopped me from going any farther.

I got out of the car. Someone yelled for me to put my hands on my head. I did as I was told, and I walked back to the first cop car.

"I need help," I said. "I was following the black Lincoln Town Car. It belongs to Luis Salzar, and he's kidnapped my brother."

"That's pretty original," the cop said. "Usually we just get PMS stories."

"It's true!"

"Radio for a female," he said to his partner. "We're going to need to search her for drugs." He snapped a cuff on my wrist. He brought it to my back and snapped the second cuff on my other wrist.

"You're making a big mistake," I said. A tear trickled down my check. I'd totally screwed up.

"Oh man," the cop said. "I hate this part." He swiped the tear away with his finger. "Lady, you shouldn't be doing drugs. You're real cute in your little pink skirt and hat. You don't need drugs."

"Thanks," I said. I was obviously a loser, but at least I

looked cute. I tried to tell myself that was worth something, but I wasn't convinced.

One of the cop cars left. Two stayed. The two that remained had their lights flashing, and I suspected there would be a big rush at the hospital for strobe-induced seizures. Traffic slowly moved around the police circus, gawking at me in cuffs, gawking at the cops who were standing, hands on gun belts, in case I made a run for it.

After a couple minutes I realized there was one more cop car involved. It was an unmarked car parked behind the two cop cars to my rear. It had blue grille lights flashing. I couldn't see inside the car. Too far away and too much glare on the windshield. One of the uniforms had walked back and was talking to the driver. The uniform turned his head and looked over at me. He turned back to the driver and shook his head. More discussion. The uniform went to his car and got on the radio. After a five-minute radio conversation the uniform returned to the unmarked cop car. The uniform didn't look happy.

"What's going on?" I asked one of the cops.

"Looks like a fed pulling rank," the cop said.

After a short conversation between the uniform and the government car, the driver's door to the unmarked car opened and a guy got out and walked over to me. It was Slick.

I instinctively edged closer to the cops.

"You're being released into my custody," Slick said.

"No way!" I pressed myself against a uniform. "I don't want to be released. I demand that I stay arrested."

"Not my call," the uniform said, uncuffing me.

225

Slick wrapped his hand around my arm and tugged me toward his car. "Just shut up and come with me," he said. "The last thing we need is for you to get arrested. Although it wouldn't bother me much to see you behind bars. You've been a real pain in the ass."

"Who are you?"

"Federal agent. One of those three-letter organizations. I'd tell you, but then I'd have to kill you."

The only thing more frightening than thinking this buffoon was working for Salzar was knowing he was on my side. "You're not exactly competent."

"You're not exactly a model citizen."

"Are you kidding? I'm a good citizen. And I'm thinking I might report you to somebody. You shot Hooker."

"I tranked him. And just for the record, your friend Felicia shot me when I didn't have a weapon drawn. That's a little illegal."

"I thought you were trying to kill me."

"I asked you to step aside so I could talk to you. How does that translate to kill?"

"When you came up to me at Monty's you said you'd kill me."

"I'm supposed to be undercover. Don't you ever go to the movies? Don't you watch television?"

"You shot real bullets at my car last night."

"Okay, I admit it. I got carried away. Hell, you ran over me. What did you expect me to do, yell *thank you?*"

"You're lucky I didn't back up and finish the job."

"Tell me about it."

Slick was driving a sedan. He opened the back door for me, and Gimpy looked over his shoulder from the shotgun seat.

"Look who's joining us," Slick said to Gimpy. "Devil Woman."

"This is a bad idea," Gimpy said to Slick. "She's deranged."

"She's all we've got."

Slick got behind the wheel, shut his grille flashers off, and hit the door locks.

"I had them take the cuffs off," he said to me. "I'd appreciate it if you don't try to climb out a window or strangle me while I'm driving."

"Where are we going?"

"Early lunch. My pain pills are wearing off, and I don't want to take more on an empty stomach."

"My brother and Hooker . . ."

"Would have been fine if you hadn't stolen a car. We were staking out Salzar when you bumbled in . . . like always. All we ever wanted you to do was butt out."

"Why didn't you say that? Wait, I know, because then you'd have to kill me."

Slick slid a look at me in the rearview mirror. "Yeah. Doesn't seem like such a bad idea anymore."

"You'd better be nice to me, or I'll kick your ass again."

"Lady, this has been humiliating enough for two lifetimes. And painful. It'd be a real treat if you kicked someone else's ass for a while."

"We need to do something about Bill and Hooker and Maria."

"There's not a lot we can do right now. We lost the Town

Car. I got stuck in the police roadblock, so I went to Plan B and rescued you."

Slick pulled into a fast-food drive-thru, and we all put in an order. I got a burger, fries, and a chocolate milk shake. Slick got a burger and a diet soda. Gimpy sulked in the front seat. Slick parked in the fast-food lot, and we ate our food with the motor running and the air-conditioning on.

"Here's the deal," Slick said. "You and your brother have screwed up this whole operation and now you're going to have to help us salvage it."

I sucked some milk shake up the straw and slanted a look at him in the mirror.

"There are things about Calflex that you don't need to know. . . ."

"That's not a good way to start," I said.

Slick washed two pills down with some soda.

"Where's the pain?" I asked him.

"Cracked rib."

"Sorry."

"Yeah, right," he said. "Change places with my partner so I can see you without twisting. The looking-in-the-mirror thing is getting old."

Gimpy got out and held the door for me. His foot was still bandaged. His knee was still in the brace. His face was a mess of cuts and bruises. And he was bent.

"Do you have a cracked rib, too?"

The line of Gimpy's mouth was thin and tight. "Just get in the car, okay?"

228

Slick grinned. "It's his back. He tore a muscle when he tried to get off the gurney to choke you."

I did more milk shake sucking. "Tell me about Calflex."

"Salzar has been negotiating a Cuban land deal for Calflex. Prime real estate that will be used for a variety of purposes. The deal is being made with a member of the Cuban politburo who has large aspirations."

"Large aspirations?"

"He wants to be king."

"Would he be king through the normal chain of events?"

"He would not."

"A coup?"

"Possible. He needs money for the coup."

"This would be supplied by Calflex in exchange for the land?"

"Yeah. Unfortunately, this is not an individual who would be a good neighbor. In addition to Calflex money, he's demanded an item that would give him military leverage. Salzar has been shopping for such an item without much success. These things are available, but the purchase requires time and connections. When the agency learned Salzar was making inquiries, we got involved. We've spent the past year penetrating Salzar's organization."

"A year's worth of work shot to hell," Gimpy said from the backseat. "Shot to hell by a blond in a pink skirt."

Slick helped himself to some of my French fries. "Just for the record, you look great in the skirt."

"What's the Salzar connection to Calflex?" I asked Slick.

"Salzar *is* Calflex. It's not widely known. The ownership goes through holding companies and filters back under his wife's maiden name. If the deal goes through, Salzar will not only get land, he'll also get significant behind-the-scenes political power. Maybe even a seat on the politburo."

"Scary."

"You bet. He's a ruthless sociopath. And he's not aging gracefully."

"The Maria connection?"

"Maria arrived in Miami four years ago. Just another boat person washed ashore. Only it turns out she's more than that, and she blipped onto Salzar's radar screen a couple months ago. We had a man on the inside, and he said Salzar saw Raffles mentioned in a newspaper article. Salzar asked around Little Havana and found out Raffles came to Miami when her mother died. And then he found out she was a diver and that she had charts of Cuban waters.

"I don't think Salzar knew anything for sure until Maria took off in Hooker's boat with her charts. Once she took off, his gut instincts told him she was going to the wreck. He had the helicopter working overtime looking for her. And somehow, he knew there was more than gold down there. Our man inside overheard Salzar talking about the canister. Salzar knew the canister went down with the gold. The gold is worth millions, but it's the canister he really wants. With Russian help we were able to identify it. And it's not good. It's exactly what Salzar's politburo friend needs."

"Why didn't you go to Maria and get the canister first?"

"We want to catch Salzar with his hands dirty. So far, Salzar's been careful not to directly involve himself in anything illegal. And the few times when he has become involved, people who might have been helpful have disappeared. Forever. Probably encased in concrete two miles off Fisher Island. Persuading Maria to help us get the canister is only part of the problem. Unfortunately, there's a lot of bad shit out there, and if we don't nail Salzar, he'll keep looking and eventually he'll find something."

"Yeah, and anyway, we tried and she wouldn't cooperate," Gimpy said.

Gee, let me help you out with some charges against Salzar, I thought. Kidnapping, murder, assault with a deadly weapon.

"We had a man in place on the boat when Maria was brought on board. We could have gotten Salzar on a number of charges and recovered the canister if only Maria had *stayed* on board. They wouldn't have killed her until after the wreck location was confirmed and the canister brought up. We had a team ready to move in before anything bad happened to her. Once your brother got involved things went downhill fast."

I was thinking Slick was pretty cavalier about risking a civilian life for his operation.

"Unfortunately, we no longer have a man on the inside, and there's something I don't understand," Slick said. "Maria and Bill brought the gold up. And they brought the canister up, too. I dove down to the wreck site after you left. It was picked clean. Salzar tracked Bill and Maria, shot Bill and took Maria. I got a police report. So here's what I don't understand. Why did they take Maria? Why not just take the gold and the canister? Why not kill Bill and Maria on the spot? The obvious answer is . . . because they didn't get what they wanted. So they've got Maria. They encourage her to talk to them. Why don't they go get what they're after? Why do they grab Bill and Hooker?"

"I don't know," I said. "Why?"

"Because as much as they encouraged Maria to talk she couldn't tell them something she didn't know."

I sent Slick my very best dumb blond look. I didn't trust him. And I wasn't going to tell him something *he* didn't already know.

"I don't suppose you'd know anything about this?" Slick asked.

"Sorry. I wasn't on deck at the end when Bill and Maria took off. There was water in the fuel line, and I was in the engine room trying to get the *Happy Hooker* up and running. That's why they transferred everything over to the Sunseeker. Or at least I thought they transferred everything."

Slick locked eyes with me for a couple beats. "You should work with us," he said. "We can help you."

"What happened to the inside guy?"

"Disappeared."

"Tell me about the canister," I said.

"You don't want to know about the canister."

"I can find out for myself. I was there when they brought it up, and I know what it looks like. I can go on the Net and research the markings."

There was a silent exchange between Slick and Gimpy.

"I'll give you a history lesson first," Slick said. "Because if

I just tell you the contents of the canister you're going to think I've been seeing too many doomsday movies.

"Khrushchev launched Operation Anadry in June of '62 and began sending troops and weapons to Cuba. The Soviet military deployment to Cuba by fall of '62 included medium- and intermediate-range ballistic missiles, surface-to-air missile systems, coastal defense missiles, MiG fighter aircraft, medium-range bombers, and battlefield artillery. Plus there were forty-two thousand Soviet troops on the island, operating the equipment and training Cubans.

"The warheads in place included nuclear, conventional HE, chemical, and cluster munitions that were capable of penetrating the United States and of defending Cuba.

"Khrushchev decided more was needed. So the Soviet freighter *Indigirka* left the Soviet Union on September fifteenth, 1962, and arrived in the Cuban port of Mariel on October fourth. The *Indigirka* was carrying forty-five SS4 and SS5 warheads, thirty-six FKR warheads, which were approximately twelve kilotons each, and twenty-eight warheads containing a new-generation chemical agent, SovarK2.

"Kennedy went nose to nose with Khrushchev on October twenty-second, and in November the Soviets started pulling their strategic weapons out of Cuba. To date, twenty-seven of the SovarK2 warheads have been accounted for and removed. The twenty-eighth SovarK2 warhead was smuggled out of the country, along with one hundred bars of gold from the bank of Cuba, hours after Kennedy enforced the blockade of Soviet ships en route to Cuban ports.

"Intelligence indicates that this was a back door for Castro, should he need to leave the country. He'd have money, and he'd have a bargaining chip. The gold and the canister of SovarK2 were secretly given over to Maria's grandfather for transport to possibly Grand Cayman, and from there it would go by plane to South America.

"We're not sure what happened, but the fishing boat never reached its scheduled destination."

"The story I heard was that Maria's grandfather was bringing gold *into* Cuba," I said to Slick.

"When the gold and the canister of SovarK2 went missing Castro launched a search, and that was the cover story. It wouldn't have done much for his image if it became known he was planning to flee in case of invasion. The part about Maria's grandfather being a smuggler is probably true. There was money to be made off the Russians. In fact, the advance information Enrique Raffles had that night might have been the story circulated. It's possible Raffles didn't know until the very last moment, when the truck arrived on the dock with the gold and the SovarK2, what the true mission would be."

"And this canister of SovarK2?"

"Is essentially a bomb. It contains somewhere between forty-six to fifty-three pounds of liquid SovarK2. SovarK2 is similar to the nerve agent Sarin used during the Gulf War, but SovarK2 is far more potent. It has an indefinite shelf life and is highly volatile. It's colorless and odorless in both gas and liquid forms. Skin absorption can cause death in one to two minutes. Respiratory lethal doses kill in one to ten minutes. Liquid in the eye kills almost instantly. And you want to hope for a lethal dose of this stuff because the pain and suffering and permanent neurological damage will make you *wish* you were dead.

"The agent in the canister in question is in relatively stable form unless the canister is accidentally pierced or intentionally combined with a device to disperse. On a modest estimate, the canister has the ability to deliver six million lethal doses. If disseminated over Miami there would be tens of thousands to hundreds of thousands of people killed. And under the right conditions, millions could be incapacitated beyond help."

"So, if Salzar got his hands on this and turned it over to his friend in Cuba, they could use it to persuade us to accept their government?"

"Or possibly to persuade Castro to step down and allow them to take over."

"Would they actually use it? Are they that crazy?"

Slick shrugged. "Hard to say. The original intent was that the canister would be the payload on a warhead, and it would be exploded over a target area. But it might be possible to put a dispersion mechanism on the cylinder that would allow dissemination of a small amount and hold the rest in reserve. It would cause a lot of damage, and Salzar and friend would still have cards to play."

The thought that this stuff even existed made my skin crawl. And the realization that we'd had it on board the *Happy Hooker* took my breath away.

"Here's the thing," Slick said. "We need to get to the canister before Salzar. And don't for a minute think that Hooker won't talk. Salzar will make him talk.

"And by the way, I don't suppose you'd know anything about an explosion that sunk *Flex*?"

And here's *my* thing, I thought. I'm with two guys who impressed the police enough to get me released into their custody but won't show me any identification. They could tell me anything. How would I know fact from fiction? Call me a cynic but I have no reason to trust them. And no reason to like them.

"Wish I could help you," I said. "But I don't know anything."

We were back in Little Havana, and I wanted to put physical distance between me and Slick and Gimpy. I was going to move the canister. I'd made up my mind. I wasn't entirely sure how I'd do it, but I'd find a way. And I'd find it fast before Salzar beat me to it. I'd do what I could to check up on Slick and Gimpy. In the meantime, I'd work independently.

"I'm feeling stressed," I said to Slick. "I have a headache. Maybe you could drop me at a hotel."

"Do you have a preference?"

"I remember one on Brickell. The Fandango. It looked nice."

"The Fandango's expensive," Slick said. "You sure you don't have a gold bar hidden away?"

"I have Hooker's credit card."

I turned my back on Slick and Gimpy and entered the Fandango lobby. The floor was polished black marble. The vaulted ceiling was two stories above me, painted a soft blue and white to simulate sky and clouds. The support columns were cream-colored marble that had been carved into floor-to-ceiling palm trees. Fred Astaire and Ginger Rogers could have tap tap tapped their way through the lobby and looked perfectly at home. Registration counter at the far end. Concierge desk to one side. Couches and chairs and potted plants were scattered around, arranged in conversation areas.

I thought I'd performed well in the car. I held it together, and I didn't show a lot of emotion, but deep inside I was ruined. I'd left the car with Slick's cell phone number and a promise that I'd call him if Salzar contacted me. I kept my head down and walked to an unused conversation area on the perimeter of the room.

Hundreds of thousands of deaths from the disbursement of a vile liquid into the air over a city filled with kids and puppies. It was horrific and disgusting. I wasn't on a career track to save the world, but I was going to move this one canister out of harm's way.

I gave a startled yelp when my cell phone rang.

"Miss Barnaby?"

"Yes."

"You're missing the party. Everyone else is here . . . your brother and your boyfriend. Wouldn't you like to join them?"

"Who is this?"

"You know who I am. And you know I'm looking for something, don't you?"

"Mr. Salzar."

"I will make life very unpleasant for you and the people you care about if I don't get what I want. Never in your worst nightmare could you imagine how unpleasant life will become. Do you understand?"

I disconnected and searched through my purse for Chuck DeWolfe's card. My hands were shaking and I couldn't find the card. It was in there, somewhere. I dumped everything into my lap and fingered through it. I finally found the helicopter pilot's card and punched his number into my cell.

DeWolfe answered on the third ring. "Hey!" he said. "Chuck here."

"Hey," I answered back. "It's Barney. I need help."

THIRTEEN

I chose to get dropped at the Fandango because I'd driven past a bunch of times since I'd been in Miami, and on a couple of those passes I'd noticed a helicopter coming and going off the roof. It was a huge, expensive, high-rise hotel, and it made sense that it would have a helipad. Chuck DeWolfe had confirmed my suspicions.

My plan was basic. Get the canister before anyone else. Figure out what to do next when the canister was safely hidden. It wasn't hard to come up with the plan. It was obvious. Everyone's welfare hung on the canister . . . Bill's, Maria's, Hooker's, the world's.

I got off the phone and crossed the lobby to the hotel gift shop. My heart was beating with a sickening thud, and I was doing my best to ignore it. I bought a pair of shorts and changed out of the pink skirt. I went back to the chair, and I called Rosa.

"I've been thinking about Salzar's property," I said to

Rosa. "Some of his financial transactions go through holding companies and then filter back to his wife under her maiden name."

"Gotcha," Rosa said. "I'm on it. I'll dig around for the maiden name and I'll check for more properties."

"I'm especially interested in property north of the Orange Bowl Stadium." That was where I lost the Town Car.

After an hour I went out to the pool and sat in the shade, waiting. Forty-five minutes later, I heard the *wup, wup, wup* of the approaching chopper. I quickly walked to the elevator and I took it to the rooftop. I stepped out just as the chopper was touching down.

Chuck was at the controls. He smiled at me and gave me a sign that I shouldn't approach. He had a guy in the seat next to him. The guy got out and ran over to me as the blades slowed.

The guy was my age and reminded me a lot of Bill. Sandy hair and freckles. Ratty sneakers, baggy rumpled red-and-white shorts, washed out T-shirt. Lean and muscular.

"I have a harness," he yelled. "I'm going to strap you in."

I was holding my hat on my head with both hands. "Sure," I said. "Whatever."

Minutes later I was buckled into something that looked like a full-body chastity belt. The guy tugged on the straps, and when he was satisfied everything was secure he threw an arm around me and moved me forward. "Show time," he yelled. "Come with me."

We hunkered down and ran to the helicopter and climbed in. I was directed to the seat next to Chuck and given a headset with a microphone. The second guy took a seat behind me. Chuck revved the engine, and before I had a chance to throw up, the chopper lifted off. It's amazing what you can force yourself to do when you're saving the free world.

I could hear Chuck talking in the headset.

"This is Ryan behind you," Chuck said. "He's going to help us. We need a third person for this kind of a maneuver."

I nodded. I was disoriented, fighting panic, not wanting to look like an idiot in front of the two men. My lips were numb and there was a lot of clanging in my head. I leaned forward and put my head between my legs. I felt Chuck's hand on my back.

"Breathe," he said. "You'll be okay as soon as we get away from the city. I'll be flying over water and you'll lose the vertigo."

I kept my head down and concentrated. I thought about Bill as a kid. No help there. I thought about Hooker. Hooker thoughts were better. I got him naked. Okay, I was on to something. Here was an image that could compete with the panic of flight. I had the naked Hooker walking around in my head, and I realized we were over open water, and Chuck was right about the vertigo. It disappeared when we left Miami.

I could see the reef below us as we skimmed along the Keys, passing over pleasure boats and schools of fish. And then we were over ocean, flying toward Cuba, heading west of Havana.

My stomach rolled when the three islands appeared in front of us. The boot, and the bird in flight, and a third island that looked like a cupcake iced in bright green frosting.

"There it is," Chuck said over the headset. "The island is coming up. It's the one shaped like a boot. I'm going to do a couple flyovers to make sure nothing is going on down there."

We took a straight route to the island and flew over high enough to get an overview.

"No boats in sight," Chuck said. "That's good."

He circled the island at a lower altitude and then he followed the stream, buzzing the treetops.

"Okay," he said to me. "This is it, Barney. Tell me where you want me to drop you."

"What?"

"That's the plan, right? You want to go down to pick up the canister."

"Yeah, but not me!"

"You're all we got, honey," Chuck said. "That's why we've got you in the harness. I have to fly. And Ryan's the drop-and-pull man. You can't do either of those."

"Omigod."

"You said this was important. And that we had to get the canister up fast," Chuck said to me. "Life or death?"

I swallowed and nodded.

"Then do it. Ryan's going to hook you up to the cable. Don't make a move until he tells you. He'll drop you to the water. He's a pro at this. He does search-and-rescue and adventure diving. I'm not flying my usual sightseeing mosquito. This helicopter is designed for this sort of thing. We're going to give you a collar and an extra line for the canister.

When you get into the water I'll give you some slack. You said the canister was only about fifteen feet down?"

"Yes. At the mouth of the estuary, dead center."

"You're not going to have great visibility. The blades are going to move the water and churn up sediment. Don't waste time. Get down there and try to find the canister. Ryan's going to take your headset and put you into some foolproof scuba gear. You're going to have a flashlight on your wrist. Shine the light at us if you want to get pulled up, or just follow the cable to the surface. Once you get the canister secured we'll bring you in. We'll bring the canister up after we get you on board. There's not a breath of wind today. This should be pretty easy."

Here's the truth. I was beyond scared. I couldn't believe I'd actually come up with this stupid idea. And I couldn't believe I'd talked two other men into being accomplices. The phrase *not thoroughly thought through* came to mind.

Chuck looked over at me. "Are you breathing?"

"No."

"You're going to have to remember to breathe. It's hard to pull someone in when they're dead weight."

We were directly over the stream, slightly above treetops. I looked down and caught a glimpse of the canister in the swirling water.

Chuck was smiling. "I see it," he said. "Piece of cake. Go back with Ryan, and he'll suit you up."

I crawled back and Ryan sat me on the floor and started walking me through the equipment.

"This is a no-brainer," he said. "Try to enjoy yourself. It's not every day you get a chance to swing from a helicopter."

I did an inadvertent whimper.

Ryan was grinning. "You're going to be great," he said. "I'm going to take your headset off now, and replace it with a full face mask. All you have to do is remember to breathe. When I get the mask on, you're going to scoot over to the door. You'll feel me holding you. Don't worry about anything. I'm going to take good care of you. Stay as still as possible while you're dropping. Look down so you know when you get to the water. Keep concentrating on the water and stay focused on your goal." And then he took the headset and fixed the mask over my face. I felt his hand at my back, and I knew I was supposed to scoot to the door, but I was paralyzed. My heart was pounding so hard it was shaking my whole body. I turned and grabbed hold of Ryan's shirt with both hands. We're talking genuine death grip, my fingers curled into the fabric, possibly drawing blood. I was shaking my head *no, no, no,* and I was babbling gibberish into the mask.

Ryan tapped a finger on the visor to get my attention. He pried my fingers loose from his shirt, and he eased me over in a crab-walk to the open doorway. And then somehow, I was dangling from the cable, slowly dropping to the water.

I have a dim memory of screaming. My screams getting lost in the whoosh of air in my mask and the beat of the chopper blades. I was swinging under the chopper, and I was choking on a fresh wave of panic. I tried to conjure up Hooker naked, but I was way beyond that as a mental health aid. Water was whipping up from the chopper's downdraft and spraying onto my mask. My mind was scrambling. I didn't realize at first that my feet were splashing in water. Ryan was holding me at stream level, waiting for me to get calm and give him the signal to drop me farther.

I started an internal dialogue. Okay, Barney, it's up to you now. Get it together so you don't screw up when you're under water. Remember to breathe. Focus. Do the job.

I waved at Ryan, and he started letting out more cable. I was in water up to my knees, my waist, my chest, and then the water was over my head. More panic. Push it away, I thought. Trust Ryan. Get the job done. I realized I was breathing underwater and the panic became manageable.

The water was murky. I flashed my wrist light around, but I didn't see the canister. I was disoriented, and I was reluctant to move from my drop point. And then I saw a slim, fluorescent green laser beam cut through the water in front of me. Ryan could see the canister from the air and was trying to guide me. I followed the beam, and I found the canister. It had only been about ten feet away. I attached the collar and made sure it was secure. Then I flashed my light at Ryan, and he pulled me up.

This time the trip was exhilarating. The fear was gone. Or maybe I'd learned to enjoy the fear. At any rate, I was smiling when Ryan pulled me through the door and removed my mask.

"I did it," I said. "I did it!"

Ryan was grinning, too, "You were amazing!" he yelled.

I took my seat and watched as Ryan raised the canister from the water. Six million lethal doses of SovarK2 swinging below me. I closed my eyes for a moment, and my hand reflexively went to my heart. I didn't know all the mechanical details, but I suspected it wouldn't be good if the canister dropped from this height. Ryan got the canister to the door and hauled it in. His expression turned sober when he saw the markings. It didn't take a lot of imagination to figure this was some sort of bomb. He secured the canister in the back of the cargo area without comment. Before Ryan was even back in his seat, Chuck lifted the chopper, our eyes held for a moment, and then he angled off, and we were over open ocean, on our way to Key West.

I rented a car and drove it across the runway to the helicopter where Chuck and Ryan were waiting. They were sitting in the open door, feet dangling, guarding the canister. I could see the bulk of a gun on Chuck's hip, under his orange-and-purple flowered shirt.

"Do you always carry a gun?" I asked, getting out of the car.

"Need it for gators," Chuck said.

They transferred the canister to the trunk of the rental and took a step back.

"Be careful," Chuck said.

I gave them both a hug, got into the car, and left the airport behind. I took South Roosevelt Boulevard to Route 1 and began my trek through the Keys. I checked my rearview mirror from time to time to make sure I wasn't being followed. I kept the radio silent so I could listen for a helicopter. I was pretty sure I was a couple steps ahead of Salzar and Slick and Gimpy, but I was being careful.

I hadn't heard from Hooker. No messages on my cell. No missed calls. That wasn't good. It meant Bill and Hooker were still being held captive . . . or worse. The sadness took over my heart and radiated out into every part of me. Not an emotion I wanted to embrace. Better to channel my emotional energy in more positive directions, I thought. Stay alert. Get the job done. That was my mantra. *Get the job done.*

The job was simple to articulate. Not so simple to complete. Rescue Bill and Hooker and Maria without letting the canister fall into the hands of the bad guys. And that meant I had to make sure the good guys weren't bad guys.

The sun was low in the sky when I reached Key Largo. I'd felt especially vulnerable in the Keys. One road in and one road out didn't leave a lot of escape routes. Scary when traveling with a much-sought-after warhead in the trunk. I drove onto the last bridge and was relieved to be back on the mainland.

I was still wearing the same clothes I'd worn diving, and I was anxious to get out of them. When I approached Homestead I made a fast stop at a Wal-Mart and got a complete new outfit, including sneakers. I got a bag of food at the snack bar. And I got a charger for my cell phone.

I didn't have much direction, other than north to Miami. I needed a place to spend the night (or at least to take a shower), and I thought I would be safer in Homestead than I was in Miami. I took the first motel that popped up. It was an affordable chain. I paid cash, and I gave a fake name. If you're going to be paranoid, go all the way. The canister was in the trunk of the rental car, in the parking lot. I couldn't do much about that.

I took a shower and dressed in the clean clothes. I flipped the television on and dug into the food.

My cell phone rang. It was Rosa.

"I just got off the phone," Rosa said. "I got another list of Salzar's properties, but there's only one property on it that's north of the Orange Bowl. It's not a good neighborhood."

I got the address from Rosa and told her I'd get back to her. I scrounged in my purse and came up with Slick's cell phone number.

"Yeah?" he answered.

"It's Devil Woman."

There was a moment's pause. I'd caught him by surprise.

"Where are you?" he asked.

"The Fandango."

"No you're not. You never checked in."

"Where are you?"

"Coral Gables."

They were probably back to following Salzar. Salzar lived in Coral Gables.

"Do you know anything about Bill and Hooker?" I asked.

"Haven't seen them."

"I know where they are."

Okay, so this was sort of an exaggeration. I knew where they *might* be located. The thing is, I needed to get Slick's attention.

"And?" Slick asked.

"And I want you to go get them."

"Have you planned out any of the details of this rescue?"

"I figured that was your arena."

"I'm not much of a break-down-doors, shoot-'em-up agent. I'm more of a sneaky, *listen*-at-doors agent."

Easy to believe from what I'd seen. "Look, I don't care how you do it," I said. "Bring in the Marines, for crying out loud. Just do it."

"All right, here's the truth. It would screw up everything. I'm after Salzar, and I'm not going to tip my hand by staging a Waco to rescue your brother."

"Here's *my* truth. I've got the bomb, and I'm going to FedEx it to Cuba if you don't help me."

Silence. "I don't believe you've got the bomb," Slick finally said.

"I'll phone you a picture tomorrow morning. You have a picture phone, right? In the meantime you should be thinking about a rescue operation." And I disconnected.

Then just for the hell of it, I dialed Hooker's cell phone and let it ring until his message service came on. I finished the food and watched more television. I slept in my clothes, waking every couple hours with a start. At five o'clock I gave up on the sleep thing and checked out. It was still dark, and the lot was eerie, lit by overhead halogens spooked up by fog. I checked the trunk for the bomb and took off. I thought I was probably less than an hour from Miami. My timing was good. I'd be able to check out the address Rosa gave me just as it was getting light.

The closer I got to the address, the more depressed I

became. Houses were squalid cinder block cells. Windows were barred. Exterior walls were covered with gang graffiti. Trash collected against buildings and on roadsides. There were no lush gardens. No rows of palms. The yards surrounding the stucco bungalows were barren, the dirt hard packed and cracked from sun exposure.

The address Rosa had given me was actually an entire block of condemned houses. They were little stucco bungalows in varying degrees of decay. Windows and doors were secured with hammered-on boards to keep squatters and users out. One of the houses had been gutted by fire. The roof was collapsed into the house and the stucco was stained with soot. A few pieces of charred furniture—a couch and two chairs—were left in the small front yard.

And one of the houses had a car in the driveway. The windows were boarded shut on the house, but the boards on the door had been removed and tossed on the ground.

I drove by the house twice, and I swear I could feel Hooker's heart beating inside. There were no other cars on the street. No one rattling off to work. No one parked at the curb. The structures on the opposite side of the street had already been razed. Nothing left but concrete slab foundations and an occasional piece of pipe that had escaped the demo.

Because there were no houses obstructing my view I was able to park a block away and watch the occupied bungalow. I had my doors locked, and I was hunkered down in my seat, trying to be invisible. I was wearing a new plain black ball cap with my hair tucked up, a black T-shirt, jeans, and black-

and-white Converse sneakers. Not especially cool in the Miami heat, but it was unisex and practical.

There were a few other cars parked at the curb and in driveways. Mostly junker pickups and rusted-out muscle cars. The rental didn't totally fit, but it wasn't glaringly conspicuous either.

At precisely seven o'clock, a silver Camry rolled down the street and parked in front of the occupied house. Two guys got out and walked to the front door. The door opened, and the guys went in. Five minutes later, two different guys came out. One of the guys was carrying a black plastic garbage bag. He put the bag into the trunk of the Nissan Maxima in the driveway, both guys got into the Nissan, and took off.

Shift change.

Okay, I was excited. I was pretty sure I'd found Hooker and Bill. And I was pretty sure they were being guarded by two guys. I followed the Maxima out of the neighborhood and dropped back when they pulled into a restaurant parking lot. They drove to the back of the lot, the one guy got out, took the bag from the trunk, and left it sitting by the Dumpster. I continued following them when they left the lot, and I lost them when they turned south on Seventeenth Street. They were heading for Little Havana, and I didn't want to go there.

I returned to the abandoned house and cruised by very slowly, taking it all in. Then I went back to the restaurant parking lot and parked by the Dumpster. Call me crazy. I wanted to see what they were throwing away. Who knows, right?

I pawed through the bag and found a bunch of large plastic soda bottles and cardboard pizza boxes. I looked at the top of the box. Pizza Time. It was one of those chains that advertise on-time delivery or no charge. The orders were taped to all the box tops. These guys were living on pizza and soda. And it was being delivered. I went through all the boxes. The day shift ordered a large pizza with green pepper, sausage, onions, extra cheese. They got a big bottle of Dr Pepper with the pizza. Yesterday the order went in at noon and again at five. The night shift ordered pizza at ten. Large pie. Plain. Large bottle of Sprite.

I took one of the day shift boxes and headed out of the lot.

I went east, looking for a safe place to call Slick. I found a spot I liked on North River Drive. It was a church with an empty parking lot. The lot was large and only partially visible from the road. I pulled in, parked in a far corner and placed the call.

Slick's cell rang five times before he answered. "Unh," he said.

"Are you awake?"

"Barely."

"I have something to show you."

"I'm hoping it's you with your clothes off."

"Not nearly."

He blew out a sigh. "Okay, let's see it."

I got out of the car, went around to the rear, and opened the trunk. I'd angled the car to get as much early-morning light as possible into the open trunk. I aimed the phone at the bomb.

252

"Fuck," Slick said.

I closed the trunk and got back into the car. "I know where they've got Bill and Hooker," I said to Slick. "I want you to go get them."

"Okay, but you have to transfer the item over to me first."

"Can't do that."

"Why not?"

"I don't trust you."

"You think I'd go back on my word?"

"Yeah."

"Boy, that hurts."

"Here's the thing," I said. "I'm not all that patriotic. What I really want is to get the two guys I care about someplace safe. So if you won't help me, I'll deal directly with Salzar."

This was a flat-out lie. I trusted Salzar less than I trusted Slick. And I had no intention of handing a deadly chemical bomb over to possible terrorists.

"Gonna call your bluff on that, Barney," Slick said.

"You're not going to help me?"

"I am helping you. I just can't do it your way. You need a little patience here. And you really need to turn that item over to me. And I'm also assuming you have the gold?"

I disconnected, immediately left the lot, crossed over the Miami River, and drove west. I didn't think there was much showing in the photo other than the trunk and the bomb, but I wasn't risking getting caught because Slick identified a corner of the church.

I found a small bakery parking lot off Seventh and hid between two other cars. I ran into the bakery and got a bag

253

of doughnuts and a large coffee. I ate a doughnut, drank some coffee, and called Judey.

"I think I found Bill and Hooker," I told Judey. "I'm pretty sure they're being held in one of those condemned houses in Northwest. I checked it out this morning, and it looks like they're being guarded by two guys. I can't see in the house at all because it's all boarded up, but two guys went in at seven and two guys came out and drove away."

"Let me guess . . . you want to rescue Bill and Hooker?"

"Yeah."

"I'm in. Do you have a plan? Are we gonna do a SWAT thing and kick some ass? What do you need?"

Good thing I watch a lot of television. If it wasn't for television I wouldn't have any ideas at all. Sometimes I worried that I didn't have a single thought in my head that wasn't already a cliché.

It was almost noon, and I was sitting in a Pizza Time parking lot. Judey and Brian were with me. Judey was holding a small vial. Brian was in attack-dog mode, alert at the back window.

"It would have been much easier if you'd wanted an erection extender," Judey said. "*Everyone's* got that. Fortunately, I happen to know a pharmacist who works out of the trunk of his car. Of course he works at night, so I had to wake him up, but I got just what we need. And he gave me instructions on use. Five drops per piece of pizza will render the diner unconscious in less than five minutes and have him sleeping for over an hour. It's the date rape drug of choice when you're in a hurry."

I dialed the Pizza Time number off the box top I'd gotten out of the Dumpster. "I want to check on a pizza order," I said. "It's going to 9118 NW Seaboard."

"Is that a large pie, peppers, onions, sausage, extra cheese?"

"That's the one. I want to pick it up instead of having it delivered."

"You got it. Five minutes."

A woman walked by the car. She had a mixed breed on a leash, and the dog was walking placidly beside her. Brian was nuts in the backseat, bouncing around, clawing at the window.

"Arf, arf, arf, arf."

Judey took a spice cookie out of his pocket. "If you're a good doggie I'll give you some cookie," Judey said. "Does 'ou wanna spice cookie? Does 'ou? Does 'ou?"

Brian stopped arfing and sat at attention, ears up, body vibrating, totally focused on the cookie. His eyes were so wide they were surrounded by white and looked like they might roll out of his head.

Judey held the cookie out and Brian lunged for it. *Snap!* The cookie broke into about twenty pieces, and Brian was nuts again, tracking the cookie pieces.

"He really likes spice cookies," Judey said.

There were two Pizza Time delivery cars parked in reserved slots by the back door. They were old Ford Escorts that had been painted pink with powder blue palm trees, and PIZZA TIME was written in fluorescent green all over the cars.

"I could use one of those cars," I said to Judey.

"That shouldn't be a problem for you," Judey said. "You and Bill have been stealing cars since you were ten years old."

"Not stealing. Borrowing. And I only borrowed cars from the garage."

I turned the key in the rental and pulled it up into the slot next to the Pizza Time car. I left the rental, walked into Pizza Time, and picked up my pizza and soda. I rushed back to Judey, and we very carefully lifted the cheese and added five knockout drops to each piece of pizza.

The driver's side door to the Escort was unlocked. I got in with my nail file and had the car running in less than two minutes.

"You are *so* clever," Judey said. "There's not a car made that you can't steal."

"Thanks, but the newer ones are impossible. Lucky this was an old Escort."

I took off in the Pizza Time car with Judey following in the rental.

FOURTEEN

I drove by the condemned bungalow once to check things out. Nothing had changed. Same car at the curb. Judey was following me. When I did my second lap around the block, Judey dropped back and parked the rental in the spot I'd vacated earlier.

Now or never, I thought. I took a deep breath and yanked the Pizza Time car into the driveway. I got out, walked around the car to the passenger side, and got the pizza box and the soda. I marched up to the front door and rang the bell. Nothing. No bell sound. The bell wasn't working. Great. I knocked as hard as I could. Still no action.

"Hey!" I yelled. "Anybody home?" And I gave the door a good kick.

I could hear someone mumbling behind the door. The door opened and a big sweaty guy looked out at me.

"What?" the guy said.

"Pizza."

"You're late."

"I would have been on time if you'd opened the door when I got here. You need to get your bell fixed. What are you doing here, anyway? It looks like all these houses are condemned."

"I work for the guy who's gonna build here. We're doing . . . research."

"That's twelve-fifty."

"I'm gonna give you fifteen 'cause you're cute."

He gave me fifteen. I told him to have a nice day. And I got into my stolen car and left. I got to NW Twentieth Street and saw flashing lights behind me. *Shit.* I pulled over, got out, and walked back to the cop car. As luck would have it, it was the same cop who pulled me over yesterday.

"Oh man," he said. "Not you again. Give me a break."

"I'm on a secret mission."

"Of course you are."

"And that's my partner behind you."

Judey was idling behind the cop car, a forced smile on his face. Brian was in the seat next to Judey, front paws on the dash, schnauzer eyebrows drawn together in concentration, staring the cop down.

The cop looked back at Judey. "The gay guy with the dog? Are you kidding me?"

"How do you know he's gay?"

"I'm a cop. I know these things. And his dog's wearing one of them rainbow collars."

"Maybe it's just his dog that's gay."

"Lady, I don't want to go there. My nuts are shrinking up in my scrotum just thinking about it."

"Listen, I sort of have things to do . . ."

"Like go to jail?"

"You're not going to make me call the guys with the blue flashy grille lights, are you?"

"Scala and Martin? No! Don't do that. I *hate* those guys."

"Tell you what. I'm done with the car. How about if I just leave it here, and you can call it in."

"Fine. Great. But you gotta stop stealing cars on my watch. Steal them on the night shift. Steal them from Coral Gables or Miami Beach."

I ran back to Judey, shooed Brian into the backseat, and buckled myself in.

"You are *so good*," Judey said.

Fifteen minutes later, we were back in front of the abandoned bungalow. I was hunkered down, out of sight in the backseat. Judey was driving. The plan was that he'd park behind the silver Camry, run up to the house, tell them he was lost, and ask directions. If no one answered after he yelled and pounded and kicked, we were golden.

"If I don't come back you have to promise to take Brian," Judey said.

I looked up at Brian sitting on the backseat. If there was a God in heaven, Judey would come back.

"He's very smart," Judey said. "If you mix up the letters in his name it spells *brain*."

I kept my head down and listened to Judey walk up to the house. He knocked. He yelled. And then quiet. I popped my head up. No Judey. I looked at Brian.

"Where is he?" I said to Brian.

Brian just sat there. He looked worried. Most likely not crazy about the prospect of maybe living with me.

Judey appeared at the back of the house, and I let out a *whoosh* of air. He'd circled the house, probably looking for an open window. He returned to the front and waved me over.

I got behind the wheel and pulled the rental into the driveway.

"I was able to look in through the back windows," Judey said. "There's some good news and some bad news. The good news is that both goons are out for the count. The bad news is, it looks like they shared the pizza with Bill and Hooker."

I got a tire iron out of the trunk.

Judey was looking over my shoulder. "What's that thing in the trunk?"

"Bomb. Probably a warhead, to be more precise."

"I wouldn't expect any less," Judey said. "You never disappoint."

I hustled across the yard with the tire iron and wedged it between the jamb and the door, just below the doorknob. I put my weight behind it, the jamb splintered away, and the door popped open.

The inside of the bungalow was even more depressing than the outside. The air was stale, smelling of poor sanitation, mold, and cold pizza. The furniture was Dumpster pickings. The light was dim.

Salzar's men were face down on the floor, having fallen off their chairs at the rusted chrome and Formica kitchen table. The empty pizza box was open on the tabletop. Nothing left in the box but smudges of tomato sauce and a few scraps of cheese.

A short hallway opened off the living room, dining room, kitchen area. There were two bedrooms and a small bathroom at the end of the hallway. The bedroom doors were open. Bill and Hooker were handcuffed together in one of the bedrooms. They were sprawled on the bed, out like a light. A half-eaten piece of pizza was stuck to the threadbare yellow chenille bedspread, inches from Hooker's open hand.

"Hey, wait a minute," I said. "Where's Maria?"

We looked in the second bedroom and bathroom. No Maria.

"She's probably at a different location," Judey said.

Neither of us entirely believed it, but it was a good thought for now. Worry about one thing at a time.

"How are we going to get these big boys out of here?" Judey asked. "They're hooked together, and together they must weigh about three hundred and sixty pounds. And then we have to get them through the door."

I ran to the kitchen and checked the goons' pockets for a key. I did a fast scan of the house. No key. I looked back at the bedroom door. Not wide enough to drag them through side by side. "We're going to have to make them into a sandwich and pull them through."

We wrestled Bill and Hooker off the bed and onto the floor, trying to be careful with Bill's gunshot wounds. We took the ratty chenille spread off the bed and worked it under Hooker. Then we put Bill facedown on top of Hooker.

Judey and I grabbed the chenille spread and pulled Hooker and Bill through the bedroom door, across the living room, and out the front door. We got them as far as the rental car, and we were stumped again.

"I guess we have to try to sit them up in the backseat," I said.

We pushed and pulled and managed to get them more or less sitting in the backseat. Hooker was hanging in the shoulder harness, head down and drooling. Bill was leaning on Hooker, looking like Zombie Bahama.

Brian had retreated to the front and was peeking between the seats, not sure he was liking what he saw.

"You know what we should do?" Judey said. "We should take one of the goons. And then we can interrogate him and maybe find out where they've got Maria."

We went back to the house and took the smallest of the two men. We dragged him out the door to the car and around to the trunk. I opened the trunk and threw the spare tire away. Now I had room for the goon *and* the warhead. I took a good look at the warhead to make sure it'd be safe back there with the goon. It didn't look like anything could break off. We heaved the goon into the trunk, folded him up, and closed the lid.

"Now we need a good porn store," I said. "One that sells

devices. Handcuffs have a universal key. I know that from watching *Cops* on television."

"I *love* that show," Judey said.

I drove across the Miami River, went south on Seventeenth Street and into Little Havana. After a few blocks I saw what I was looking for. Adult Entertainment. I swung into a strip mall parking area and came to a stop in front of the store.

"I don't want to buy an expensive pair of handcuffs just to get a key," I said to Judey. "See if you can borrow one."

Judey ran into the store and a couple minutes later came out with a guy who looked like Ozzie Osbourne on a bad day.

"Whoa," the guy said when he saw Hooker and Bill. "Kinky."

We got the cuffs off, and the porn guy shuffled back into the store. Judey and I made a half-hearted attempt to revive Hooker and Bill. Hooker opened one eye halfway, smiled at me, and went back to slumberland.

"We should put those cuffs to good use," Judey said.

We got out of the car, went around to the trunk, and made sure no one was looking. We opened the trunk, twisted the goon until his arms were behind his back, and cuffed him.

"Much better," Judey said. "It's a little creepy to have him back here with the warhead."

I know this is weird, but I was getting used to carrying the warhead around. I wouldn't go so far as to say I was going to miss it when I got rid of it, but I wasn't nearly as freaked out that it was back there. It was sort of like . . . luggage.

Judey and I got back into the car and watched Hooker and Bill. They seemed to be comfortable, breathing normally, good color. Still, I was worried. It would be a relief when they came around.

"I appreciate your help," I said to Judey. "Probably I should take you and Brian home."

"You'll do no such thing. I'm staying with you until these bad boys wake up."

So we sat there in front of the smut shop, waiting for Hooker and Bill to wake up.

"This is just like when we were in school," Judey said, smiling. "We were always getting Bill out of scrapes. And usually they involved young ladies."

Sometimes the more things changed, the more they stayed the same.

After an hour, Hooker opened an eye again. "Did I miss something?" he asked.

"We rescued you," I said.

"The last thing I remember I was eating pizza."

"Yep," I said. "I did the old date-rape-pizza-delivery routine."

"What's this big wet spot on my shorts?"

"Drool."

"That's a relief." He glanced out the window. "And we're parked in front of adult entertainment, why?"

"We needed a key for the handcuffs."

Bill opened his eyes. "Adult entertainment?" He put his hands to his head. "Wow, killer headache."

"Your sister delivered poison pizza to the bad guys, and we ate it," Hooker said.

"Did I tell you? Barney always comes through," Bill said. "She's been rescuing me for years."

"Not a minute too soon for me," Hooker said. "Things were about to get really ugly."

"Hooker sang like an *American Idol* wannabe," Bill said. "They tied him to a chair, gave him one punch in the face, and he told them everything they wanted to know."

"Yeah," Hooker said. "I told them we buried the canister about ten feet into the jungle about an eighth of a mile upstream. I thought that would keep them busy. Bill was sure you'd ride in with the Marines and save our asses."

"The Marines were booked," I said. "Fortunately, Judey was available."

"I figured this was the day Salzar would find out I sent him on a wild goose chase, and he'd order his goons to come back to beat the living crap out of me," Hooker said. "He wants that canister real bad."

"It's filled with a chemical nerve agent," I said. "SovarK2. It's estimated that it contains about six million lethal doses. If dispersed as a gas over Miami it would kill tens to hundreds of thousands of people. It turns out Slick and Gimpy are with one of those three-letter government agencies, and they've been trying to retrieve the canister and nail Salzar."

"Had me fooled," Hooker said.

"Me too. And I don't entirely trust them. I could use their help, but they worry me."

"I don't know anything about this," Judey said. "Nobody tells me anything."

"When Maria dove down for the gold, she also found a

canister. We didn't know it at the time but it turns out it's a chemical bomb."

"The bomb we've been carrying around in the trunk?" Judey said.

Hooker looked over at me. "In the trunk?"

"I was worried about Salzar finding it. So I went back and got it and it's . . . in the trunk."

Everyone turned and looked at the backseat, as if they could see through it into the trunk.

"This trunk?" Hooker asked.

"Yep."

"You've been riding around with a chemical bomb in the trunk?"

"Yep."

"I hate to change the subject," Bill said. "But they still have Maria."

"I don't know where she is," I told him. "We ran through all Salzar's properties, and we didn't turn anything up. No Maria and no gold bars."

A car parked next to us and a middle-aged, balding guy got out and walked into the smut shop.

"I know him!" Judey said. "That's my dentist."

"Wait a minute," Hooker said. "I want to go back to the bomb in the trunk. How did you get it out of Cuba?"

"Chuck helped me. And his friend Ryan."

"They flew to the island, got the bomb, brought it back, and put it in your trunk?" Hooker said.

"That's the big picture."

I put the car in gear and pulled out of the lot, into traffic. I had no idea where to go next, but it seemed like it was time to move on.

"I might know where they've got Maria," Bill said. "When they first brought us out of Salzar's office there was some confusion about where we were going to go. They were talking about a garage on the Tamiami Trail."

Bill wasn't looking great. His face was ashen and there were dark blue smudges under his eyes. Blood had seeped through the bandage around his ribs and stained his shirt.

"How are you feeling?" I asked him.

"Fine," he said.

"You look awful."

"Bad pizza."

"Here's the deal," I said to him. "I'm sending you back home with Judey. If you promise to stay in bed, Hooker and I will look for Maria."

"Not good enough," Bill said. "You have to promise to *find* her. And you have to help her get her father out of Cuba."

"I'll do my best," I said.

There was some thumping and muffled yelling from the trunk.

"The goon is awake," Judey said.

I turned to Bill and Hooker. "I almost forgot. I have a goon in the trunk, too."

"We thought it might be helpful to be able to interrogate one of Salzar's men," Judey said. "So we put him in the trunk . . . with the bomb."

"It was Judey's idea," I said. "He's a crime fighter mastermind."

"Some people think I look like Magnum," Judey said. "Do you think I look like Magnum? Maybe around the mouth a little?"

"I'm awake, right?" Hooker said. "This is real?"

FIFTEEN

By the time we got to Judey's condo building, the guy in the trunk had quieted down.

"What's Salzar like?" Judey wanted to know. "I only know what I read in the paper."

"He's scary," Hooker said. "Obsessed with the canister. Obsessed with one last grab at power in Cuba. I think at this point he might not be playing with a full deck. I think what probably started out as a smart political move has turned into a last-ditch nightmare. Castro's time is coming to an end, and the politburo is in a power scramble. If Salzar doesn't come through with that canister, I'm guessing he's lost his place in history."

"I got a creepy phone call from him," I said.

"He got your number out of my cell phone. He went nuts when he found out you'd escaped," Hooker said.

It was late afternoon. There were big puffy clouds in the

sky and the wind was picking up. It would have been a nice day to be on the beach or drifting around in a boat. A couple blocks over, the almost naked sun worshippers were packing up, and the Ocean Drive waiters were arriving for work. And here I was wearing day-old underwear, sitting in a parking lot with a bomb and a goon in my trunk.

"All righty then," Judey said. "Let's get Bill upstairs and comfy. And you're welcome to come up, too. I could put a pot of coffee on. And I have a cake."

"Anybody have any ideas about the goon?" I asked.

"He can come, too," Judey said. "I have plenty of room. We can lock him in my powder room. And before we put him in the powder room we can put on a salsa CD and beat the crap out of him."

"That sounds like fun," Bill said.

We opened the trunk and hauled the goon out. He was wild-eyed and soaked through with sweat.

"It's Dave," Hooker said. And then he punched Dave in the face.

"Stop that!" Judey said, clutching Brian to his chest. "I was kidding about the beating." He put his hand over Brian's eyes. "Don't look."

"I owed it to him," Hooker said.

NASCAR Guy was back in the saddle.

We dragged Dave up to Judey's condo, locked the door behind us and propped Dave up against a wall.

"We need to know where Maria's hidden," I said to Dave.

"Eat shit," Dave said.

"Can I hit him again?" Hooker asked.

"No!" Judey said. "He'll bleed on the carpet."

"This is your last chance," I said to Dave. "Or else."

"Or else what?" he asked.

"Or else we'll turn Brian loose on you," Judey said.

Brian was running in circles, happy to be home. "Arf, arf, arf, arf."

"Yeah, that's gonna worry me," Dave said.

Judey took a spice cookie out of his pocket and held it out, waist level. Brian rushed over, jumped into the air, and *SNAP!* The spice cookie was dust.

Hooker was smiling. "Allow me," he said, unzipping Dave's slacks. The slacks slid down and pooled at Dave's feet, leaving Dave standing there in his tighty whities.

Judey scooped Brian up and tiptoed over with Brian under his arm. With his free hand, Judey dropped three spice cookies into the front of Dave's briefs, crushing them up a little, releasing a lot of spice cookie fragrance, making sure the crumbs settled in the pouch.

"Rawffff!" Brian said, watching the spice cookies disappear from view.

Judey held Brian out so he could better smell the cookies. And Brian started to salivate. Brian's ears were up and his legs were treading air. He was squirming and running in place, eyes bugged out of his head, and schnauzer spittle was flying everywhere. "Arf, arf, arf, arf!" Brian was in a spice-cookie frenzy.

"Okay, now I'm going to put Brian down," Judey said.

"Jesus, no!" Dave said. "You people are freaky."

"So, what about Maria?" I asked him. "Do you know where she is?"

"Yeah," Dave said. "I know where she is. Get the dog away from me."

"Where's Maria?" I asked again.

"Salzar's got a garage on the Trail. She's in the garage," Dave said.

"She's alive?"

"Yeah. She's alive."

When we were done questioning Dave we pulled his pants up and shoved him into the powder room.

"Hey," he said, "you can't leave me in here like this with my hands cuffed behind my back and cookies in my drawers. And what if I have to use the facilities?"

Judey smiled at him. "Just give me a holler, big boy, and I'll be glad to help you."

We closed the door on Dave, and Judey rolled his eyes.

"Wouldn't touch him with a long stick," Judey said, "but I couldn't resist scaring him one more time. Now if you'll all get comfy, I'll make some coffee, and we can sit down and plan out the rescue operation."

"We need help," I said when we were at the table. "We need someone in government that we can trust."

"I know a guy," Hooker said.

Hooker called his assistant and minutes later had a phone number. Hooker dialed the phone number, made some required small talk when the connection was made, and then got to the point.

"I found something that might be dangerous," Hooker said to the person on the phone. "I want to turn it over to the authorities, but I'm not sure how to go about it. I think giving it to the local police isn't the route we want to go." There was some talking on the other end. "I don't want to go into details on a cell phone," Hooker said. "Let's just assume the government would like to gain possession of this item that's chemical in nature. I've been approached by two losers who claim to be feds."

"Scala and Martin," I said. "Working out of Miami."

Hooker repeated the names to his connection. "And something else," Hooker said. "I want to get someone out of prison in Cuba. Maybe buy him out." There was some more small talk, and Hooker hung up.

"He's going to get back to me," Hooker said.

"He have a name?"

"Richard Gil."

"Senator Richard Gil?"

"Yeah. He's a real good guy."

"And a NASCAR fan?"

"That too."

"Let's make a list of everything we have to accomplish," Judey said. "We have to rescue Maria. We have to get the gold and use it to buy Maria's father out of Cuba. We have to give the bomb over to the authorities."

"It would be good if we could neutralize Salzar," Hooker said.

"Neutralize?" Judey said. "You mean like whack him?"

"NASCAR Guy doesn't whack people," Hooker said. "NASCAR disapproves of whacking. Neutralizing is broader in scope."

Brian was whining at the powder room and sniffing under the door. He wanted the cookies.

"Now let's review what we know," Judey said. "We know the location of the garage on the Tamiami Trail. We know what it looks like inside and that there are always four guys there. We know they have the gold crated for shipment to Cuba."

"We know the helicopter can land in the parking lot out back of the garage," Bill said.

"I think my man can help facilitate things like swapping out an old Cuban guy for a shitload of gold," Hooker said. "And I think he can coordinate this with canister pickup. What he's probably not going to be able to do is round up the goods. We're going to have to round up the goods. And then we're going to have to deliver them."

"I don't want to be left out," Bill said.

"You look awful," I told him.

"I can deal," he said.

It was midafternoon, and by six we had a plan pretty much in place. It sounded ridiculous on paper. Straight out of a bad movie. But it was the best we could do. We couldn't move on the plan until we heard from the senator.

The phone rang at seven-thirty and Hooker answered. It was Senator Gil. Hooker took notes while he talked. His face was flushed when he got off the phone.

"It's a go," he said. "Everything will be in place tomorrow at ten AM." He turned to me. "NASCAR Guy's a little flummoxed."

We were all flummoxed.

"Gil says Slick and Gimpy are part of a combined agency task force that keeps tabs on international arms sales. He didn't know much about them. They've been with the task force for three years. Before that they were ATF, pushing paper. Gil's sending them over to help us. He thought we could use some extra firepower."

This set off a mental alarm. "They're coming here?"

"Yeah. Is there a problem?"

"I don't know. There's something about those guys that doesn't feel right. Maybe we should do something with the bomb."

"Damn," Hooker said. "We left the bomb in the trunk. I forgot all about the bomb."

We all trooped out and got in the elevator and rode to the garage. Judey had a blanket so we could wrap the bomb and bring it upstairs unnoticed.

Hooker opened the trunk. "It's gone!" he said.

We all gasped.

He winked at me. "Only funnin'."

NASCAR Guy humor.

Hooker wrestled the bomb out of the trunk, we wrapped the blanket around it, and Hooker headed for the elevator.

"This is like carrying a giant eighty-pound watermelon," he said. "Somebody hit the button. Barney'll be all disappointed if I get a hernia from this. She's got plans for me."

Bill grinned at Hooker. "A hernia's the least of your problems if Barney has plans for you, you poor dumb sonnovabitch."

We got to the condo and Judey ran ahead clearing the way. "Put it in my closet. It'll be safe there. No wait, not on the Gucci loafers. Right there, next to the Armani dress shoes."

We closed the closet door on the bomb and the doorbell sounded. Slick and Gimpy.

Judey looked out at them through the peephole.

"They don't look happy," Judey whispered to me. "And they look like they've been run over by a truck . . . several times."

"Guess it's tough being a federal agent," I said.

Judey opened the door and I introduced Slick and Gimpy to Judey and Bill.

"So, you gentlemen are *agents*," Judey said, making quotation signs with his fingers when he said *agents*. "That must be pretty exciting."

"Whatever," Gimpy said. "I'm hanging on for my pension. I don't know why . . . it's a freakin' pittance."

"Yes, but the job must be rewarding."

"Real rewarding. We sit on our ass for a year watching Salzar, trying to set him up, and then some politician calls our boss and we're told to take orders from a NASCAR driver."

"Gotta go with the flow," Slick said, sliding a cautionary look to Gimpy.

"I haven't got a lot of orders," Hooker said. "I figure we'll all meet downstairs in the garage tomorrow at nine AM and we'll take it from there."

"Cake anyone?" Judey said. "I have a coffee cake."

"Things to do," Slick said. And Slick and Gimpy left.

"I'm going out for stone crabs," Hooker said. "I didn't get to eat them last time." He draped an arm around me. "C'mon, Barney. I'll take you for a ride."

I followed him into the hallway and into the elevator. "Since we had decided to move out at five AM and you told

Slick and Gimpy to show up at nine, I'm assuming you don't trust them either, do you?"

"They're not on my list of favorite people." He tossed me the keys when we got to the car. "You drive, and I'll run."

As usual, there weren't any parking places by Joe's. I double-parked and watched Hooker jog off. Eye candy, I thought. Hooker always looked relaxed . . . as if motion was effortless, and all the body parts were working perfectly in sync. He had a nice gait when he ran and when he walked. I was betting his stroke was good, too. Holy cow! Did I just think that? Okay, truth is I've been having a lot of erotic thoughts lately. I'm sexually deprived. My love life is a barren wasteland. And I'm locked in an adventure with a sexy guy. Yes, he's sort of a womanizer, but he's a *nice* womanizer. I think his heart might be in the right place. And the rest of him seems to line up pretty good too. Damn. There I go again.

I wasn't paying a lot of attention to what was going on around me. I was watching Hooker through the big windows in the take-out section. He was standing in line with his hands in his pockets and his shorts were pulled tight across his butt.

So by the time I saw Puke Face, it was already too late. He had the door to the rental open. He reached across, released my seat belt, and yanked me out of the car like I was a ground squirrel and he was a grizzly.

I was tumbled into the back of a Town Car, Puke Face got in next to me, and before I could scream or kick or even haul myself off the floor, the Town Car was in motion.

No one said anything. No music from the radio. A driver.

And a man on either side of me. Everyone stared straight ahead. Although, the truth is I could see only one of Pukey's eyes, the fake one. I wasn't sure where his other eye was going. We crossed the bridge into Miami and took Route 1 south. When we got to Coral Gables the driver turned off Route 1 and took a road that ran along Biscayne Bay. It was a service road, leading to a small marina. There were no other cars on the road. We stopped before we got to the marina entrance, and I realized there were lights shining in the rearview mirror. A car had come up behind us.

Pukey opened his door and yanked me out. Headlights blinked off on both cars, and I could see that the second car was a black stretch limo. Six seater.

I thought I was going to die. My chest felt constricted, and I had a sick feeling in my stomach. Beyond that there wasn't much. No tears, no diarrhea, no fainting. Maybe girls who grow up in a garage in Baltimore aren't real fragile. You learn early on that parts are recycled. Even scrap metal has some worth. Maybe that was my religion. Junkyard reincarnation. The soul as a rebuilt carburetor.

I was walked back to the stretch, Pukey opened the back door, and I was shoved in. There were two bench seats facing each other. Luis Salzar sat on one. A man Salzar's age sat next to him. There was enough ambient light that I could see the men clearly. Both were dressed in expensive summer-weight suits, white shirts, and conservative ties. Their trousers were pressed. Their shoes were polished.

"We meet again," Salzar said. "Please sit down." And he gestured to the seat across from him, where Maria was sitting.

But then maybe sitting is the wrong word. Maria was so rigid she seemed to be levitating, hovering a fraction of an inch above the cushy black leather.

"You've caused me some inconvenience," Salzar said to me. "Perhaps I can rectify that now."

Some inconvenience. I supposed he was talking about his boat going down in a blaze of nonglory. Plus there was the canister.

"I believe you've already met Miss Raffles."

I looked over at Maria. Her hair was unwashed, pulled back from her face, and held at the nape of her neck with a rubber band. Her face was pale. Her eyes were rimmed in dark circles, slightly sunken. Her expression was pure unadulterated rage. Her hands were cuffed behind her back, probably to keep her from ripping Salzar's eyes out of his head. She barely acknowledged me. She was concentrating every scrap of hatred she could muster on Salzar.

"Pig," she said to Salzar.

"She's unhappy with me," Salzar said. "She's just received some unpleasant news about her grandfather and her father."

"You killed my grandfather," she said. "And you had my father imprisoned."

Salzar showed a brief, slightly loopy smile. "True. But it wasn't much of a loss. Your grandfather's passing was a nonevent. Unfortunately, my gold and my SovarK2 were lost with your worthless grandfather. And your dim-witted father preferred beatings to divulging the location of the wreck."

Maria spit at Salzar, but it fell short.

"Allow me to finish my introductions," Salzar said,

returning his attention to me. "This is Marcos Torres, my very good friend and the next President of the Council of State and Ministers of Cuba. You have something that belongs to me . . . and to Marcos. Would you like to tell me where our property is located?"

I didn't say anything.

"I was hoping Miss Raffles would encourage you to cooperate."

Neither Miss Raffles nor I responded.

"Very well," Salzar said. "It's only a matter of time. And it's always much more rewarding when you have to beat information out of a woman. Plus, I have some men who would enjoy you." He turned his attention to Maria. "What do you think of my men?"

Maria continued to give him the death look.

"You killed Maria's grandfather?" I asked Salzar.

"I was his partner many years ago in Cuba. I changed my name when I came to this country. I erased my past. Now I am going to reclaim it. In Cuba, I was a government officer, attached to the Council of Ministers. It was a good position, but not especially well paying, so sometimes when the occasion presented itself, I would supplement my income with an entrepreneurial enterprise. Maria's grandfather and I had a very profitable, but short-lived entrepreneurial enterprise."

"Smuggling?"

Another of the crazy half smiles. "Yes, but it was women we were smuggling. The Russian sailors wanted women, and we would supply them. We would run them out in the fishing boat. Maria's grandfather and I were common pimps." He gave a bark of laughter at that.

Maria continued to glare at him. No laughter from Maria.

"When the blockade went up, and Castro wanted to hide some things away for a rainy day, our fishing boat was the perfect choice," Salzar said. "I was a trusted aide, and the boat wouldn't raise suspicions. Unfortunately, Maria's grandfather and I had a difference of opinion. He thought we should follow orders. And I thought we should take the gold and the SovarK2 and never look back. Marcos was the silent partner, the partner Enrique knew nothing about, really the mastermind of the plan. Even then, Marcos had a taste for power, eh Marcos?"

There wasn't a lot of light in Marcos's eyes. They were focused on me and they weren't smiling. And it occurred to me that Marcos was probably crazier than Salzar.

"Enrique and I were arguing on the little fishing boat and not paying close attention to navigating and somehow we hit a reef," Salzar said. "The boat began taking on water, so I shot Maria's grandfather in the head and left him for dead. Then I set out in the dingy we carried and watched for the boat to go down. I knew exactly where we were. Salvage would be easy. But the boat didn't go down. Maria's grandfather didn't die fast enough. He managed to get the boat moving away from the reef, leaving me behind. I don't know how he did that with a head wound. A hard head, I guess.

"Can you imagine? There I was in the dingy and I had to watch the boat cruise off away from me."

"You must have felt pretty stupid," I said.

Salzar's eyes narrowed, and I thought he might hit me, but he reined himself in and continued. "We searched for that boat for years without finding it. Who would have thought it could have gotten so far away? When he left me he was moving toward Havana. Those were the waters where I concentrated my search."

"You disgust me," Maria said. And she spit at him again. This time scoring a direct hit on his perfectly polished shoe.

Salzar flicked his arm out and caught Maria on the chin with his fist. Her head snapped to the side, and a small trickle of blood appeared at the corner of her mouth.

Maria was concentrating so hard on hating Salzar, I wasn't sure she felt him hit her.

"Where were we?" he said, settling back in his seat, forcing his cold, thin-lipped smile on me. "Oh yes, the gold and the SovarK2. Isn't it interesting that it's been returned to me after all this time? True, I don't have the SovarK2 in my possession, but that's just a technicality." He leaned close to me. "Where is it?"

"Uh . . . I don't know," I said.

Salzar rapped on the tinted glass window and Pukey opened the door.

"Miss Barnaby and Miss Raffles are going to the garage now," Salzar said to Pukey.

I cut my eyes to Maria, and she gave an almost imperceptible shake to her head. Going to the garage wasn't a desirable thing to do.

My hands were cuffed behind my back, and Maria and I

were transferred to the Town Car. There was a guy driving. And there was Pukey. Pukey looked like he had a different opinion of the garage. Pukey was looking forward to it.

Once we got on the Trail there wasn't a lot to see at night. A lot of dark. Occasionally rectangles of light from a house. A few headlights from cars en route to Miami or points south. Maria didn't say anything. She'd lost the angry energy and was slumped in her seat, smaller than I'd remembered her.

Hard to keep track of time when you can't see a watch, but I was guessing we drove for somewhere between thirty to forty minutes before slowing and turning onto a dirt road. After maybe a quarter of a mile we reached our destination. I was pulled out of the limo, and I stood for a moment looking around. I was in a large hard-packed dirt field, and beyond the dirt was tall grass and swamp. A large cinder block building with a corrugated metal roof hunkered in the middle of the dirt field. The *Flex* helicopter was parked behind the building. A large military-type helicopter was parked beside the *Flex* chopper. A couple cars were parked in the front of the building, not far from where I stood. A single light burned over a door at one end. A bunch of bugs were beating themselves senseless against the light. Not a good omen, I thought. Four portable latrines sat off to one side. Another bad omen.

The building was large enough to hold maybe eight eighteen-wheelers. Only one was parked at the rear of the building. The floor was poured concrete, stained with oil drips, transmission fluid spills, and the rest of the crud that accumulates when cars and trucks are involved. Plus, I thought there were some stains I'd rather not identify.

There were no windows. A large fan droned on the far wall, providing ventilation. Lighting was overhead fluorescent. The air was damp and tasted metallic. The door was solid metal. Heavy-duty fire door. Two garage doors were built into the far end. Again, heavy duty. This wasn't a mechanic's garage. This was a storage garage, reinforced to serve as a bunker.

A wood crate sat on a forklift. The gold was ready to go. A motley assortment of chairs had been gathered around a rectangular scarred wood table. A single can of Coke had been left on the table. A small television tethered to a wall outlet had been placed on a folding chair. A makeshift kitchen with a rusted refrigerator, coffeemaker, and hot plate occupied an area behind the table.

We'd been told by Dave that there were four men in the garage keeping watch over Maria. This evening there were twenty. The men were working, cleaning out the garage, moving crates of guns, massive amounts of consumer goods that probably had been hijacked, and several metal file cabinets into the eighteen-wheeler. Dave told us that Salzar had a small army of dedicated men, and that almost all were illegal immigrants, handpicked by Marcos Torres, brought over one at a time on *Flex*. This was obviously some of that army.

I didn't see any rooms partitioned off. No bathroom. No office. A wood bench had been placed more or less in the middle of the floor. It was long and narrow and it had heavy metal rings screwed into the seat.

Maria and I were handcuffed to the bench.

"What are we supposed to do with them?" one of the men asked.

"Nothing," Puke Face said. "Salzar wants them left alone until he gets here."

After several hours my ass was asleep and my back ached. Thank God I didn't have to use the latrine because I'd already been told that wasn't one of my options. I had both wrists shackled, which meant I couldn't lie down. I now understood the sunken eyes and dark circles on Maria. She was exhausted. Probably the sunken eyes had other sources as well, but I didn't want to dwell on that. I was making a large effort not to freak.

No one came near Maria or me. Not complaining about that. Only occasionally Puke Face. He'd look down at us, drool a little, and move on. Hours passed. Once in a while the door would open for someone to use the latrine, and I'd look out to see if the sky was showing signs of light. I dozed off very briefly, head between my legs. When I awoke the men were still working, but the garage was close to empty of goods.

Another horn sounded outside the garage bay. The bay was opened and the stretch rolled in, followed by an SUV. Beyond the open garage door, the sky was still dark, but I thought it had to be almost daybreak. I looked over at Maria.

"I'm sorry," she said. "This is all my fault."

I knew that Hooker'd had a plan. It was pretty straightforward. Go into the garage like gangbusters and overwhelm whoever was in there. He couldn't get help from law enforcement or military. Too much process involved. Too much chain of command to wade through. Hooker's plan was to use a few friends. That was before I was captured. That was before Slick and Gimpy sold me out. I figured it had to be them. Senator Gil gave them the address. And they gave it to Salzar. There was no other way Salzar would know to follow Hooker and me from Judey's condo. No one knew about Judey.

Salzar and Torres left the limo and crossed the garage. They stopped to talk to Pukey and then they moved to me.

"Are you ready to talk to me?" Salzar asked.

I didn't say anything.

"You're not going to get rescued," he said. "We know all about the plan, and we'll be long gone before anyone reaches this garage on your behalf. All they'll find is an empty garage."

"Let me guess. Scala and Martin?"

"Very good. I'm impressed. They were unhappy with the way their lives were shaping up and decided they could use one of my gold bars. Of course, down the line they'll get one of my bullets."

"No honor among thieves, hunh?"

Salzar motioned Pukey over with a crook of his finger. "We need to persuade Miss Barnaby to talk to us," Salzar said.

Pukey looked down at me. "My pleasure."

I was thinking now would be a good time for Hooker to show up. Although, I wasn't sure how that would play out, considering the number of armed men in the garage.

I heard a roll of thunder in the distance, and I knew it was starting.

Salzar heard the thunder, too. "A storm," he said to Pukey. "Make sure the helicopters are secure."

That's not a storm, I thought. That's NASCAR.

Two men ran to the door to secure the helicopters. They

opened the door and stood momentarily dumbfounded. They slammed the door shut and yelled something to Salzar in Spanish.

I looked to Maria.

"They say we're under attack," Maria whispered.

And then there was chaos. Footsteps and shouting overhead on the corrugated roof. Salzar's men firing off rounds at the ceiling only to have them ricochet off the metal and embed themselves in the concrete floor. There were a couple heavy thuds on the roof and then the unmistakable sound of acetylene torches at work. Dave had told us the doors were impenetrable. Hooker knew the roof was vulnerable. Especially since he had access to a mobile metal shop. NASCAR did on-site body work. I couldn't tell how many people were on the roof, but it sounded like a lot. When Hooker put the call in for help, after we'd come up with the plan, he didn't know exactly what he could muster. We knew we could bring in the people at Homestead on short notice, but it sounded to me like all of NASCAR was overhead.

Salzar was shouting instructions in both English and Spanish, attempting to organize his men. He and Torres were at the side door that opened to the dirt helipad. Puke Face was in front of me, working at my cuffs. "You're going with them," he yelled over the noise and confusion. He released me from the shackles and jerked me to my feet. I dug in and refused to move. He gave me another jerk and I went limp, down to the ground. I wasn't going to make this easy. Hooker was on the roof, trying to get in. I just needed to last long enough. I could see the outline where the torch had carved into the metal. They were almost through. A second crew was working at the other end of the building.

Puke Face picked me up like I was a sack of flour and ran to the door with me. There was the sound of ripping sheet metal and a crash. Puke Face turned to look, and I saw that a big piece of roof had crashed to the floor. The torches were still whining overhead. The second piece was about to go. Ropes dropped through the hole in the roof and guys with guns were sliding down the ropes. I had a moment of disorientation when I thought the men were in SWAT dress. Where had Hooker gotten a SWAT team? And then I realized they were in leathers. Hooker had recruited a biker club. The second piece of roof went down, and Hooker came down with it.

Puke Face turned away from the chaos in the building and ran through gunfire to the big military helicopter. A handful of Salzar's men were defending the helipad area. The helicopter blades were in motion, picking up speed, kicking up dust in the predawn darkness. Salzar was already on board. Torres was at the helicopter bay door with an aide. They were waiting for me. I was their hostage. I was their last chance to get the canister.

Pukey had me at the door, trying to hand me off to Torres and the aide, but I had my feet braced on the lip of the open door. I heard Pukey do something like a grunt and a sigh in my ear, and then he released me and went over on his back with a crash. I curled my fingers into Torres's expensive suit jacket, gave a hard shove with my legs, and pulled Torres out of the helicopter. We both went flying and hit the ground hard, Torres on top of me. I was stunned and simultaneously utterly revolted. Having Torres sprawled over me was right up with spiders and leeches in my hair. I did a full body grimace, rolled Torres off and scrambled to my feet.

Salzar yelled for the chopper to *go* and the bird lifted.

There was a volley of gunfire from the ground, aimed at the departing helicopter. I shielded my eyes from the swirling dust, but even through the dust, I could see the flames shoot out from the chopper's undercarriage. The chopper hovered in place for a couple beats and then spiraled off, like a crazy airborne top. It went up and then it went down, crashing in the swamp. There were two explosions and fire jumped high in the sky and then settled into the water grasses.

Hooker came up behind me. He grabbed me and hugged me to him. "Are you okay?" Hooker yelled.

"Just got the wind knocked out."

"I was worried you were dead. It would have been terrible. I would have cried in front of all these guys."

"There's no crying in NASCAR?"

"Hell no. We're manly men."

And then he kissed me with a lot of tongue, and his hand on my ass.

"Your hand's on my ass," I said when he broke from the kiss.

"Are you sure?"

"Well, *someone's* hand is on my ass."

"Guess it's mine then," he said.

I shoved Puke Face with my foot and rolled him over onto his stomach. He had ten darts in his back. The darts were big enough to take down a moose. Torres had three in the chest.

"I see you used the tranquilizer darts like we talked about," I said to Hooker. "Someone's a real marksman."

"Darlin', this is NASCAR. We're beer-drinkin', skirt-chasin', speed-crazy rednecks. *And we can shoot.*"

Someone threw a switch inside the garage and the outside was flooded with light, letting me see for the first time the full extent of the operation. I'd counted twenty-three men with Salzar. It looked to me like Hooker had sixty men. Maybe more. Hard to tell in the activity.

NASCAR uses big tractor trailers to transport their cars and equipment. One of Hooker's eighteen-wheel transporters was parked back by the garage doors. His service truck was next to the transporter. There was a herd of Harleys and half a dozen big-boy customized pickups parked in the same area. There are three sounds that give me goose bumps every time. NASCAR starting their engines, a well-tuned Porsche, and a Harley with Python pipes. The Harleys in the lot were totally pimped, Pythons included. No wonder it had sounded like thunder when they rolled in. A second transporter and service truck from another race team were backed up to the side of the building. Men were working, moving the welding equipment off the roof and onto the trucks.

The stench of burning aviation fuel hung in the air. The dust was settling over the helipad, and the frenzy of the attack was reduced to ordered confusion.

"It's over," Hooker said. "Salzar's gone, and we have Torres. We're turning Salzar's men loose in the swamp. Good luck there. Except for Puke Face. We have plans for Puke Face and Torres."

Hooker and I went back inside the building and watched Bill motor the forklift over to a rental van. Bill loaded the crated gold into the van and pulled away from the pallet. Hooker and I closed and locked the van doors. Then Bill drove around the building, and we loaded the still unconscious Pukey and Torres onto the forklift and dumped them into a crate in Hooker's transporter. Bill backed off with the forklift and jumped in to help Hooker nail the crate shut.

The deal Senator Gil made with his contact in Cuba was that they would trade Juan Raffles for the gold or for Salzar. Our choice. Senator Gil's Cuban contact had made it known that Cuba considered Salzar an enemy of the government, and the government would be happy to trade him for Juan. I suspected the Cuban contact would be even happier to open the crate and find Marcos Torres. Sort of like Christmas come early. One less political piranha for Castro to worry about. Castro would open the crate in the dark of night in Havana and maybe dispose of the contents. Not my problem.

We carefully tucked the canister, still wrapped in Judey's blanket, beside the crate containing Puke Face and Torres.

Judey was doing his nurturing thing for Maria. He had her in a chair, drinking coffee, eating a granola bar. I walked over and sat with them, taking a cup of coffee for myself.

"Are you okay?" I asked Maria.

"No permanent damage. Older and wiser."

"We've made arrangements for your dad."

"Judey told me," she said softly.

Maria's eyes filled, but she didn't cry. More than could be said for me. I was on emotion overload. I was willing to cry at the least provocation. I drank a cup of coffee in one gulp and ate a granola bar without even realizing it. I looked at the empty wrapper in my hand. "What's this?" I asked Judey.

"Granola bar," he said. "You ate it."

The garage doors were open, and I could see the motorcycle guys were leaving. The NASCAR guys were staying to help with cleanup, scouring the area, picking up darts that missed their mark, and collecting spent casings from real bullets. Police would be responding soon, chasing down the smoke that was still billowing from the downed helicopter. We wanted to be out before they arrived.

Hooker's public relations car had gotten rolled out of the transporter to make room for the crate containing Torres and Puke Face.

"I came in the transporter," he said, "but we can go back in the dummy car."

"Okay," I said, "but I get to drive."

"Are you crazy? I'm not letting you drive my car. You're a maniac."

"I'm *not* a maniac. Besides, it's just a dummy car. And *I* should get to drive because I've had a very traumatic experience."

"*I* should get to drive because I rescued you. I'm NASCAR Guy."

"If you want to get lucky you'll let me drive."

Hooker looked a little like Brian when presented with a spice cookie. "Really? All I have to do is let you drive?"

"Yep."

He wrapped his arms around me. "I'd get lucky anyway, even if I didn't let you drive, wouldn't I?"

I smiled at him. "Yep."

"Here's the deal," he said. "You can drive, but you have to be careful. No cowboying around. This is a race car. It drives different from a regular car."

"Really?"

"Have you ever seen the inside of one of these?"

I levered myself in through the window and flipped the switch. *Driver, start your engine.* "Just get in," I said. "I think I can manage."

Hooker's transporter pulled out first, followed by Hooker and me in the PR car. Bill and Maria were behind us, driving the van with the gold. Judey and Hooker's crew chief were behind the van in a pickup. Everyone else was already on the road. The sun was visible on the horizon. The garage was deserted. Tendrils of smoke curled from far off in the swamp. So far, there was no indication that the swamp police were investigating. Hell, maybe helicopters crash there all the time and they only clean them up once a week.

We were all headed for Homestead Air Force Base, where we'd make the swap. The plane that brought Maria's father to American soil would carry Torres and Pukey back to Cuba. The military would take possession of the gas canister, and hopefully the SovarK2 would go to gas heaven. Juan Raffles would go home with Maria . . . and so would the gold.

We were almost at the juncture of Route 997 when a blue Crown Vic blew past us. Slick and Gimpy. Late for the party.

I whipped Hooker's PR car around, hung a U-turn, and dropped the hammer.

"Oh man," Hooker said. "Here we go again."

I caught Slick and Gimpy and pulled out to pass. I looked to the side and saw the horror on their faces as they stared into the PR car at Hooker and me.

"It's all in the timing and placement," I said. Then I jerked the dummy car and clipped the Crown Vic, sending it careening off the road. It caught some air, hit the water with a *splash*, and settled into the swamp.

"Darlin'," Hooker said. "We need to talk. I get the feeling you've done this before."

EPILOGUE

Hooker was grilling barbecued ribs on board his boat. He was dressed in his usual rummage sale shorts and ripped motor oil T-shirt. His nose was pink and peeling. His eyes were hidden behind his Oakleys. He looked happy. I don't usually brag, but I thought I had something to do with the happy part.

Judey was in the fighting chair, watching Hooker grill. Brian was dancing in place, focused on the ribs. Bill, Maria, and Juan Raffles were in deck chairs. Actually, Bill and Maria were in the same chair. It was almost embarrassing, but hey, this was my brother Wild Bill. Todd was lounging on the rail with Rosa and Felicia.

We were having a party. We were celebrating the fact that we weren't dead. We were celebrating Bill and Maria's new two-million-dollar boat, which was tied up in the neighboring slip. And we were celebrating Juan's freedom.

"Cigars for everyone," Rosa said. "I rolled them myself."

I took a cigar and lit up.

Hooker smiled at me. "Darlin', that's damn NASCAR."

"Special occasion," I told him.

"You are *such* a charm," Judey said to me. "Just look at you in your brand-new little pink skirt and adorable blond hair. Who would think you smoked cigars and overhauled carburetors? It's like you take metro-sexual to a whole new level. It's like you're Metro Girl."

Hooker rocked back on his heels, his cigar clamped between his teeth. "Yeah, and Metro Girl's gonna kick ass on my racing team."

Overhead, the sky was a brilliant blue. The hot Miami sun warmed hearts and minds and points south. A late-afternoon breeze rattled in the palms and caused the water of Biscayne Bay to gently lap against the boat hull. Life was good in Florida. And okay, so I was going back to working on cars. Truth is, I was pretty happy with it. I was looking forward to working on Hooker's equipment. I'd seen his undercarriage and it was damn sweet.

Evanovich, Janet.
  Metro girl

✏	DATE DUE		